THE BIG MISTAKE

A STELLA REYNOLDS MYSTERY

LIBBY KIRSCH

Sunnyside Press

Sunnyside Press
PO Box 2476
2075 W Stadium Blvd
Ann Arbor, MI. 48103
www.LibbyKirschBooks.com

Publisher's Note: This is a work of fiction. Names, characters, places, and incidents are a product of the author's imagination. Locales and public names are sometimes used for atmospheric purposes. Any resemblance to actual people, living or dead, or to businesses, companies, events, institutions, or locales is completely coincidental.

Cover art by LibbyKirschBooks.com

The Big Mistake/ Libby Kirsch -- 1st ed.

ISBN 978-1-951184-01-8

Created with Vellum

1

Stella Reynolds wandered around the opulent hotel room in downtown Chicago, bleary-eyed and fuzzy-brained. She shifted her long auburn hair over to one side of her neck and made a conscious effort not to rub her tired eyes. She blinked several times instead, then blew out a sigh when she felt a chunk of mascara fall to her cheekbone.

"Lala, what's going on over there?" Conrad Sellars, her photographer for the day, looked up from a light stand he was assembling and made eye contact through the mirror she was now leaning toward, tissue out, dabbing gently at her cheek.

"Nothing new, Conrad." She smiled. "Just tired."

He glanced at his wristwatch and grimaced, then went back to work by the pair of chairs they would use for the interview. "And no wonder. You came from Seattle, right? You must have left there in the middle of the night. Sleep on the plane at all?" He pulled an elastic tie from his pocket and gathered his shoulder-length dreadlocks into a bundle at the nape of his neck, then took out the final light stand from the case at his feet.

"Oh, you know. A bit." Stella walked to the window and glanced out at the Chicago cityscape that unfurled below. The sun was just glaring out from behind the nearest skyscraper. At 9:20, the morning was frosty, still, and cold. Stella had only just warmed up from the walk between the taxi and the hotel lobby. According to the calendar, spring wasn't too far off, but no one had bothered to let Chicago know. The icy wind that gusted off the lake in late February felt like a mid-winter gale.

Stella's flight had landed at Midway a mere two hours earlier. The taxi had dropped her off at the Westin on Michigan Avenue, and she'd spent the better part of the last hour removing all traces of exhaustion from her face with assorted makeup products. Now she swayed along with the skyscraper as they waited for their celebrity guest to arrive.

Conrad guided her to one of the chairs. "I need to fix the gel on this light, so you might as well sit and be useful. Any consultant ever tell you to wear green eyeshadow to match your eyes?"

"Believe it or not, purple does it best."

"Huh. Go figure. So what did you cover yesterday, anyway?" He cocked one ear toward her, but his eyes were glued to the colored sheet of cellophane he nimbly clipped to the side flaps on a light.

As a network correspondent for NBC News, sometimes Stella traveled with a photographer, and other times NBC hired a photographer from her destination city. Conrad was a perennial favorite in Chicago, and she had been delighted to see his face when she got to the hotel.

"It was a tough one." Stella closed her eyes for a moment, remembering. "CO2 poisoning. A whole family."

"As bad or worse than when we last worked together?" Conrad asked.

"That house fire in the West Loop?" she asked. "The one that killed three kids?" She peeled one eye open and frowned when Conrad nodded. "Mmm. I don't know if I could rank them, but..."

He stopped fiddling with the crinkly red paper that clipped to the light and laid a hand over his heart, remembering. "Both terrible." He gave her a moment to collect herself, then, his tone more upbeat, said, "From that to Sophia Thomas, huh? Crazy world."

"Crazy is right." Stella looked down at her press packet for the A-list Hollywood actress who was supposed to have arrived fifteen minutes ago for a no-holds-barred sit-down interview. Nominated for an Oscar three of the last four years, she'd agreed to sponsor a scholarship for one worthy student at a charity gala that Stella was emceeing this upcoming weekend.

Stella pursed her lips and looked at the door, wondering if they were getting stood up.

"And I don't think I ever thanked you afterward," Conrad said.

Stella turned her gaze back to Conrad with a frown. "Thanked me for what?"

"I went to the boss the day after that fire and said, 'Put me in Special Events or I quit.'"

"Did you really? And that's how you ended up here?"

He nodded. "I've been in the Specials department ever since. Lighting celebrities instead of victims. Covering concerts instead of protests."

"Well, congratulations. That must have been a big promotion."

Conrad chuckled. "My wife doesn't think so. It's still a lot of nights and weekends. And, of course, I do still freelance for news from time to time. But generally, life is much less stressful, so I call it a win."

They smiled at each other, knowing that only people who'd worked in news could understand the stress behind covering one tragedy after another. "We've come a long way, Lala. Although..." He looked pointedly at his watch and then the door. "Maybe not that far, huh? What do you think? Is this one going to show? Or is your boyfriend going to have to find us another celeb to interview?"

Stella scrunched up her nose. Her boyfriend, Lucky Haskins, was a NASCAR living legend, and it was his charity event that Stella was going to emcee just across the street at the Hancock on Saturday night. The network brass had given her a few days in town before the gala to record some interviews that would air during the event.

"You know these big shots. They run on their own schedule." Stella flipped through the press packet, reminding herself about all of Sophia's accomplishments, then groaned when the pages slid right out of her hands. She scrambled to pick them up from the floor and reassemble them into some sort of order.

A newspaper clipping settled on top and her brow furrowed. "John Stevenson is engaged?"

"Is that the news guy out in LA?" Conrad asked.

"What? Oh... yeah." She hadn't even realized she'd spoken aloud, but now Conrad studied her with interest.

"He's the one who saved a whole family trapped in their car when a road washed out after a storm, right? How do you know him?"

"We used to work together. Years ago, back in Montana." Stella glanced involuntarily down at her naked ring finger. It had been a long two years in her job as a national correspondent, but life didn't stop just because she was too busy to live it. And her ancient-history ex-boyfriend was now engaged. She had no stake in the matter at all. None. In fact, she was dating a really great man.

"Easy there, Lala. Can't read it if it's crushed."

She glanced at the article now neatly clenched inside her fist. Had she just crumpled it up? Huh.

"I swear that man's been with more supermodels and singers over the last year than—well, than a movie star," Conrad said conversationally. "Funny to think he's finally ready to settle down. This one used to model for Victoria's Secret, didn't she?"

Stella rubbed her fingertips along the bridge of her nose. Why was this article in the press clippings for Sophia Thomas? She flattened the crumpled strip against her thigh, suppressing her irritation that the newspaper editor had thoughtfully included a picture of the gorgeous couple. Jarissa Headley, what a dumb name. She flipped the article over in disgust.

Another picture caught her eye, and she snorted when the dots connected in her overtired brain. The article on the *other side* was about Sophia Thomas. That was the clipping she was actually supposed to be paying attention to.

Determined to push all thoughts of John Stevenson out of her mind, she focused on the other column. Stella had already known that Sophia was from the Chicago area, but apparently her old high school theater teacher was getting ready to retire.

The article mentioned how close the teacher, a former soap

opera star named Madeline Mowery, had been to Sophia, and how proud she was of her former student.

Stella tucked the stack of papers back into the folder and closed her eyes, aware of a sudden pounding behind her right eye that was sure to turn into a twitch if she didn't stop and take a few deep breaths.

A light tap on the door jerked her back to the present. She leapt up from the chair and bounded across the room, suddenly wide awake. Flinging the door open, she forced a welcoming smile onto her face when a woman who was clearly *not* Sophia Thomas stood at the threshold.

"Hi, Stella? I'm Louise Barr, Sophia's assistant. May I?"

Stella moved aside so the tall, almost criminally gorgeous woman with skin like fresh espresso and deep brown eyes could step inside.

"Sophia is running a few minutes late but should be ready to join us very soon." She shifted her glance across the room toward the photographer. "Can I help get things ready in any way while we wait?"

Conrad stared at Louise with his jaw nearly on the floor.

A spontaneous giggle slipped out of Stella's mouth, and Conrad shot her a glare from across the room. Louise, to her credit, pretended not to notice any of it as she crossed to the refreshment cart by the windows.

"Oh, good, this looks perfect. I know water and hard-boiled eggs seem like a strange combination, but Sophia likes to have quick, healthy food on hand if she needs it." Louise smiled at the room in general, and then glanced at her watch, almost involuntarily.

"Any idea on an ETA for Ms. Thomas?" Stella asked. The movie star was already a half hour late, and they only had the room until noon.

"No, in fact, I'm a bit concerned—" Louise broke off, and it was only when she licked her lips that Stella realized the other woman was flustered. "Not concerned." Louise forced a light laugh. "Confused is a better word. I'm certain I briefed Ms. Thomas on the day's schedule last night, but I'm sure if there's any confusion, it's on my part. Like I said, she'll be here soon. I'm certain."

Louise's tone was anything but certain, and Stella and Conrad exchanged a look while Louise studied her perfectly painted nails.

Stella broke the awkward silence. "Have any plans for the weekend, Louise?"

In the few minutes that they chatted amiably, Louise looked at her watch at least twice. The assistant's nerves were stoking Stella's own concerns about the interview.

Stella's phone buzzed and she declined the call, knowing that Kenny Decker, her executive producer, was likely looking for an update on the Sophia Thomas interview that she didn't have to give.

But then it immediately buzzed again, and Conrad's phone rang seconds later, then the hotel room phone trilled loudly.

Stella's stomach tightened as she answered the call.

"We've got a shooting just north of the city," Kenny barked, already impatient to be off the phone. "We need all crews to head that way. Are you almost done with the Thomas interview?"

"Haven't even started it yet, Kenny. She's running late."

"Then reschedule it stat. I need you to head to Rivermoor. Conrad will work with you for the day. Go!" He clicked off before she could ask any follow-up questions. Across the room, Conrad was writing an address down on a notepad, ending his own call.

"Louise, I'm so sorry, but we'll need to reschedule with Sophia." Stella began packing up her briefcase, her mind already thinking ahead to what she might need out on the scene. She added two pencils and an extra notebook to her bag, then looked up at the other woman. "Is she free at all later this week?"

Stella's heart rate increased, and the last vestiges of fatigue wore off. Louise, in contrast, seemed to relax knowing that the interview was off. She handed Stella her card, then undid the buttons at the bottom of her sleeves and rolled them twice. "Just call me to reschedule. We'll try to make it work."

All three left the room together, and Stella and Conrad waved goodbye to Louise at the elevator.

"What do you know?" Conrad asked when they were alone, descending to the lobby.

Stella read from an email Kenny had just sent. "Shooting at Rivermoor High School. Multiple people down, suspect unknown and at large."

The air in the elevator seemed to evaporate and Stella mentally steeled herself. The next few hours would be tense, emotional, draining. But she had a job to do. She always did.

2

"Sorry, Stella. This is going to be it, I think." Conrad slowed his Chevy Blazer to a stop alongside the road, several hundred yards away from the high school. They'd lucked out on the traffic front; it had taken them less than half an hour to get to the mid-sized suburb called Rivermoor.

Conrad took a few minutes to load up his vest with extra batteries and video cards, then as the pair started walking, Stella dug her press pass out of her bag and slung it around her neck. She turned the dial on the portable police scanner Conrad had handed over, trying to find the right emergency channel, then took the tripod from Conrad. He'd need both hands free to shoot video.

Dozens of police cars from Rivermoor and beyond lined the streets, ambulance lights flashing in the distance. How bad was this going to be?

Stella took a deep breath and scanned the road ahead as the school came into view. Police tape was already strung around the entire perimeter, but the scene was anything but orderly.

"Press? That way. Stay out of the way or you'll be escorted from the scene," an officer barked at them. Stella grabbed the back of Conrad's vest with her free hand and guided him around a pile of abandoned backpacks on the ground. He already had the camera up on his shoulder filming, and she didn't want him to trip as they moved to the press area.

The structure that came into view was impressively large. The left side of the building was solid, a two-story brick wall with no windows and "Rivermoor Theater Arts" written in fancy silver letters. Curved beams flared down from that section toward the main entrance, all shiny steel and glass. Then a huge two-story complex furled out to the right that likely contained all the academic classrooms.

Stella couldn't see it from her vantage point at the edge of the parking lot, but she guessed the gyms and athletic fields would be in the back.

From a quick Google search on her phone in the car, she'd learned that the student population at Rivermoor High School was more than 3,500. Currently, every single one of them appeared to be streaming across the parking lot in groups and alone, moving on and off the street as they located friends, teachers, and worried parents. Half the kids were crying; the rest wore blank looks of shock and horror.

Emergency lights flashed from all sides, and even though there appeared to be more police officers present directing people and car traffic than any single department had on staff, they were no match for the endless number of students and parents present.

A man in a black Ford Explorer honked impatiently for the officer standing guard at the parking lot entrance. "I need to find my son," he called out his open window. "I want to take him home now!"

"Sir, you need to follow the directions to the waiting area across the street," a Rivermoor police officer said as he approached the car, his hands resting on a bulging chest pocket in his ballistics vest. "We are working to match up all the kids with their parents away from the scene."

The father shook his head. "But I—"

"We need to clear the scene before anyone is released. Go that way. Now." His tone cut through the father's panic, and the man blew out a breath and nodded.

"Okay. Thank you."

The father executed a clumsy three-point turn and disappeared down the road back toward the main street.

"Anyone, Lala?" Conrad had the camera up on the tripod now and hadn't stopped recording since they arrived.

Stella shook her head. "No. I can't grab a student without their parent's permission, and police won't talk just yet. You keep recording."

Conrad nodded, then panned the camera to the right and zoomed the lens in. Stella stepped closer to see what he'd noticed. A boy with white-blond hair and baggy pants with a dangling wallet chain curving from his front belt loop into his back jeans pocket crept closer to a Dumpster to the right of the school.

While they watched, he looked furtively in each direction, then tossed something up into the air. It arced away from him and landed neatly into the Dumpster without a sound—at least, no sound reached them.

Stella and Conrad looked at each other, surprised. What was he getting rid of?

The boy turned on his heel and nodded innocently to an officer who walked by. Stella tried to follow his progress, but he melted away into a crowded line of students, lost to her among all the other floppy-haired, baggy-pants-wearing boys.

Conrad's brow furrowed. "Should we tell someone...?"

Stella blew out a sigh. She knew what Conrad meant. In a situation like this, where the shooter was still at large, every student was a potential suspect. Had that boy just thrown away evidence? Or was he just tossing out a gum wrapper? It was impossible to know, and before she could come to any decision, the scanner still clutched tightly in her fist crackled to life.

"We need another ambulance at the entrance. Send in Unit Eight."

Stella instinctively looked toward the main road as one of the waiting ambulances lurched forward, lumbering off the shoulder and heading toward the road.

Right behind it, a dented silver Toyota Tercel tried to slide onto campus. Two officers stepped into the roadway, blocking the path.

"Ma'am, you can't come in here! All parents are to wait in the parking lot across the street. Children will be released as they are cleared and it's safe to send them on their way."

The woman behind the wheel nodded, her face a mask of concern. "It's just—my daughter—"

"Please wait across the road and we'll be escorting children across very soon."

The officer's attention was diverted by a squawk on the scanner clipped to the shoulder of his uniform. He listened intently for a moment, then his gaze swiveled around to Stella and Conrad. "Gather the troops. Chief's coming to give you all an interview." Then he looked up the drive toward the main road and spoke into the radio, "You need to stop the parents before they come this way. There's nowhere for them to go when they get here!"

An affirmative response came through and he and his partner walked down toward the school.

The woman in the silver Tercel hadn't moved yet, and now with the officer gone, she pulled her car over to the side of the street and put it in park, waiting with her window down. Her face was creased with worry, and her eyes scanned the parking lot, no doubt trying to find her own kid.

Stella followed Conrad to a small grouping of local media. All the TV stations, several of the major Chicago dailies, and a few smaller local suburban papers were all represented.

A group of commanding officers approached, the chief easy to identify by the four gold stars centered between the top and bottom seam of the collar on her white button-down shirt. Two lieutenants flanked her.

"Morning, everyone. I don't have a lot of time so let's get to it. My name is Renee Sterling. I am the police chief for the city of Rivermoor."

The assembled media scrambled to hold their microphones out. She didn't wait, just launched into a short description of what happened.

"Shortly before ten o'clock this morning, an unknown assailant entered the building and opened fire. Our school resource officer was shot from behind before she even knew there was a threat. Three other students were injured. All four were or are being transported to the hospital. We are not releasing the conditions of any victims at this time, other than to say that all are alive and expected to stay that way. We are still trying to identify and locate the shooter."

"Did security cameras capture anything that went down in there, Chief?" a print reporter asked from the back row.

"No comment."

"Is the shooter a student?"

"No comment."

"Do you have any leads on the identity of the—"

"The only identifying feature we've been able to confirm from multiple witnesses is that the shooter was wearing a blue hoodie. Obviously our detectives are still talking to students and staff, hoping for a more robust description moving forward."

"Can you ID the victims?"

That question from a local CBS affiliate earned a dirty look.

"Obviously we cannot and will not identify the victims until their families have been notified. That's all."

Chief Sterling pivoted and moved away from the crowd of reporters, ignoring the continued questions being shouted at her. The lieutenants flanking her led her to the other side of the driveway.

Conrad muttered a curse word and when Stella looked over, he was glaring at his camera. "Something's wrong with the power supply, and before you ask, I don't think I got the chief's whole interview. It just happened. Give me a minute, okay?"

Stella swore under her breath and started moving toward the chief. She needed to get that information on the record again, as it might be the only official sound for the story that day.

As her colleagues scattered, each hoping to find the best witness soundbite, she stopped a few feet away from the chief, who was in deep conversation with her subordinates. She caught snatches of conversation.

"Haven't been able to get in touch with her parents..."

"The girl said she won't leave..."

"Ma-tie-ka-what?" one of the lieutenants asked.

"Matykiewicz. Find them. Now." The chief dismissed both men and without looking at Stella said, "What do you want?"

"Chief, Stella Reynolds, NBC News. We had a technical problem earlier. Can I get your statement on camera one more time?"

The chief shook her head. "No time, sorry." She walked away.

Stella bit back another curse word and rolled her neck to loosen the tension that had been steadily building behind her shoulder blades since they first arrived.

This wasn't good, but it wasn't a crisis. She scanned the crowd, searching for a teen who looked like they might be eighteen. She opened her mouth to call to Conrad, when a throat cleared nearby.

"Excuse me? Are you with the school?"

Stella looked down at her business suit and heels and realized how easy it would be for someone to mistake her role at the scene. "No, I'm not. Sorry."

"I—I'm just trying to get information on my daughter. Maybe you can help?"

"Was she inside the building?"

"Yes, and she's not answering her cell phone, and her friends across the street haven't heard from her and I can't get any of the officers to even let me ask a question before they're barking at me to move my car, and..." The woman sucked in a quick breath that sounded like a strangled sob.

"I'm with NBC, and from what the police chief just told us, three students were injured and are heading to the hospital. She said everyone is still alive."

Stella's words didn't have the soothing effect she'd hoped for. The woman's face paled at the phrase "still alive."

"Oh, oh...okay. Thanks for that. I'll just try and ask...someone..." She turned and walked to the silver Tercel from earlier, clutching her cell phone in one hand and her keys in the other. A sticker above the license plate read "Matykiewicz Mobile."

Stella sucked in a breath of recognition, then called out, "Mrs. Matykiewicz?"

The woman turned. "Do I know you?"

"No. But come with me." Stella headed for the police line, where the chief was talking to a patrol officer. Sterling wasn't happy to see her again.

"Ms. Reynolds, I said no, and here in Rivermoor, that still means no, five minutes later. If you haven't seen, we're in the middle of a crisis, and I won't—"

"Chief Sterling," Stella interrupted. "This is Mrs. Matykiewicz. She's been unable to contact her daughter and I thought you might have some information for her."

"Oh." Sterling's mouth snapped shut and she looked at Stella with grudging respect. She softened her expression when she turned to the mother. "Mrs. Matykiewicz, we've been trying to call you."

The woman gripped her phone tightly. "New number just this week."

"No matter. Please come with me. Your daughter is ready to be transported and you're just in time to ride with her to the hospital. Her injuries are not critical."

The woman's pale face drained of any remaining color, and she swayed unsteadily toward Stella. "I don't...I can't believe...Not critical? What does that mean, exactly? Is she okay?" Still clutching her car keys in one hand, she reached out with her other to grab hold of the nearest person, which happened to be Stella. "My car—it's in the way, I should move it...Or...I don't know?" She turned her dazed eyes toward Stella.

"Of course, Mrs. Matykiewicz, you go be with your daughter." Stella took the keys from her outstretched hand and a patrol officer escorted the mother down a short grassy hill to start what would feel like a very long journey across the parking lot. "Do you have a second set?" Stella called. "Should I just leave them inside the car and lock it up?"

Mrs. Matykiewicz didn't answer, just kept walking toward the last remaining ambulance in front of the school like she might fall over at any minute.

Stella blew out a sigh, then turned away from the chief, who was still assessing her baldly, to call to Conrad. "I'll be right back. Keep shooting. See if you can find anyone to talk."

Before she could turn to walk to the Tercel, though, Chief Sterling's radio blasted three short squawks. A dispatcher's calm voice announced, "Shooting at the Dempster Stop N Shop. One victim down. Suspect described as wearing a blue hoodie."

"Oh, shit," Stella breathed, at the same time as Sterling. They looked at each other for a beat, then took off in opposite directions.

3

The Dempster Stop N Shop might never have been as busy as it was when Stella and Conrad pulled up five minutes later. Surrounded by police cars and with one officer unfurling caution tape around the perimeter, the small convenience store's exterior was unremarkable, with four gas pumps, an ice cooler, and an air pump. The store itself looked to be only a couple hundred square feet.

Medics worked furiously on a woman laying half inside the store. Conrad's camera rolled, capturing the moment when they lifted her onto a board, then hefted the board up to a gurney.

"Three, two, one," a medic said, signaling to her partner that it was time to raise the gurney to hip height. The pair then ushered their patient to a waiting ambulance. Was this a victim? Or was it the shooter?

While Conrad got video of the scene, Stella approached a patrol officer.

"No comment, ma'am," he answered, his hands up as if she had a weapon.

Stella glanced down at her microphone, tucked under one arm, and realized he must think that she did. "Oh—off the record, I promise! See?" She showed him the power switch set to the "off" position.

"I think the chief is on her way for the official sound. I'm just wondering what's going on."

"Hmm." His lips scrunched together while he considered the reporter. After a quick scan of the scene, he said, "Off the record, the lady who worked here was shot once and went down. You just saw her go into the ambulance. Suspect still at large. But you didn't hear that from me." He patted his breast pocket with a practiced hand, then shook his head. No cigarettes allowed on the job. He turned and headed to the other side of the parking lot.

Stella looked around with a critical eye. The Dempster Stop N Shop was only a few miles from the high school. The shooting here happened just over a half hour after the high school shooting. If it was the same person, what had they been doing? Did they have a car? Run or walk between the two locations? And what was the connection?

"Hey." The voice came from behind Stella and she turned to find a tall handsome stranger with dark hair and olive skin holding a microphone with the local NBC flag. "Conrad said you're with the network?" She nodded and he raised an eyebrow, considering her. "That was fast. When did they send you?"

She steeled herself mentally. Working with local reporters usually went one of two ways. They were either starstruck and delighted to help, or they felt like she'd stolen their opportunity to be on national news. Which way would this guy lean?

She introduced herself with a friendly smile. "I was in town for another story when this broke, so my executive producer sent me over."

He nodded, his face not giving anything away.

"I'm happy to share any interviews I get with your station, of course."

"That's so kind of you. I'm sure they can work that out behind the scenes." He smiled, but it didn't reach his eyes. "Well, I'm going to go poke around. Try out this reporting gig."

He looked her up and down before turning on his heel. She bit her lip. It was possible she'd just unintentionally offended him.

"Well, that was fun," she said.

Conrad spoke from her other side. "So you met Malcolm McCoy. What'd you think?"

"Oh. He seems...nice." She tried out the word, but it didn't quite sit right on her lips as she considered the reporter's retreating figure: tall and lanky, with a definite designer cut to his dress pants and button-down. He turned back to look at her and their eyes met. Before she could attempt a smile, he looked away.

Conrad snorted. "Hmm, nice isn't the word I'd have used. I've worked with him for more than ten years now. He is...I guess I'd call him a massive, pulsating pain in the—"

Before Conrad could finish his colorful description, Stella's phone rang. The boss.

"Kenny, we're at the gas station now. Not much going on. We'll get a quick soundbite from the police chief, then head back to the school."

"Are the shootings connected?"

"We'll ask the chief, but no matter the answer, the story is definitely back at the school."

"Good. Tell Conrad that I'm sending the satellite truck there for him. A local stringer for NBC will run camera so Conrad can operate the truck. Name's Art." He disconnected without saying goodbye

A stringer was a daily hire employee, and it wasn't *necessarily* a bad thing...but if someone was really good at their job, station management would usually lock them down with a contract. Which likely meant that this Art guy was still a stringer for a reason.

"You know any of the stringers at NBC?" Stella asked Conrad.

But just then, a blue Crown Victoria pulled up.

"Here we go," Conrad said.

Chief Sterling climbed out of the passenger-side door, her face drawn, eyes tired. She headed directly for the officers standing guard by the convenience store. Stella and Conrad moved toward the rest of the media, who'd gathered at the corner closest to the intersection. By Stella's count, all the local TV stations, a few local print reporters, and at least one radio reporter were there. Soon, the chief adjusted her hat and walked toward the assembled media.

"Guys, I've got some basic information, but not much."

Almost a dozen microphones jabbed out toward the chief and she stepped back, barely concealing a frown.

Stella's phone, clenched in her fist, rang, and she silenced it with barely a glance at the screen. Of all the times for her mother to call!

She looked up to find Sterling staring at her. "Everyone ready?"

Stella's cheeks heated. She pressed her lips together and nodded.

"Officers were dispatched to the 500 block of Dempster Street at 10:32 this morning on reports of shots fired. When the first officers arrived on scene, they found a thirty-eight-year-old woman down with a gunshot wound. She is a long-time employee at the Stop N Shop, and before you ask, we do not yet know if this shooting is related to the shooting at the school. Initial reports suggest similarities between the suspects. We are investigating the matter now and hope to have more information out to the public later today. At this time, we hope that surveillance video from both scenes will help us determine the suspect's identity." Sterling paused to take a breath, and an explosion of questions tumbled toward her.

"Is the victim connected to the school?"

"Are there any eyewitnesses to the shooting?"

The chief ignored them all. "Our office will send out any new information via press release later today. Right now, we're asking the public for help. We have one shooter, maybe two out in the community. They are armed and dangerous. If you know something, please contact our 911 dispatchers immediately. We accept anonymous tips. That's all."

Sterling turned and ignored a handful of final questions shouted at her as she walked back to her officers by the store.

"Back to the school, Lala?" Conrad asked. He held one hand out on the lever that would detach the camera from the tripod, waiting on Stella's word.

Stella surveyed the scene. The story was definitely back at Rivermoor High. "Yes, let's head back."

He nodded and unclipped the equipment, and they turned to walk to the car together.

Stella's phone rang again, and she answered it. "Hey, Mom. It's not a good time right now. Can I call you back?"

"Well, when can you talk, then? I'd love to know." Stella's mother sniffed, her tone injured. "It's never a good time, and if I waited for you to call me, I'd be dead."

Stella blew out a silent breath and screwed her eyes shut. "You're not the first to say that to me, believe it or not, Mom. But I'm right in the middle of something here. I promise I'll call you tonight when I get to the hotel."

"Listen, honey, Carol's granddaughter is in a bad spot, and I told her you'd be happy to help out."

"Caro—" The name died on her lips, and Stella searched through her memory bank to make sense of her mother's request. "Carol who?"

Beth Reynolds groaned. "Carol who? Carol Miller! My best friend since before you were born?"

"Oh, right." Stella's heart squeezed at the thought of the Miller family. One tragedy after another for them. "Well...I mean, I don't even know her granddaughter, do I? I'm not sure—"

"She goes to St. Agnes College in a small town near Chicago. Fran is a communications major and she's having a hard time in school. I told Carol you'd swing by her dorm room and give her a pep talk."

"Oh...well, Mom, I mean—"

Her mother's answer sounded like one long, frustrated word. "Stella Reynolds you can find five minutes to help out my oldest friend even if that means skipping dinner, do you understand?"

Stella chuckled under her breath. Her mother's disappointed tone hadn't changed in all Stella's twenty-seven years. Flipping open her notebook, her pen poised over a blank page, she said, "Okay, Mom. How do I find her?"

She took down the information and then hung up on her mother mid-sentence when Conrad gunned the engine.

"Hold on!" He peeled out of the parking lot in a small break in traffic.

She looked at the clock on the dash. It was just before noon. She likely wouldn't get a break until after the evening newscast six hours from now.

"Stella?"

"What?"

"Your phone. Looks like Kenny."

"Oh, thanks." She answered the call. It was going to be a long day.

4

"So...how long are you going to be in town?" Art Werrick batted at his amber-brown hair, which stood up at the ends like a well-used Brillo pad. Two blotches of red lit up his pale cheeks like stoplights, and he wore only a lined denim jacket against the freezing temperatures. The photographer with the local NBC station didn't seem fazed to have been pressed into service for Stella's live shot.

"I'm not really sure." She glanced down at her notes one more time, then plucked a flyaway hair out of her freshly glossed lips.

He pressed a finger to his earpiece and squinted. "Oh, standby. You're live in forty-five."

She nodded, trying to concentrate on her script. She had interviews with the school principal, the police chief, and two students who'd fled the building when the shots rang out. Kenny wanted her to find a student who'd actually seen the shooter, but Stella had struck out.

"Ten away." Art adjusted the key light and touched the zoom button on the camera. "In five, four..." Art's fingers finished the countdown, and when he pointed at Stella, she started talking.

"Good evening, Hank. We are live at Rivermoor High School, where students and the community are in shock over this morning's shocking violence. And even as school officials call on counsellors to come to campus to help students process what happened, police have started an all-out manhunt to track down the elusive shooter."

"Clear, back in one forty-five."

Stella's attention turned from the camera in front of her to the monitor on the ground as she watched the story she and Art had already written and edited play on the news.

"Back to you in four...three..." Once again, the countdown ended silently.

"Hank, the big question on everyone's mind is 'Who?' Who is the shooter, and why did he target Rivermoor? So far, according to police, no one on campus recognized him as a former or current student, and police say they are frustrated with the school surveillance system, which appears to have failed at the time of the attack. They are also investigating whether a second shooting down the road might be connected. Much more to find out here in Rivermoor, and we'll be on the ground getting you the latest information. Reporting live, I'm Stella Reynolds. Back to you."

Art held a hand up, signaling that Stella should wait. When Hank moved on to the next story in the newscast, Art's hand fell to his side. "And, clear. Great job."

The photographer took the camera off the tripod and picked up a small backpack by his feet. He connected a cable from the pack to the camera, then hefting it onto his shoulder, picked up the awkward tripod with practiced ease and walked a few steps away. "Ready, Malcolm? They want you live at the top of the hour."

Stella stared at the backpack in awe. Long gone were the days of dangerous live trucks with huge antennae masts that could hit power lines overhead. Now all reporters needed in the field for local news live shots were small high-tech backpacks. No cables spooling out to a TV van, no limits to where you could broadcast live.

She took a minute to appreciate how easy it was to be a reporter these days where technology was concerned.

Her focus shifted with a movement to her right, and she caught Malcolm McCoy staring at her—his expression not exactly friendly.

She stared back, curious, and after a moment, he broke off the connection and spoke to Art.

Stella continued to look, though, wondering what she was dealing with when it came to McCoy. She liked to think she was on the same team as her local counterpart, but it didn't seem like McCoy thought the same.

She blew out an irritated breath when her phone buzzed.

"Reynolds."

"Terrible. Piss poor, in fact. I expect to see a level of attention to detail from you, and a burning desire to break news, not just follow along with the herd of other wannabes and imposters. If you cannot put one hundred percent into this job on a daily basis, then you need to find another one."

Stella knew from experience that Kenny Decker was only getting started. She steeled herself and tried to tune out as much as possible. Her face must have registered some level of distress, though, because when she looked up, she caught Malcolm staring at her again. When their eyes met this time, he was the one who didn't look away.

"Are you listening?" Kenny barked.

"Yes, I—yes. I hear you, Kenny."

"Good, because I'm not paying you to be out there mooning over a lost love. Is that what happened out there today?"

Stella had been walking back to the satellite truck as Kenny ranted, but now she froze in her tracks, utterly confused. "What—what are you talking about?"

"One of the APs here told me about your ex-boyfriend's engagement, and I absolutely won't tolerate your personal problems getting in the way of my—"

"Excuse me. You are mistaken." A flush worked up from her neck, and she had trouble getting in a full breath. "No matter what crackpot theory an associate producer might have told you, nothing in my personal life impacted my work life today, nor will it ever." She could just imagine some nameless AP—probably someone who'd never even met Stella—hoping to get ahead by sharing gossip as fact with her boss in the New York newsroom. "Now if you'll excuse me,

I've got a line on one of the injured students that I need to check out." When she disconnected the call, she was so angry her fingers were shaking.

"Whoa. Lala, you okay?" Conrad stopped, a cable he'd been winding up suspended in his hands.

"I'm fine." Stella rolled the tension out of her neck and blew out a slow, quiet breath to calm herself.

"Did I hear you say you've got a line on a victim? You need me to take you somewhere?"

Stella looked at the photographer fondly. "No, but thank you. I've got my own ride." His eyebrows shot up and she grinned. She looked to the far side of the school parking lot at the Matykiewicz car, still parked where the mother had left it, then patted her front pocket and felt the key tucked safely inside.

She would drive it back to the family and then order a ride to get back to her hotel. Surely there was insurance information inside the car listing the family's home address. And while she was there, she'd see about getting Kenny his interview with a victim. She only hoped the family would talk. But first—first, she needed some food.

THE LAST HOUR had felt like ten. Driving an unfamiliar car—stick shift, no less!—in a new city was proving to be a challenge. The map on her phone locked up just as she eased through a traffic light, and it wasn't until a huge semi in front of her eased down a ramp that she realized she was on an onramp for the highway. She flipped on her blinker and tapped the brakes, but no one would let her over. Before she knew it, she was merging onto the interstate, heading toward Chicago.

With a frustrated groan, she decided to roll with it and head to her hotel for some food. Heck, a meal might give her the energy she needed to face the Matykiewicz family. However, as soon as she'd tossed her bags and keys on a table in her hotel room and fell onto the uncomfortably squishy couch, she realized it was going to be hard to go back out again.

She was exhausted and determinedly avoiding her mother's repeated phone calls. Even though her stomach grumblings had turned into a non-stop dull ache, she suddenly felt too tired to go scavenge a meal.

When her boyfriend Lucky called, it was like a spark of light on a dark foggy night. She answered on the first ring.

"Hey, Bear." His husky voice lifted her spirits better than a bag of chocolate.

"Hey." She didn't have the energy to say anything else but was glad to be on the line, nonetheless.

"You need a vacation," Lucky observed.

"I agree."

After a moment of stunned silence, Lucky said, "Wait, you're agreeing with me? You'll go on a vacation?"

She laughed. "Yes, I'm agreeing with you. I need a vacation. Desperately. Want to come with me?"

"Do I—Yes, yes I do! But, uh...forgive me for looking a gift horse in the mouth—"

"Am I the horse in this scenario?"

"Don't interrupt, darlin', cause what I want to know is why you think you need a vacation. Not that I'm not thrilled, and don't think that I don't already have five ideas brewing and two booked."

She laughed in earnest then. "You can't possibly have two vacations booked already!"

"And yet I do." The background noise ended abruptly, and she pictured him moving from a crowded room into an empty one. "But what's going on?"

She toyed with the zipper of her jacket while she considered how to answer. "It's just...some days are hard, you know?"

He made a noise in the back of his throat, and she knew he did. "Anything specific?"

She rubbed her fingers against her lips trying to come up with a succinct answer, finally blowing out a loud breath. "I covered a school shooting today, and it's just..." She sighed. "It's a lot to take in. Luckily, it looks like everyone at the school will survive. But then I got chewed out by my boss—"

"Again?" Lucky growled, but she went on as if he hadn't interrupted.

"—for not getting a scoop that no one else got either, by the way, but his ten-minute recitation of all of my failures gave me time to think, and in the end, I think I need a break."

"I'm so tired of that boss of yours. He is a piece of work, and I hope someday you'll give me five minutes alone in a room with him."

"I know. And I love you for it. But, of course, *that* wouldn't help my career." She stared at the bland picture hanging at a slight angle on the wall across from her.

He sighed. "And I know that too."

They sat in companionable silence for a bit, and the background noise suddenly morphed into something familiar. "Wait...are you on a plane?"

He chuckled. "Got me. I'm headed your way. We land in thirty minutes. But I promise not to seek out your boss, how's that?"

"He's not here, anyway," she finally replied, her voice faint from surprise.

"Well, he better not be in your hotel room, Bear." After a moment he added, "Good surprise?"

"The best, Lucky. I'll see you soon."

"Love you."

"Love you."

As they disconnected, her stomach reminded her with a sudden side pain that she hadn't eaten since breakfast. Did she have time to grab something, or would such an errand mean missing Lucky when he got to town? As she considered the logistics of deplaning a private jet and a chauffeured drive to the hotel versus a takeout run, a crisp knock had her up and across the room.

"Yes?" she called through the door. Peeking into the security lens, she made out a man in a delivery uniform. The rich, familiar smell of freshly cooked pizza made her mouth water.

"I got a delivery for Lucky Haskins."

Stella opened the door and fumbled for her purse on the nearby table.

"Don't worry, miss, all paid for, with a nice tip to boot." He handed a large pizza box across the threshold, then stooped to pick up a bag by his feet. "Enjoy!"

Inside the hotel room, she unpacked a bottle of wine, a six pack of beer, and a tray of brownies from the bag, a slow grin spreading across her face. She tapped out a quick text to Lucky. *You're the best.*

I know. The answering text was so fast, it was as if he'd pre-typed it, waiting for her message.

She laughed out loud, and before she could answer, he'd sent another text. *You never leave time to eat when you work. I can't work like that.*

What work are you *planning?* she typed, a smile turning the corners of her mouth up.

You'll find out when I get there.

Suddenly, instead of hunger pangs, her stomach felt pleasantly hollow at the thought of Lucky working on *her* after dinner.

I can't wait, she typed, then opened the pizza box and pulled out a slice.

5

Stella awoke slowly but inexorably, even though she could tell by the nonexistent light in the room that it was well before dawn. Lucky stirred but didn't wake, and she envied his steady, even breath and respite from life's problems.

She extracted herself from Lucky's arms and checked the time on her phone. Just after five in the morning. She set the device down, refusing to check email or texts, then reached overhead, thoroughly stretching her neck and shoulders before rolling onto her side to stare at her boyfriend.

Lucky's blond hair was tousled in sleep, his whiskery two-day growth of beard like soft velvet. She reached out to stroke his face, and his hand caught hers neatly against his cheek.

"What are you doin' awake, Bear?" His voice rumbled from disuse. "Sun's not even up yet." His eyes blinked slowly open, and he stroked his thumb across her knuckles. Gooseflesh prickled down her arm and she shivered, pulling the covers up around her shoulders.

"Not a very feminine nickname, is it? Bear? Sounds like a lumbering beast." She smiled to show she didn't mind. He'd given her the nickname years ago—long before they started dating—from an old NASCAR saying.

"Well..." He rolled over onto his back, pulling her onto his chest in the process. The covers slipped and he rubbed his hands lingeringly down her spine. "You cold?"

She shook her head. She suddenly felt decidedly hot.

"I guess I could call you Lady Bug, or Sugar, but they just don't seem to fit." He cupped her shoulders with his big calloused hands and squeezed lightly. "Bear."

She rested her chin on his chest with a smile.

"And you're as fierce as a bear when you think someone's done something wrong."

The small fire that burned in her stomach grew bigger, spreading heat waves all the way through her fingertips. "Mmm."

"And stubborn as a bear." She pinched his arm and he chuckled, then the sound cut off when the movement slid their bodies enticingly against each other from toes to throats. "And soft in all the right places."

She muffled a snort as he shifted so that she was lying under him, and he reached between their bodies and rested his open palm against her chest. "You've a heart of gold, Bear. And that's one of the things I love about you most."

She blinked and looked away. How did he do that? Move her so completely with so few words that the mere inches between their bodies felt like a terrible gulf of separation? Lucky raised a finger and gently lifted a teardrop from her cheek and licked it. It was unexpectedly sensual, and she reached for him with an urgency that left her breathless.

Some time later, they lay next to each other, limbs heavy and damp, staring into each other's eyes.

"You know," Stella said, breaking the silence, "I'm supposed to be the one with all the words, yet somehow you always manage to leave me speechless."

He ran a hand lightly down her arm, a smug smile on his face. "I go for the win every time."

They smiled at each other again, and she felt her heart speed up. He raised his eyebrows in surprise when she reached for him again.

They both swore when her phone chirped.

"Ah, well. It was going to be good."

"Yes, it was," Stella said with regret, her legs already swinging over the edge of the bed. "Reynolds," she barked into the phone. It wasn't even six in the morning yet; who could be calling?

Lucky groaned and then climbed out of bed. She watched appreciatively as he walked naked to the bathroom. "Uh, sorry, what was that?"

"I said this isn't a vacation, you know! It's work, and I need to know that you're working! Hank and I both want to know: what's your plan today?" Kenny said, impatient already.

Stella grabbed a robe from the closet and pulled it on as she walked to the bar area, where the single-serve coffee machine beckoned. "I'm going to visit one of the victims. See if she and her family will talk about what happened inside that school yesterday." She dropped a coffee pod into the machine and pushed a button to start it brewing.

"Oh." Kenny obviously hadn't been expecting an answer, and he wasn't sure how to respond. "And just how do you think you'll figure out where she lives? No one has released any information on the victims at all—"

"I've already got her address." *And her mother's car*, Stella thought guiltily to herself. In the excitement of Lucky's surprise arrival, she'd completely forgotten about returning the car to its owner last night.

Kenny muttered a distrustful "Hmm," then cleared his throat. "Art will be working with you for the duration. I emailed you his contact information."

"Th—" But it was no use thanking Kenny. He'd already hung up, the wannabe drill sergeant jerk. She saluted the phone. She'd get the whole story, and she'd get it first.

"You thinkin' of changing careers, darlin'?" Lucky's drawl was stronger in the morning. "I sure would like to see you in uniform. Or better yet, I'd like to take one off of you." He patted her rear and reached for the coffee cup just as the final drops splashed in. "Mmm." He took a slow sip and smiled. "Perfect."

She couldn't be irritated at him after the way they'd started their morning together, so she smiled indulgently and dropped another pod into the machine without taking her eyes off his rangy lean muscles—on clear and thoughtful display as his robe was open and Lucky was only wearing a pair of black athletic boxers.

"What's your plan today?" She ran a hand up his washboard abs and he choked on his drink.

"Ow—shoot, that's hot." He set his mug down on the countertop behind her and she slipped her hands inside his robe and around his back.

"Uh, what did you ask?" he asked sheepishly.

"What are you doing today?"

"Ah, right. I've got to do some prep work for the gala Saturday night. Shouldn't take me too long. Dinner?"

"Mmm," she murmured and planted a kiss in the middle of his chest. "Perfect."

He pulled away from her and looked around the room, assessing the love seat and quickly dismissing it as not long enough. "Come back to bed? Surely there's no news to gather before the sun comes up." He reached out a hand in invitation. She took it without hesitation.

"Lucky?"

He looked back, eyebrows raised.

"I love your heart too." He narrowed his eyes and she grinned widely. "And your abs, and your arms, and your—"

He scooped her up with a whoop and she squealed when he dropped her from waist height onto the mattress. "I *am* the wordsmith in this relationship," he said, then covered her mouth with his. There was no more talking.

6

Flowers, candles, and cards flowed down the front steps and spilled onto the flagstone walkway of the blue stucco home where Anna Matykiewicz lived.

Art parked his beast of a rusted-out old jalopy behind the Matykiewiczes' own car, and as Stella climbed out of the silver Tercel, she held out a hand, warning him to stay in place for now.

She headed up the walk and knocked on the door, consciously tamping down the nervous feeling that sliced into her gut. In an unpredictable job, worried parents hit the top of the list for erratic behavior.

A younger boy opened the door, maybe ten or eleven years old. "Yeah?"

"Hi, is your mom or dad home?" Stella asked, looking over and around the kid for an adult.

"Who are you?"

Stella introduced herself, and his eyes grew large. "Wow, are you going to ask us about the shooting?"

Stella licked her lips. First rule of thumb when speaking to minors—don't. Nothing pisses off a parent more than if they think a reporter's trying to pump their kid for info without permission. "Well, I'd like to talk to your mom or dad if they're home."

He shook his head. "Nope. They're at the hospital with Anna."

"Oh, of course. Is she okay?"

"Yup, coming home any minute, actually. Want to wait inside?"

"No—no thank you. I'll just wait out—"

"There they are!" The boy pointed happily to Stella's right. She turned in time to see a white Chevy Equinox pull slowly into the driveway. She hurried down the front walk toward the driveway.

"How's Anna?" she called as soon as the front passenger door opened.

A wide, stocky man with overlarge weary eyes turned to stare at Stella. "Who's asking?"

"Stella Reynolds, NBC News. There are a lot of people worried about her." She hovered at the side edge of the apron of the driveway, stopping just feet away from the SUV.

The man narrowed his eyes for a brief moment, then his face softened when the rear door opened and a girl climbed carefully out onto the pavement. "Let me help, hon."

"Thanks, Dad." A girl with a pale heart-shaped face and lank dirty-blond hair looked over at Stella with interest. "What's she want?"

"Anna?" Stella asked, certain that this was the girl, but needing to make sure. Just as Anna answered "Uh-huh," her bandaged arm caught the door as she tried to ease past and chaos erupted.

"Easy!"

"Dad, seriously!"

"Wade, is she okay?" Mrs. Matykiewicz ran around the front of the car.

"Good question." The narrowed eyes were back. "I'm sorry, it's not a good time, obviously." He stepped between Stella and the girl. "Elise, get the door for us, will you?"

Stella moved back, not wanting to crowd, but also not wanting to let the Matykiewicz family slip away.

"Have police told you how the shooter managed to escape?"

Wade stopped along the path and turned back to Stella. "No. Nothing from police. Nothing at all. It's...it's very frustrating."

"According to the timeline in the Rivermoor Police press release, the first shot rang out at 9:54 a.m. First officer arrived on scene approximately three minutes later." Stella licked her lips, amazed that Wade was still listening. "The chief said a cruiser was just a couple of blocks away when the alarm sounded. They locked down the building and completely searched it using police K-9s, but... nothing. I can't figure out how the shooter escaped. No one saw them leave the building, right?"

Wade sighed and scratched his head. "No one that I've heard, anyway." He pulled the front door open and Anna walked in. Before her mother could follow, Stella called out, "Mrs. Matykiewicz! I brought your car back!"

Elise tore her eyes away from her daughter for the first time since they arrived home. "Oh! Oh, Wade, this is the nice woman I told you about." She made sure that Anna got through the door safely, they turned and headed back toward Stella. "Thank you. For everything yesterday."

Stella handed the keys over. "It was nothing. I'm just glad I was able to help."

Elise smiled faintly, then shook herself and hurried back up to the house after her daughter. Just before Wade disappeared into the house after them, he turned back. "Well, come on."

Stella turned and motioned to Art. He'd already gathered the camera and tripod, and at her cue, they walked inside together.

The foyer was bright. Twin skylights in the ceiling brought in as much winter sunlight as several 120-watt bulbs. Stella's eyes drifted back down past a maze of framed photos showing off what looked like a very happy family, years in the making. Annual pictures, professionally taken, lined the steps to the left, and a bank of photos on the wall ahead showed Anna and her younger brother at various stages in childhood.

"So, what do we have to do?" Wade squinted at them from the end of the hallway. At a glance, he looked exhausted—just as you'd imagine a parent would look some twenty-four hours after getting word that their daughter had been shot.

"Well…I mean, you don't *have* to do anything. I want you to know that." Art stiffened beside her, but she didn't acknowledge him. "People here in this community are worried about your daughter. They want to know if she's okay, they want to know if they can help, but they don't want to bother you—"

"*You* don't mind bothering us?"

"Not usually," Stella answered with a smile, ignoring the dig. "Even though it might not feel like it from your perspective, I'm helping organize the community outreach into something you can handle. Does that make sense?"

"Nothing has made sense since approximately 9:54 yesterday morning. But yeah…I get it." Wade turned down the hall and called over his shoulder, "Well, let's get this over with."

Several minutes later, Anna and her parents were sitting shoulder to shoulder on the couch. Her little brother hovered nearby, and Stella sat across from them in a blue swivel chair near the TV.

"I was sitting in art class. We were—we were working on block printing. I don't know if that matters?"

Stella nodded at Anna. "It all matters, Anna. Just tell me what you remember about yesterday morning."

"Okay, well, we had just gotten to our tables and I was still organizing my supplies, when the door banged open. Before I could even turn around to see who was late—the second bell had rung a couple of minutes before—I fell off my stool, and my arm was just burning."

"The impact of the bullet knocked her clean off her seat," Wade interjected, his face both stern and wary.

"I didn't even really get that I'd been shot yet, you know? It just seemed so…I don't know, random? Anyway, Cece started screaming, and then I started screaming. The teacher dove under her desk, and I heard a few more shots before it was just suddenly, like, *so* quiet." She took a tremulous breath. "I mean, I don't think I've ever heard silence so…utterly *complete* there at the end."

"And then what?"

"I guess the guy left the room, because suddenly the teacher was tying something around my arm, and I was trying not to cry, but man, it hurt."

"That woman used her scarf as a tourniquet around Anna's arm. The doctor said it might have saved her life. We haven't even been able to say thank you yet." Tears pooled in Elise's eyes and spilled over.

Stella directed her next question to the parents. "And when did you get the call that there was a shooting at the school?"

"It's an emergency system that automatically sent out the text. But we didn't know Anna was injured until I got to the school."

Stella nodded, considering her next question. "So, Anna, what's the prognosis?"

But it was Wade who answered. "Anna suffered a single gunshot wound to her left upper arm. The bullet went straight through her bicep, but amazingly, missed her arteries. She'll need six to eight weeks to recover."

"And according to Chief Sterling, three others at the school were shot. Did you know any of them?"

Anna nodded. "Well, sure. I mean, it's a big school, but we all know each other. I heard the security guard took one in the leg, and then two other students in the art room with me were injured. But everyone will l-live." The stutter at the end was the only crack in Anna's otherwise stoic countenance. "I heard at the hospital that they'll all be okay."

"Anna, did you see the shooter? Recognize them?"

Anna shook her heard. "I was shot before I'd even turned all the way around. I didn't see him."

Elise bit her lip. "It could have been so much worse."

"But it was bad enough," Wade added, a frown stitched back into his pale features.

"Anything on your mind now that you're all home and Anna's safe?" Stella's gaze moved from Elise to rest on Wade. "Anything you'd like to say to the school, the police?"

Wade's muscular arms crossed over his chest as he leaned forward. "Anna's safe. I like the sound of that. But I'll tell you what. There's either an evil or unstable person out there, running around with easy access to a gun, and until he's locked up, I won't feel safe—we won't *be* safe. I want to know who dropped the ball to not only let this maniac into the school, but then to let him out again. This kind of thing doesn't manifest itself overnight. Who knew this kid? Who let him get a gun? How in God's name did he get away?" Wade's eyes snapped in the camera light, and the zeal of his anger made him seem more alive than before. His gaze shifted from Stella to the camera for his final words. "How did this kid escape?"

Elise gripped his arm and murmured soothing words under her breath, and he seemed to remember himself. He shook his head and after a moment of ringing silence, he added, "None of us are really safe until he's behind bars."

Ten minutes later, Stella stood in the foyer, saying goodbye to the Matykiewicz family, when Art shuffled back up the front steps from loading his gear into the car. He looked meaningfully over his shoulder as another news car slowed to park alongside the curb.

Stella handed her business card to Elise. "Please call if there's anything I can do for you."

"Thank you, Stella. We will. Chief Sterling said she'd be in touch with updates, but we haven't heard anything yet."

"I think it's a good sign that she's busy. Hopefully they're making progress in the case," Stella offered.

"We'll see." Elise looked past Stella, her brow furrowed. "Who's that?"

"I think it's another reporter."

"Oh—oh no. I can't do this again." Elise clutched her chest and backed away from the door.

Wade shook his head. "Tell them to leave. We don't want to talk to anyone else right now."

Art blew out a soundless breath and Stella nodded. It seemed the least she could do.

When the door closed, Art said, "Malcolm's gonna love *that*."

She turned and assessed the tall, wiry reporter as he climbed out of his car. He had the requisite strong jawline and perfect teeth that seemed made for—or at least corrected for—TV, and an artificial smile that didn't quite soften the way he cataloged the scene with narrowed eyes.

McCoy locked eyes with Stella again, and she shrugged off a feeling of unease in her belly. The Matykiewiczes' decision to not talk to another reporter had nothing to do with her.

Art raised his eyebrows, answering her unspoken defense. "He would have no problem shooting the messenger."

7

Stella ignored Malcolm McCoy's angry glare as she walked into the Rivermoor Police Department conference room and took a seat, as far away from the irritable man as possible. She made a point of relaxing her expression into one of extreme indifference as she waited for the press conference to begin.

McCoy had pushed past her at the Matykiewicz house after she'd explained their wishes, and she'd heard him knocking on their door as she climbed into Art's car.

Based on their joint arrival times at the police station, she guessed he'd struck out on interviewing Anna, and now he appeared intent on melting her with his eyes.

Stella turned at a tap on her shoulder. "Ms. Reynolds? Here are the reports you requested."

Stella tucked the papers into her briefcase before anyone else could see them. "Wanda, thank you so much. I ordered you up a picture of Hank. He said he'd sign it himself and drop it in the mail."

Wanda's pale face flushed pink from her cheeks to the roots of her gray-blond hair. She was the chief's administrative assistant, and when Stella had gone hunting for old police reports just a few minutes earlier, she'd found out the woman was a huge fan of the evening news anchor, Hank Smith.

Wanda backed out of the room without a word when a string of uniformed officers filed up to the front of the conference room. Chief Sterling took center stage and adjusted the microphone to the proper height. She wore an identical uniform as the day before: crisp white button down with several bars and patches on the chest, with standard-issue black uniform pants. The chief's straight dark hair was pulled into a low no-nonsense ponytail under the edge of her police hat, and her dark blue uniform jacket was smooth and crisp. Stella bet a wrinkle wouldn't dare touch it. Chief Sterling looked directly into the bank of cameras at the back of the room as she spoke. "I have a short opening statement, then I'll take a few questions before we get back to work."

A small twitch of her fingers against the side of the podium gave her nerves away. There couldn't have been many other occasions where tiny little Rivermoor had been in the unrelenting glare of the spotlight before.

"Despite a tireless night of investigative work, our detectives have been unable to identify the person responsible for the violent and senseless shooting yesterday at Rivermoor High School."

From the front row, McCoy raised his hand as he spoke. "Any surveillance video of the shooter, Chief?"

Sterling grimaced, either at the interruption or the answer she was about to give. "We are also investigating whether the shooting at Rivermoor High is connected to another shooting at a second location, just thirty-six minutes after the first shot was fired at the school." She shook her head when McCoy opened his mouth again. "As I said, please hold your questions. The school district was in the middle of a contract switchover with two video surveillance companies. It pains me to report that we have no video from inside the school Monday morning. Likewise, the gas station has no video to share from the shooting there. However, the description given by several brave students loosely matches the description we have of the suspect from the Dempster Stop N Shop shooting. While we can't say yet that the shootings are related, we are investigating both with equal fervor today." She cleared her throat and looked up from her notes, focusing on the TV camera in the middle of the row. "I'd now like to turn things over to the Rivermoor superintendent of schools, Niles Wright. Dr. Wright?"

Sterling stepped to the side and a tall, lanky man with blond hair and pale skin took her place at the podium. His voice was low and monotone, and Stella found herself—instead of listening to him describe the protocol for when school would resume and how many counsellors would be on hand—wondering how it was possible that there was no surveillance video from either shooting. Most schools were wired up like sports arenas these days. And even the dingiest convenience mart or gas station invested in cheap but reliable video security systems. You could buy a doorbell camera for 150 bucks and have around-the-clock access to recordings for a small monthly fee.

She refocused on the press conference when Sterling spoke again. "Are there any questions?"

McCoy's voice rose above the fray. "Chief, are you investigating the possibility that the shooter is a current or former student?"

Sterling's face remained a mask, not revealing any clues. "At this point, we don't know the identity of the shooter, so I can't say with any certainly who he is or isn't."

"Are you looking for any accomplices?" That one came from a newspaper reporter in the front row.

"We are open to any and all scenarios as they present themselves. Our priority now is finding the shooter."

Stella waited a beat, then said, "Can you give us an update on the medical conditions of the victims?"

The chief gripped the sides of the podium stand. "One student is already home. Two more are improving by the hour with non-life-threatening injuries. Our school resource officer will require extensive surgeries to repair her leg, but we hope she will make a full recovery.

"We can now release the name of the victim from the Dempster Stop N Shop shooting. Dana Scott was transported from Rivermoor General to Northwestern Memorial Hospital's Level I Trauma Center this morning. We have very few leads and hope that someone will come forward with information about the shooter." Chief Sterling blew out a slow, quiet breath and looked, unblinking, at the bank of cameras at the back of the room. "The gunman did his best to kill five people. He clearly has no conscience or remorse. He is a threat to this community and others as long as he is walking free.

"Someone out there knows him. Someone out there heard his plan before it happened or heard him talk about it afterward." She looked down at her notes briefly. "We're in this together now; the gunman, all of you out there in our community, and me. You're my eyes, my ears. I need your help. We all do."

After a pregnant pause, Stella asked, "How did he escape from the high school?"

The chief's answer was clipped. Angry. "We don't know. But we're investigating the possibility that he had help. That's all."

She turned on her heel, and ignoring the other questions being shouted at her, led the group of officials and bigwigs out of the room.

Stella stared at the empty dais. There it was, the lead for her story. Police believe the shooter had help.

"Phone."

"Huh?" Stella dragged her eyes away from the empty podium and looked up at Art, confused.

"Your phone. You must have it on silent, but there's a call coming in, see?" He pointed to her device, and sure enough, Kenny's name and number lit up the screen.

She picked up the phone. "Hello?"

"I told you to call me when the press conference ended."

"It literally just—"

"Don't want your excuses, Stella. The AP's reporting that the school shooter had help. I want that confirmed and in your story, got it?"

"Got it." Stella disconnected and took a deep breath, gathered her bag, and followed Art outside.

As they left the building, Stella spotted McCoy chatting up a deputy. A pang of worry sliced into her stomach. What new information was he getting? She shook herself. No matter. Despite what Kenny said, she couldn't spend all her time worrying about the competition. She had her own story to get that day.

~

WHEN ART SLOWED his car to park at the gas station, Stella tapped him lightly on the arm. "You come with me, and make sure you're rolling. We might only get one chance at this."

Inside the small store, crowded with racks of snacks and candy, a hulk of a man stood behind the counter. He scowled when he caught sight of the TV camera and immediately put up a hand.

"No comment, and no recording allowed."

Art dropped the camera and leaned against a drink cooler, but Stella continued forward, glancing at the cashier's name tag before she spoke. "Max? Listen, we just wanted to check on your coworker who was injured. The police think the shooting might be related to another shooting at Rivermoor High—and I don't want your colleague's condition to get lost in the confusion. Is she okay? Can we help at all?"

He snorted. "First of all, I'm not Max. This is just the shirt that fit. Second, you don't want to help, you just want to gawk at her. Exploit her."

She shook her head. "That's not true. We can link our story to her Go Fund Me page if she needs help with medical bills. We can help publicize security footage from nearby stores that might help identify the shooter. We can do a lot for her. But we need your help too. *She* needs your help."

"She needs to get better so she can come back to work and support her kids."

"No partner at home to help?"

"No." He looked up sharply, angry with himself for sharing any details about the victim. "Listen, lady, I told you. No comment."

As she turned to leave, her eyes caught a camera perched high in the corner by the ceiling. She took a moment to obviously scrutinize the room before turning back to Not Max. "Four cameras, and no surveillance video for police?" She pulled the stack of papers that she'd gotten at the police station out of her briefcase. She'd paged through them on the ride over. "According to these police reports this business has been robbed a dozen times in the last year, and each time you've been able to give police crystal clear surveillance video of the crime. But now an employee is shot, and suddenly all four—wait, five? Is that one behind you?" Not Max ignored her, and she continued. "All five cameras are down at the same time?"

The man shrugged. "No. Comment."

Stella's lips puckered, and after a moment, she slid her business card across the counter. "Let her know I'd like to help. That's my cell phone number. She can call me anytime."

She and Art left together, and she gave him the address for the dorm where Fran, Carol Miller's granddaughter, lived. It turned out St. Agnes was in Rivermoor, so this trip was hardly out of the way. It was time to appease her mother.

She spent the short ride across town trying to remember all she could about her mother's friend's family.

Carol's youngest child was the same age as Stella's much older sister, which is how Carol's granddaughter came to be only a few years younger than Stella.

She rubbed the bridge of her nose, remembering when tragedy had struck the Millers. Carol's oldest son and daughter-in-law had been killed in a car accident. Carol and her husband had taken their granddaughter Fran in when the girl was in middle school...from somewhere around Chicago, actually. Taken her back to Cleveland to live with them. Now the girl had made it back closer to her hometown and was struggling. No wonder, really.

"This it? What are we doing here, anyway?"

Stella put a hand on the door handle. "Just a quick errand, actually. I'll be about twenty minutes, okay?"

He grumbled something about not being a car service, but agreed to find a parking spot until Stella was ready to leave.

She walked away briskly, zipping her coat quickly against the snappy gusts of winds that never seemed to falter.

She stood back from the main entrance of the dormitory, wondering how she was supposed to get in. She didn't think the girl knew she was coming, and she didn't have her phone number.

Suddenly, the door opened from the inside; a student apparently late for something hurried past her, still bleary-eyed from sleep at eleven in the morning. The student stumbled down the stairs and Stella snuck into the building without a second thought.

"Room 333," she muttered, looking down at her phone to double check the number her mother had texted her last night. She stepped over a stray sandal abandoned in the hallway and found a door to the stairwell at the end of the corridor. Huffing loudly as she ascended to the third floor, it took a few steps before she heard yelling and cursing over her own loud breathing.

Several disgruntled students peeked out into the hallway, faces turned toward the argument, their expressions guarded and curious at the same time.

Stella would have smiled at the memory of having to live so closely to so many people, until she realized she was headed right for the argument.

The door to Room 333 stood wide open, and as she hesitated a few feet away, a large textbook flew into the hallway, smacking the opposite wall with a *thwack* that made her jump.

Before she could change her mind, she picked up the book and walked into the room.

8

"Who are *you*?" A girl with wild yellow hair said, another textbook frozen in her hands. Her full curly hair bounced as she spoke, her face red from the exertion of her angry fit.

"Fran?" Stella ventured. The girl nodded even as her eyes narrowed suspiciously. Stella pushed into the small room. There was a total of about two feet of open floor space. The college had crammed in two beds and desks, and Fran and her roommate had added a large flat-screen TV and a small refrigerator.

"I'm Stella. Your grandmother asked me to check in on you." She held the textbook-turned-missile out gingerly. "Is this yours?"

Fran snatched the book from Stella and tossed it into an open backpack hanging off the end of the closest desk chair. Her lips pressed together like she wanted to say something, but the sound of someone clearing their throat lightly from the far side of the room drew Stella's attention. A girl with straight dark hair sat on the floor, tucked in next to the wooden bedframe. Her shirt was tattered at the collar. It was either a fashion statement or very old. A deep baritone hummed tunelessly, and when Stella took another step into the room, she saw a man—boy, she supposed—sitting between the roommate and the wall. Dark goggle-like glasses covered his eyes and he stared straight ahead without acknowledging Stella.

She looked from the strange couple to her mother's best friend's granddaughter. "Should I come back?" She raised an eyebrow delicately, and Fran's red face flushed a brighter shade.

"No. No—I was just leaving anyway."

Fran grabbed a jacket from the back of the closest desk chair, slung the backpack over her shoulder, and turned without a word toward the door.

"Bye, Fran," the roommate called. "See you at dinner?"

"Bye, Tandy," Fran mumbled.

Tandy shot Stella an apologetic smile. The guy—a friend? Her boyfriend?—continued to stare at the opposite wall ahead. A flash of light and a muted *tut-tut-tut* pierced Stella's subconscious. The roommate raised a shoulder and dropped it with a wry smile, then turned her attention forward too. Understanding clicked into place with the next burst of machine gun fire. A second, small TV lit their faces as the young man manipulated the controller of a gaming system in his hands.

She smiled and stepped out into the hallway, gently closing the door behind her. Fran waited at the end of the hallway by the stairwell door.

"Gram sent you?"

"Well," Stella clarified, "she and my mother combined are a force to be reckoned with." Fran's lips quirked up, even as her eyes filled with tears. "Hey, why don't you tell me what's going on? It's probably not as bad as you think it is."

Stella's phone buzzed deep inside her pocket. She took it out as they made their way down the steps to find a message from an unknown Chicago area code. *I know what you did. And I'll get you back.*

Her stomach lurched. *I know what you did*? Was this from Malcolm, still angry over her interview that morning? Her finger hesitated over the screen. Her first instinct was to call the number immediately to confront whoever sent the text, but something stopped her. She tucked the phone away; probably better to ignore it.

At the bottom of the stairwell, Fran led the way to a bustling cafeteria off the back of the lobby. "Coffee?"

Stella grimaced, thinking about the kind of coffee likely available in a college cafeteria, but followed Fran to a clean counter with a massive espresso machine and milk frother.

Fran placed her order with the barista and swiped her card. "Did you want anything?"

"Wow. This is just—included?" Stella remembered back to her own dorm cafeteria, with its limp salads and lukewarm baked-potato bar. Nothing like this high-end café in the mix.

"Well, not included, per se, but part of my meal plan. They don't take cash, so if you want something..." She looked over her shoulder at Stella, and her face broke into a legitimate grin at Stella's expression of joy.

After the two women were settled with their drinks, Stella leaned forward toward Fran. "So, what's going on? My mom said you were having trouble with a class or something?" Fran's eyes dropped down to her drink and she didn't answer. After a minute, Stella said, "Are you failing a *few* classes?" Still no response. "Pregnant?"

At that, Fran choked on her drink, shaking her head decisively. "God, no! No—not pregnant." She laughed shakily, then added under her breath, "If only it were so simple."

Stella set her coffee cup down. "Is there anything I can do to help, Fran?"

Fran placed her mug on the table too, but kept her eyes glued to the milky brown liquid. She turned the cup so the handle was set to nine o'clock, and her expression was so troubled that Stella's own stomach squeezed painfully.

"Did you ever find yourself in a situation that felt...impossibly real, but also decidedly fictional?"

Stella's lips twitched. She'd forgotten the overblown dramatics of college life. "Well...not really, no. Not a lot of fiction in my life these days." Fran's eyebrows knitted together uncertainly, and Stella explained, "I'm a reporter. It's all research and facts, you know?"

The girl nodded slowly and made a sound in the back of her throat that could have meant acknowledgement or despair.

Stella reached out impulsively and laid her hand over Fran's. "What I do know is that most things aren't as bad as they initially seem, if you just address them head on. Face up to it. Can I help you do that in any way?" Her phone buzzed again, but she ignored it.

Fran's teeth pressed into her bottom lip, leaving white slash marks when she finally spoke. "I don't think...I mean, I don't know..."

"Is it classes?"

She snorted. "No. Classes are fine."

"Friends?"

"What are friends?" Fran snatched her hand away and stared moodily at her drink again.

Stella suppressed a sigh. Friends, then. The transition from high school to college could be difficult. Some people made their friends in kindergarten and their group never changed again, all through high school. To suddenly be thrown into a whole new ocean of people at college could be a harsh adjustment.

Fran's lips pursed as she thought. "I think I know what friendship looks like, and even friendly people, but what I'm encountering here..."

Stella's phone buzzed again and she slipped it unobtrusively out of her pocket and read the screen under the table so Fran wouldn't notice. Three texts had come rapid fire from the same unknown number. *You're on my turf now. Payback will be swift. Justice complete.*

Stella must have made a face, because Fran stopped mid-sentence, flustered.

"You think I'm crazy."

Stella shoved her phone between her leg and the seat cushion and looked up. What had she missed? "Umm—no. Fran, you're not crazy, okay?" She hoped that was true. "Why don't you start from the beginning?"

Fran blew out a frustrated breath and sat back in her seat, her springy blond curls bouncing for an extra second after her body stopped. "There's...there's something strange going on with a...a friend here. And...my gut tells me that what they're doing is dangerous, and that someone might get hurt." She swore, her eyes finding Stella's and holding them steady. "I don't know, maybe someone already is hurt. But when I brought it up with my...friend...I guess it sounds like *I'm* the one with problems."

"Okay." Stella drew the single word out for an extra beat, still not understanding Fran. Was there actually a friend, or was she trying to hide the fact that she was talking about herself?

"My friend makes me feel crazy whenever I bring it up, and well..." She stared off over Stella's left shoulder, deep in thought. "It's true, I'm sleep deprived, and yes, occasionally I party too much, and yes, college is much harder than high school ever was. But really! None of that surprises me. But the fact that I'm questioning my own mind, I've just never..." Her eyes snapped back to Stella's, suddenly sharp and focused. "How do you know when to trust your gut, and when it's just your imagination running away with you? How can you possibly tell the difference?"

Wow. Stella hadn't been expecting such an abstract but searching question away from work, and she was glad to have her coffee as an excuse for a couple extra seconds to think. She drank deeply, finally coming up for air when the tears pooling in Fran's eyes threatened to spill over.

"I'm no expert, Fran, but it sounds like you need to go see someone official." Stella was thinking about the school's mental-health professionals; surely they had counsellors on hand to talk with students overwhelmed with all the changes to their lives as they entered university. "I'm sure the school has loads of people, ready to..."

Fran stiffened, her face losing what little color had returned over the last ten minutes.

Stella felt her own back straighten out, too. This girl had spent the last five minutes speaking in barely veiled riddles about her own mental health! She was a grown woman—or at least close to it, and maybe no one had ever told her that before. Stella girded her loins; after all, she'd promised her mother she'd do her best to help. "Fran, it's time you act your age."

The girl drew in a sharp breath.

"If you're having trouble, you need to address it head on." Stella frowned, thinking of her anonymous texter, and a sense of rightness filled her chest. If only everyone had a mentor who could speak so frankly to them, life would be easier. "Take responsibility for your actions. Trust *yourself* to know when you should seek out the authorities for help. You're what? Eighteen? No one expects you to do all of this," she motioned to the room at large, "on your own!" Fran opened her mouth to object, but Stella spoke first and louder. "There's no shame in asking for help, Fran. Act now. My advice? Don't mess around with questioning what you know to be true."

Fran's mouth snapped shut and she stared past Stella for a long moment, then she nodded slowly. "You're right, Stella. Of course you're right." She suddenly pushed her chair back with a screech and pulled on her coat, not meeting Stella's eye. "I'm late for class. I—I've got to go. Thanks, Stella. Thanks for trying to help."

She left her mug on the table in her haste to leave, and Stella watched her heave the heavy glass door open. The girl's breath blew out in a white cloud and her shoulders rounded into themselves as she moved quickly across the diagonal path.

Stella collected their trash and carried it to the nearest waste station, feeling unsettled. She hadn't really helped, and the girl seemed just as—maybe more—distraught as ever.

As she turned to leave, though, someone tugged at her sleeve. "Oh!" Stella exclaimed, surprised by how close the person was. On second glance, it was Fran's roommate. "Is it...Sandy?"

"Tandy Scarborough. Nice to meet you." Fran's roommate's eyes never met Stella's, staring instead through the wall of windows, her eyes following Fran. "Where's she going? Is she going to be okay?"

"Ummm." Stella buttoned her coat and stepped away, unsettled by Tandy's proximity. "I don't know." The girl wore an oversized tattered sweatshirt over black leggings, and her long dark hair was now pulled back into a low ponytail.

Tandy turned her large unblinking eyes on Stella, and she felt her throat close up. The girl had an unnerving directness in her gaze, and frankly, Stella was delighted when another text gave her a reason to leave.

"I've gotta take this," she said, holding up the device.

Tandy didn't nod or blink, just stared at Stella as she turned and walked away.

~

BY THAT AFTERNOON, Stella was struggling to come up with a new exclusive angle for the story that would make her boss happy.

"Kenny says you'll lead the newscast with a live package wrap here at the school after a quick VO pop from Hank," Art said.

Stella nodded at this jumble of familiar letters and words, understanding immediately what it all meant, and bent over her story, her back not happy with the hard springs in the seat of Art's car. They were parked in the high school parking lot with permission from the superintendent, waiting on Conrad to arrive with the satellite truck. At a sharp knock on her window, she turned.

"Oh. Malcolm," Stella muttered, then hesitated, not reaching out for the door handle. He'd used his cell phone to get her attention, and still held it in front of his body.

"You're not gonna talk to him?" Art asked incredulously.

"No, I just don't know—oh, is this it?" She saw a shiny silver arm near the door handle and started cranking. The window rolled down slowly. "What's up?"

McCoy's eyes narrowed. "I just want to set the record straight."

Stella steeled herself mentally, then climbed out of the car, having no desire to allow Malcolm to stand over her. As she slammed the door shut behind her, she tapped the screen of her cell phone and called the number that had been leaving her threatening text messages all day. She figured if McCoy's phone rang in his hand, she could confront him.

But it didn't, and Stella was so surprised—she'd been so certain that he was the one texting her anonymously—that she missed the beginning of his rant, only tuning in when her phone call disconnected. Whoever had been sending her angry text messages didn't even have voicemail set up.

She glanced up at McCoy when Art cleared his throat uncomfortably.

"I let my bosses know that you screwed me over with that interview." McCoy's head tilted to the side, like he was thinking about what to say next. "And I think you already know that you took away my chance to get on network. I should have been live Monday night with this story, not you. You know what they say, Stella." He drew her name out, two distinct syllables. "Payback's a bitch."

She rolled her eyes. "I was just the messenger on that interview, McCoy, and your bosses only care that they had access to it; which they did, since I shared it with your station, despite your unprofessional attitude toward me. As for ruining your network debut, you can call my boss." Stella smiled without humor. "It's so cute that you think I have any say over how I spend my workdays. I don't care if you don't want to work together on this story, McCoy, but please, stay out of my way."

He spluttered, his face turning a shade of red that bordered on purple, and opened his mouth, but it was Art who spoke.

"Watch it," he warned.

McCoy's lips snapped shut; he pivoted and stalked in the direction of his photographer, turning after he'd gone only a few steps. "I can tell they think the world of you over at NBC, Reynolds. Parking you with a crappy stringer for your time here. Good luck with *him*," he sneered, leveling an angry glare at Art.

McCoy disappeared around the other side of his news car. Stella's insides squirmed uncomfortably. She was like an island out here, a reporter without a team. No one but Art, and he was a man alone as well. And if it wasn't McCoy who'd been leaving her harassing text messages, then who was it? The phone hadn't gone to a voicemail, so she couldn't even put a voice with the number.

Her shoulders slumped; she could never have imagined how isolating this job would be when she'd signed on two years earlier. At the time, she'd been a weekend anchor, with a news team that she mostly enjoyed spending time with. Now she was alone most of the time or working with someone she'd only just met.

A metal clanking sound from the school building was just the distraction she needed from her infuriatingly woebegone attitude. A woman in a stylish black wool winter coat walked out of the school, her gait awkward from the burden of two heavy-looking file boxes.

"Oh!" Stella muttered under her breath as the woman's foot hit the uneven seam of a sidewalk and she stumbled, the boxes flying out of her hands, the papers scattering in the wind. The woman splayed forward on the walk headfirst, her hands barely making it up in time to protect her face.

Stella pushed away from Art's car and hurried across the empty lot, around the makeshift display of flowers and balloons, and crouched down by the heap on the ground.

The woman moaned, more papers fluttered, and then the muffled ring of a school bell sliced into the otherwise still air.

"Last bell," the woman said, pushing herself up to sit cross legged on the sidewalk. She tucked a silvery lock of hair behind her ear, then fingered a tear in her pant leg. "My favorite jeans," she said ruefully.

"Are you all right?" Stella asked. When the woman nodded, Stella jumped up and started gathering the papers, stomping on one to keep it from flying away.

"Don't bother. I was taking them to the Dumpster anyway."

Stella continued to grab at the slippery pages and eventually the other woman joined in. Soon they had both boxes full to bursting, the papers shoved in willy nilly. Each woman carried one toward the large metal trash container at the edge of the property.

"I didn't know anyone was here today," Stella said. "You going to make it home all right? It looked like you knocked your head pretty hard."

"I'm fine. A fitting end to this day, actually."

Stella raised her eyebrows and the other woman shrugged lightly. "Meaning it's been a terrible day, obviously." She tilted her head to one side, her eyes narrowed. "I never forget a face, and I certainly recognize you, but I'm not sure why."

"I'm Stella Reynolds, NBC News. Here to cover the shooting."

"Of course."

"And you are?" Stella asked. The woman was small and thin, with beautifully applied makeup. Despite her recent encounter with the sidewalk, her silver hair glistened in the winter sunlight, falling in soft waves past her shoulders in a style that looked effortless, but Stella knew from experience took at least thirty minutes to pull off with a fancy curling iron and finishing spray. Not a usual look for a high school teacher.

"Madeline Mowery. I'm the theater teacher here."

The name shook something loose in Stella's brain. "Right, of course. I read about you in the paper. You're getting ready to retire, right? You taught Sophia Thomas when she was younger."

"One of many students with talent, but more importantly, determination and heart. If you don't have that, you won't excel at anything. Would you agree, Stella?"

Stella felt an unusual weight to the teacher's words, and she considered the question thoughtfully. "These days talent and luck can get you pretty far...but yes, I agree. To go from good to great, you've got to be able to shift to another gear."

"A driving analogy?" Madeline asked, a twinkle in her eye. Stella flushed slightly, and the teacher smiled. "I read the papers too, Ms. Reynolds."

"Then you know I spend more time at the track than most." Stella shifted her attention to the file box in her arms. "Preparing for retirement?"

Madeline grimaced. "Yes. You'd be surprised what one can accrue in a classroom over a career teaching. I'm trying to clean out a bit as I go. Of course, this week's events have certainly given me more time for that than I'd expected. Not," she looked up at Stella, her eyes narrowed again, "that I'm calling it a silver lining or anything. We're all devastated by what happened Monday morning. Just devastated."

"Of course."

"And we're not supposed to talk to the media, although God

knows the school could use someone with a bit more personality to go on camera and plead for help identifying the shooter."

Stella nodded, thinking of the boring and monotonous superintendent from the press conference at the police department.

"However, Ms. Reynolds, I'm afraid our principal made it very clear that no one from the school is allowed to comment to anyone in the media about anything."

"Fair enough."

Madeline lifted her box up to rest on the top edge of the Dumpster and then gave it a shove. It banged to the bottom of the metal box with an echoey boom. She brushed her hands together, fixing Stella with an unblinking stare. "I'm sure we'll meet again, Ms. Reynolds."

Stella watched Madeline Mowery walk to a sleek black sedan, lower herself elegantly into the driver's seat, and start up the engine. It actually purred. Wow. Either Mowery was making some kind of residual money from her long-gone days as a soap star, or being a teacher paid more than it used to.

Stella stared after the car as it pulled out of the parking lot and disappeared around the corner, then, checking to see that no one from the school was looking, she nonchalantly tucked the second box of papers under her arm and headed back to Art's car.

Was Madeline Mowery doing a little pre-retirement cleanup as she'd said, just thirty hours after a school shooting? Maybe. But maybe there'd be something interesting in the file box.

She hefted the box up as she walked and spoke aloud, just to hear her own voice say it. "This. This is why I'm here. To find out who's hiding what and why."

Art got out of the car with his lighter and a pack of smokes. Stella took the time alone in his car to pluck a page out at random and smooth the creases flat against her pants. Her heart rate accelerated, her stomach clenching like it always did when she was working on something new, something only she might have. She scanned the first sheet, then the second, her brain attempting to draw out any significance from the words.

Then she lowered the papers, a sense of disappointment

speeding time back up again. It didn't look important: an old essay along with teacher evaluation pages, the name of the teacher missing.

She felt disproportionally disappointed for the loss of something that never was.

"Stella?"

She turned toward Art's voice, hastily tucking the pages back into the box, feeling suddenly guilty at having them. "Yes?"

"We've got a problem. Kenny wants to talk to you. Now."

9

"Of course we can incorporate the picture into the story. We have plenty of time." Stella walked laps around Art's car, wishing that Conrad would show up at the school already with the satellite truck.

Kenny Decker growled his next words. "The problem is, we don't have the picture yet. Your police chief out there says she'll send it to us, but we can't know if it will come in time."

"Leave that to me. I'll make sure we get it and send it back so graphics can work something up."

"Make it happen, Stella." Kenny disconnected and Stella climbed into the passenger seat of Art's car and immediately called the chief's admin.

"Wanda, I hear you're releasing a picture of the shooting suspect?"

"My, word does travel fast," Wanda said. "Yes. Chief Sterling is finalizing the details now, and we should be able to send the picture out to all media outlets by six o'clock tonight."

Stella squashed a groan. Chicago was in the Central time zone, and that meant that network news was live from five thirty to six p.m. She needed that picture sent to her by five—five fifteen at the latest—so the graphic designers in New York would have time to plug it into the newscast.

"Wanda," she said, "I know Hank wants to have the very latest information available on his newscast, and I'm sure the other networks feel the same."

"Chief Sterling wants the local stations to have it first."

"Why?"

"She's working under the assumption that the shooter is still here in town, so that's where her focus is."

"But, Wanda, we have incredible reach! We can get that picture in front of three million people within two minutes of our newscast starting. That's a lot of eyeballs to skip over." Stella waited a beat, hoping she'd persuaded Wanda.

"Hank needs it?" Wanda asked.

"Yes."

"If *he* asked me for it, I don't know how I'd be able to refuse."

Stella wanted to groan. "Hank can't ask you himself, but I'm asking you for him. We need that picture, Wanda!"

Silence met her final request, but Stella waited. Sometimes the best strategy was to say nothing at all. Sure enough, after thirty painfully long seconds, Wanda blew out a sigh.

"I'll email it to you now, Stella. You let Hank know that we did our best for him tonight, okay?"

"I definitely will, Wanda. Thank you! Hey, how did the chief get the picture anyway? I thought all the cameras were down at both the Stop N Shop and the school?"

"Apparently the owner of the convenience store was able to get one still shot out of his system."

"Huh." Stella frowned; either the system was broken or it wasn't. It didn't make sense that a single frame of video could be salvaged, but not the rest of the data from Monday morning. Those were questions for another day, though. She gave the admin her email address and cell phone number, not wanting to take any chances that a miscommunication could derail her live shot, then set about rewriting her story.

Art tapped the window to get her attention. "Conrad's here."

Stella nodded and kept working, refreshing her phone every few minutes, waiting on the picture.

Eventually, she moved from Art's car to the satellite truck, glancing across the parking lot as she walked. McCoy leaned up against a news car, chatting on his phone. He leisurely smoked a cigarette, his stance relaxed. She wondered if he knew about the picture yet.

Usually she'd share the information; after all, a reporter working for the same affiliate was technically on her team.

But not this guy. She assuaged her guilt by reminding herself that his station would get the email at six, according to Wanda. Plenty of time to get it into their newscast.

During her career, time occasionally dragged on. Stella couldn't even count the number of city commission or zoning board meetings she'd had to cover in her local news days where two hours felt like ten. But today, each minute flew by faster than the last, and no matter how often she refreshed her email, there was nothing new from the chief's office.

Stella paced in front of the truck. Time was running out. Wanda wasn't answering her phone, and now the tech team in New York was getting antsy.

After a fourth call went straight to Wanda's voicemail, Stella groaned in frustration.

The groan turned to a gasp when the silver gleam of a bumper flashed in her peripheral vision. Instinctively she stepped back, barely avoiding an oncoming car.

Malcolm McCoy smirked at her as he sped past, needlessly close to her on his way out of the parking lot.

Confused, Stella looked back. His photographer was still there, setting up lights for his live shot. Did McCoy just find out about the picture? Was he on his way to get a copy from the police station?

More importantly, should she do the same thing?

Just then, her phone pinged with an incoming email. Stella looked down. Praise the Lord! Wanda had come through.

She forwarded the email to her producer in New York, then sent Kenny a text letting him know too.

"Stella, we're ten minutes away. Are you ready?" Art asked.

She nodded, then popped in her earpiece and raced back into the satellite truck. She had just enough time to fix her hair and makeup before leading off the evening newscast live from Rivermoor High.

~

"STELLA, GREAT JOB TONIGHT," Kenny said. The praise startled her so much that she couldn't find words to answer. "The other networks didn't have that photo, and that's the kind of breaking news I want us to lead with every night. Take a break. Go get dinner. Then check back in. I want to know what your plan is for tomorrow."

As she disconnected and slipped the phone into her pocket, a car raced through the parking lot, tires squealing as it skidded to a stop. McCoy jumped out. He was too far away for Stella to hear, but she recognized the excited motions of a reporter who had an incredible scoop. Her stomach dropped. What had he uncovered? What phone calls had McCoy, with his local connections built on years of working in the Chicagoland market, been able to make?

Art, winding a heavy light cord around his arm, blew out a noisy breath. "Head on in, Stella. See what he's got. I'll take care of everything out here."

Union rules dictated that Stella wasn't allowed to help wind cords or put away light kits, but it was a kind sentiment from Art nonetheless.

She climbed the steps into the sat truck and heaved open the door.

"Hey, Lala, great job tonight. Uh-oh." Conrad froze in the middle of shutting down power to the bank of TV monitors when he caught her expression. "What happened?" He pushed the extra seat toward her with his foot. It rolled noisily on squeaky casters, and she caught it before it tumbled out the open door.

She shrugged out of her winter coat. "Can you pull up the local NBC station?"

"Sure, have a seat. I'll put it on monitor three."

He reached up to a control panel and flipped a few switches. The third small monitor in a bank of ten changed from fuzzy black and white snow to a crisp, clear image of the local anchors teasing the next block of news. The anchors cut to McCoy, with a final tease of his story before a commercial break. His words sent a chill down her spine.

"A local NBC exclusive, as someone connected to the shooting at Rivermoor High turns themself into police. I'll have the latest, right after this."

Her phone buzzed, a message from Kenny. *This should be interesting*.

She pulled at the collar of her shirt, which seemed to be constricting her breathing, even though it was a V-neck and nowhere near her throat.

After the commercial, McCoy launched right into his story.

"We have exclusive video for you tonight of a person of interest —a suspect, even—in the police investigation into the shooting at Rivermoor High."

Conrad moved closer and turned up the volume. Stella only had a picture of the shooter. If Malcolm had video of the guy, it was a great scoop.

"Take a look at this video just back from the police station."

Stella gasped. In the back of a cruiser, a *woman* stared plaintively out the window at the camera. The editor had slowed the video down, stretching the short clip of the police car passing the camera into thirty-seconds of video.

Stella shook her head in shock as Malcolm continued breathlessly.

"The shooting suspect, a student at St. Agnes College, has been transported to the Rivermoor City Jail, and my sources tell me she'll be booked into the system on unknown charges." He continued on with a recap of the shooting at the high school while Stella stared, open-mouthed, at the small TV screen.

She flicked a button after his story wrapped and rewound the feed, freezing it on a shot of the woman—girl, really—sitting in the back of a police car.

"That the school shooter, Lala?" Conrad asked, whistling low under his breath. "Don't hear about lady shooters that often, do you?"

"I don't know." She squinted up at the screen, right into the face of her mother's best friend's granddaughter. The girl Stella had met just hours earlier. She searched the frozen image of Fran Miller's face through the blurred lines of the freeze frame. "McCoy said she's a suspect in their investigation. That would be major news. If it's true."

Conrad rubbed his chin thoughtfully. "How do you think he found her? Did McCoy say she's a student here in town? Where is St. Agnes? I've never even heard of it."

Stella wasn't aware that her mouth was open until Conrad's finger pressed up under her chin. She snapped her jaw together and reached up to turn off the monitor. "I don't know how he found her, but St. Agnes is only a few minutes away from the high school."

He sighed and pushed her phone, sitting a few feet away on the desk by the door toward her. "I'd say Kenny is gonna call in three, two..."

But in fact, several minutes passed with no sound from her phone. The time did nothing except increase the tension in her shoulders and neck. What could Kenny possibly be waiting for? But perhaps more importantly, had she somehow inspired Fran to turn herself in to the police? Had the girl been planning to confess to Stella that morning? Had she somehow missed the scoop of a lifetime—or at least the week—by being distracted when she sat down with the girl? She couldn't believe that the uncertain teen she'd spoken to that morning was somehow involved in the shooting at a high school.

Finally, her screen lit up with an incoming call. As she reached out to answer and face Kenny's wrath, though, the number changed under her finger—a second incoming call—and before she could react, she'd connected with her mother.

10

"Dammit!" Stella muttered, wondering if she could disconnect the call quickly and still get to her boss.

"What?" Beth Reynolds said. "Oh, are we playing the swearing game? Okay...shoot."

"Mom, that's not even a swear word. How about sh—"

"You're not going to teach me anything at my age, Stella," Beth interrupted. "Where have you been? I've been trying to reach you for over an hour!"

"I've been getting scooped by another reporter, and I might just get fired because of it."

Conrad squeezed her shoulder and then walked out the side door of the satellite truck, giving her privacy.

Talk about getting fired brought her mother up short. "Because of Fran?"

"Yes, because of Fran."

"Oh, honey. I'm so sorry you're in this mess, but of course it's why I'm calling. Carol called right after that awful, and *awfully* inaccurate, story ran about Fran, and she's so thankful to you for your guidance and support, even if it did lead to her daughter looking like a deranged lunatic. She doesn't blame you one bit; she wanted me to tell you that."

Stella rubbed a hand over her face, belatedly realizing that she was wearing thick, heavy makeup. "Dammit."

"Stella, honey, I told you I'm not playing that game. Carol wants you to know that Fran left them a message earlier today, and she's certainly not a suspect. Good heavens! Can you even imagine?"

Could she trust Fran to be honest with her grandparents? Was she under arrest? It certainly had looked dire, but then again, Stella knew better than most people that what you saw on TV wasn't always a good representation of what was actually going on. "If she's not a suspect, then why was she in the back of a police cruiser?"

"Well, honey, you told her to go to the authorities! That's what Carol said, anyway."

"*I* told her to?" Stella shook her head, even though no one was there to see. She thought she'd been advising Fran to find a campus counsellor. So why would she go to the police? Was she involved in the Rivermoor shooting somehow? Or did she know about someone who was?

"And they were really happy to have you there to guide Fran. They're...relieved to know she's in the right place to get help. They knew something was wrong, and they worried. You know how parents worry. Anyway, now Fran tells them that she's safe."

"Safe? Safe from what?" Stella pressed her ear against the phone when her mother's words got muddled and hard to hear.

"Why, I don't know, now do I? But I imagine they'll tell you when they're ready!" Beth must have had the mouthpiece partially covered, because suddenly she was back at full volume. "Your father tells me I haven't said that we love you yet, and I told him that you already *know* that and I don't have to say it, but he says it's nice to hear anyway, so. We love you."

Stella dropped her head into her hands and nearly let the phone drop to the floor. "I love you guys too."

"How's John?"

Stella startled up off the chair. "John Stevenson? I don't know, Mom. We don't exactly talk anymore. Listen, I have to—"

"Oh, well, I guess that makes sense. Lucky doesn't want you to keep in touch?" Her mother's tone suggested that she wasn't surprised by such ungallant behavior.

"No, *I* don't want to. I mean, Lucky and I are serious."

"I know."

"Like, *serious* serious."

Her mother sighed out a funeral-dirge-sounding breath. "I just always liked that John fellow."

"Mom, I've got to go. Anything else?" She was rapidly running out of the energy needed to be kind.

"No. Just...take care, Stella."

"You too, Mom."

She disconnected, then tried to roll the tension out of her neck unsuccessfully before tapping Kenny's name in her contact list.

He let the phone ring once, twice, and on the third ring, Stella knew it was going to be bad. He wanted her to suffer. He finally picked up on the fourth ring.

"Kenny, listen, I know—"

"You obviously don't know anything," Kenny interrupted. The phone call had only just begun.

STELLA ONLY GOT a chance to break into her boss's litany of complaints twenty minutes into the call, when he finally asked a question.

"Hank and I both want to know: what's your plan moving forward? How are you going to fix this?"

"I'm going to call the Rivermoor Police chief and figure out what's going on with the girl. Then I'm going to find the person of interest's roommate and see what she knows."

"Oh." Kenny obviously hadn't been expecting an answer, and he wasn't sure how to respond. "And just how do you think you'll figure out where *she* lives—"

"Already have her address, Kenny. I've also spoken to a..." Stella scratched her nose, then settled on a completely accurate, if not misleading, statement. "A representative for the girl's family."

Certainly one way to describe her mother. "They won't talk to anyone right now, but the girl's *not* a suspect. McCoy's story was wrong, and the only thing we missed out on was having to air a retraction."

"*How* wrong?"

"All wrong. False. But the family won't go on the record yet. They're understandably shaken up by the smear against their daughter."

Kenny didn't answer, and Stella refused to be the one to break the silence. She trapped her phone between her shoulder and ear, then gathered some papers from the desk and shuffled them into order. Kenny cleared his throat. "Ah...that's fine. Keep me posted. We won't use you unless there's something new."

"Understood."

Kenny clicked off. She shoved the pages into her briefcase, then tapped the number for the Rivermoor police department from her recent call list.

"Chief Sterling's office. This is Wanda. How can I help you?"

"Wanda, hi. It's Stella Reynolds. Is the chief going to have any comment on the Fran Miller situation?" Stella smiled to herself when Wanda immediately corrected her.

"First of all, that girl was not arrested, and Chief Sterling is not happy with the media's reporting on this issue."

"McCoy's the only one who used that word, so you can blame him, not the media in general. Will she have a comment on why Fran is there?"

A long pause while Wanda considered her answer. "No." She lowered her voice. "After she stopped swearing at the TV, she started to wonder if the misinformation that's out there might help our case. Maybe the shooter will let his guard down if he thinks we're looking at someone else. But, Stella, off the record?"

"Yes."

"That girl was taken into protective custody *at her own request*. That's all I know."

"Protective custody? Does she know the identity of the shooter?" Stella pressed.

"Hmm." Wanda's tone was guarded. Stella wondered if someone else had walked into the room.

"Can you get me five minutes with the chief?"

"I'm sure I don't know. But like I said, no comment for now."

The call ended, and Stella rested the phone against her chin. Fran was in protective custody. That was new, and that made it newsworthy, but she'd gotten some of the information off the record. She'd have to get it on the record.

11

Stella woke early Wednesday morning and slipped out of bed without waking Lucky. She had a busy day; not only did she need to try and find Tandy and suss out what had happened with Fran, but Louise had left her a message, rescheduling her interview with Sophia Thomas for later that morning.

Stella dressed quietly and left a note for Lucky by the coffee machine, then ordered an Uber from the hotel lobby.

Rivermoor wasn't far from her downtown Chicago hotel, a pretty straight shot up Lakeshore Drive, but with the usual traffic snarl, it took more than thirty minutes to get to the St. Agnes campus.

Once again, Stella snuck into the dorm building without using the call button courtesy of a sloppy boy sporting a shaggy beard and torn backpack. He looked Stella up and down appreciatively as he held the door open. A sense of déjà vu enveloped her as she saw the same lonely sandal, now kicked to the side of the hallway—did no one clean this place?—and made her way up to the third floor.

This time, Fran's door was closed. Stella raised her fist to knock, but voices coming from inside stopped her. She leaned in close to the door to listen.

"You're leaving me, aren't you?" a man's voice, plaintive, spoke.

"What are you talking about?" a woman, her tone almost too innocent, answered.

"Just like before. Weeks without any calls or texts. Then you pop back up like nothing happened. I can't—I can't take it again." The man sounded broken. A hair away from sobbing.

A long pause, then the woman again. "I...life just got crazy, you know that. I can't have this discussion again, Dominic. The past is behind us. All that's important is the future. Let's just have fun now. Enjoy today. Enjoy this week!"

As the next long pause stretched into multiple minutes, Stella tentatively raised her fist.

Knock, knock.

The scratch of chair legs on tile and a burst of music came from behind the door. A minute later, it cracked open, and Tandy looked out, her expression guarded. "Hello?" Her eyes narrowed, as if she was trying to place Stella, but couldn't. "Can I help you?"

"Yes, I think you can. Tandy, right?" Stella pushed past the startled young woman with a smile. "We met yesterday."

"Oh...Fran's friend?"

Stella nodded, distracted by the state of the bedroom around her. It looked like move-out day. A suitcase lay open on the bed, full of clothes still on hangers, apparently taken straight off the closet rod. One of the desks was completely clear, the other filled with crumpled papers and a stack of books near an open backpack.

"Did you hear about what happened?"

Tandy looked at Stella for a long moment, then turned to the suitcase. "Happened with what?"

"With your roommate. Fran is in police custody."

Tandy's hands, smoothing out the folds in a shirt, froze, her body rigid. "Oh."

"Are you...going somewhere?" Stella stepped farther into the room and spotted the person with whom Tandy had been talking. "Oh, hello!" she called, determined to get as much information as possible out of her visit to the dorm. "We weren't introduced yesterday. You are?"

Tandy stepped between them, but the boy hadn't even noticed

Stella's question. He was, once again, completely zoned out in a video game, headset on, sunglasses covering his eyes.

"Does he go to class or anything?"

Tandy picked up two books and shoved them into her bag with a grimace. "When he can pull himself away."

Stella noted that the next book ready to be packed up was a fairy tale collection. She raised her eyebrows and motioned to the back of the room. "Boyfriend?"

Tandy's eyes narrowed. "So why are you here?"

Stella pulled out one of the desk chairs and sat down, intending to prolong her stay as long as possible. "I want to know about Fran. Do you know why she went to the police?"

Tandy stared at Stella for a moment, then plopped down in the other chair. Following Stella's gaze, she unclenched her right hand from gripping the fingers of her left hand and deliberately stretched them out before tucking them between her thigh and the chair. "I—I have no idea why she went to the police." The girl's clothes were ratty. Old and well-worn. A far cry from the stylish, fancy clothes of most people Stella had passed on the way in.

She tried another tack. "Did she mention anything about Rivermoor High?"

"No." Tandy looked up with wide eyes. "Did something happen there?"

Stella's breath whooshed out audibly. College was a great place to learn, but it could be so...so insulating. You only knew what was right in front of you. "There was a shooting there the other day. Gunman still on the run. And now some outlets are reporting that Fran had something to do with it."

"It was a man?"

"Huh?"

"The shooter at the high school. They know who it was?" Tandy asked, avoiding Stella's gaze.

"Well, they don't know, really. Right now all they're saying is that they believe it's a man—a boy. You know, in cases like this, it usually is."

Tandy glanced at her watch and stood abruptly, plucking the

book bag up from the desk opposite Stella and methodically adding books and papers to the main compartment. When the zipper rent the air with a loud *zurrrrp,* she finally looked up. "You're a news reporter?"

Stella blinked. Maybe not so insulated after all. "That's right."

"I hope you find out what Fran got herself into. She sure didn't confide anything in me."

"This can be off the record, Tandy. Completely confidential." The desk in front of the girl was nearly empty; only a single book and pen remained. Stella stood and moved closer, hoping her nearness might compel the girl to speak. "Just a quick interview. I can keep your identity secret."

"Uh..."

"What year are you guys, anyway?"

"Oh, ah...I'm a first year."

"Eighteen, then?" Stella asked, keeping her tone purposefully casual.

"Nineteen, actually."

"Great." Stella tapped open the camera app on her iPhone and surveyed the room. "Why don't you stand right there in front of the desk. With that lamp behind you, you're nothing more than a silhouette. Ready? Just a few quick questions." Stella wanted to make this fast before Tandy had time to reconsider.

"No!" Tandy's volume must have startled even her, because she sucked in a quick breath and tried to smile, but didn't lower the hand she'd flung up in front of her face to block Stella's shot. "I have no comment. I do not give you permission to put me on camera."

Damn. This girl knew the exact words to keep Stella from hitting record. But she couldn't leave without an interview. "Sure, no problem, Tandy. What can you tell me about Fran, then, off camera?"

"Um, Fran was—" Tandy winced. "I mean, Fran *is* very nice. Thoughtful. She's studious and doesn't really get in anyone's business."

"What do you mean?"

Tandy's eyes were glued to Stella's phone, and only when she'd tucked it into her back pocket did Tandy answer.

"I mean, she...she just did her thing, you know? Went to classes."

"Did you know anything about her connection to Rivermoor High School?"

"No."

"Did she mention anything in the last couple of days about the shooting there?"

"No."

Tandy wasn't giving her much to go on. Stella thought back to her first meeting of both women Tuesday morning, when they had clearly been in a fight. A fight that resulted in thrown textbooks and yelling. "How did the two of you get along, usually?"

Tandy blanched and glanced at her boyfriend. "Uh, fine. You know, normally fine."

"Any idea why she went to the police?"

"No. None." Tandy edged sideways. "I, uh, I have to go. To class, I mean."

"Really?" Stella looked pointedly at the suitcase and empty closet. Wherever Tandy was going, it wasn't just a classroom.

"Uh-huh." Tandy stared at her bag, her mouth open. "Right. So you should probably, uh...head out."

Stella pressed her lips together and considered Tandy for a moment. The girl was wound so tightly she was practically vibrating. She shook her head; she couldn't make Tandy open up to her, but Stella couldn't help feeling like Tandy would feel better if she just spoke frankly to her about whatever was going on. But after a moment of silence, it was clear that Tandy was done talking.

Stella turned and picked a final book up from the desk. It was a yearbook from Rivermoor High School. "Whoa. Is this yours?"

Tandy didn't even look up from her bag, just shook her head. "What? Oh—no. Must be Fran's."

"You're not the type to bring along your high school yearbook to college?" Stella asked lightly, but her mind raced. She knew that Fran had spent time in the Chicagoland area before her parents died. Had she gone to Rivermoor High School? Had her childhood friends gone there?

Tandy's tight laugh brought Stella back to the present. "Hardly.

Some years are best left behind." She hitched the bag over her shoulder and walked across the small room to the door. She held it open and waited.

Stella slipped a business card from her pocket and forced it into Tandy's hand.

"Call if you think of anything important," she said. With one last glance at the boy in the corner, she walked out into the hallway, the old yearbook tucked unobtrusively under her jacket.

She texted Art, and while she waited for him at the curb, she turned to the back index of the yearbook. No listing for Fran Miller. She flipped to the next page, and didn't see any sign of Tandy Scarborough, either. So whose yearbook was this?

Stella tucked the heavy book into her bag to look into later, and then replayed her conversation with Tandy about high school. It could be the greatest four years of your life or the worst. And for those who didn't care to remember, high school *was* best left behind. And who better to know about the typical kind of school shooting suspect, than the very people living through those hellish years right now.

Stella needed to track down the loners at Rivermoor High: the outliers, the ones living at the edges of the school society. They were the ones who might have a clue who the shooter was, how he escaped, and where he might be now.

12

"What, exactly, are we doing here?" Art looked with distaste at the group of skateboarders doing tricks around the front steps of the school.

"Looking for some color," Stella said, recalling how many news directors she'd worked for over the years who were desperate for interviews with "real" people: people who could give more colorful soundbites than the usually drab official press releases filled with carefully crafted phrases.

There were eight boys vying for attention on the school steps. Ironically, they dressed so alike in their attempt to be different that they might as well have been in uniform. Baggy low-rider jeans, wallet chains, graphic T-shirts with heavy metal band and anime logos. Only one stood out: the one with white blond hair. The one, Stella realized with a gasp, she'd seen acting suspiciously on the day of the shooting.

"Hey!"

At Stella's yell, the group looked over like lemmings. Art snorted, but she waved and walked closer, introducing herself as she went. When Art's camera came out, the boys were impressed.

Stella lasered in on the blond kid and asked for his name.

"I mean, I go by Wes, but this seems official. So yeah. Wesley."

"I just want to confirm again that you are eighteen?"

"Yeah. Just last week." The freshly minted adult swept his long bangs away from his eyes artfully, keeping the fringe molded close to his head. His black zip-up hoodie didn't seem warm enough for the winter weather, but then again, when did teenage boys ever use good judgement?

Stella retied her scarf to cover her neck more thoroughly and stepped close to Art. "Thank you for agreeing to speak with us. Look at me, ignore the camera, and I'll just ask you a few questions. We can stop anytime. Okay?"

"I—I feel weird saying this, but you feel so helpless, you know? When something like this happens. It's kind of nice to think I'm doing something...even if it is just talking."

"Wesley, can you tell me where you were when the shooting happened?"

"Sure, man. I was in the bathroom."

"When did you know that something was wrong?"

"Not until Mr. Granger came in, bolted the door, and shut the lights off. There were two of us in there, and we thought for sure we were busted—" He bit his lip. "Can we go off the record here?"

Stella's eyebrows shot up. "Sure. Uh, Art?" The photographer frowned in annoyance but pressed a button on the camera to stop the recording. Stella looked at the student across from her. "What's going on?"

"Well, it's just that me and my buddy were smoking weed, and we thought Granger was busting us for sure. That's what I was about to say, but then I realized that we might have gotten away with it, you know, with everything that happened after..." He shrugged, his guilty expression clearing after a moment. "I even threw the rest of it away in the Dumpster that morning, you know? So, you know, I don't necessarily want to bring it all up again."

Stella rubbed a hand across her mouth to cover a grin. She and Art shared a glance, and she cleared her throat. "No problem, Wes. We're not here to get you detention. Art?" When the camera was rolling again, she said, "Wes, why don't you start with what made you realize there was trouble in the building?"

"Well, we heard 'em. The gunshots. Sounded like a thunderclap, but then it happened again and again. I mean, the dude went right by our door. Granger actually passed out, from fright, I guess? Anyway, me and my buddy waited until it was quiet, then we opened the door. I crept down the hall, and then bam! More shots! I plastered myself against the wall, and the kid with the gun headed right for me!"

"Sounds terrifying," Stella prompted.

"I'll be honest, I didn't know what to think. I couldn't tell you what the kid looked like—I couldn't take my eyes off the gun long enough to see."

"What happened then?"

"The dude turned down the hall. Headed for the theater wing. And I didn't follow. I just slid down to the floor. It was like my legs gave up on me. I'm so glad I didn't have to run." Wesley's hand rested on his chest, as if trying to keep his heart rate down by touch.

"So you definitely didn't recognize the shooter?"

"No, man. The gun, I could probably draw from memory. But not the dude holding it."

Art looked at Stella, and when she nodded, he moved away to get a couple different shots of Wes as he and Stella chatted, in case they ended up using the interview in a story.

"I've never been inside the school, Wes. It sounds like the theater is in its own wing?"

"Yeah..." He drew the word out and flipped his bangs to the side again. "I mean, I guess? I don't go back there too often. There's this narrow hallway, and like, the orchestra room and the choir room and the theater are all back there. It's like a total maze, and really, only the nerds—I mean...uhhh...the people who take those kinds of classes go back there."

"Oh yeah? I wonder how the shooter made it out. Sounds like it'd be easy to get turned around back there."

"For sure. I had to do detention in the theater once; some bullsh—oh, excuse me—some dumb thing where I had to stack chairs after a show, and I'll be honest, the theater teacher had to lead me back out to the main hallway." He grinned, but then, as if he suddenly remembered why they'd been talking, arranged his face into a somber expression. "Well, anyway, is that all?"

"Yes, Wes. Thanks for your time."

He pressed down hard on the edge of his skateboard and it spun around in a tight radius, then he stepped on, and Stella was glad to see Art capture the whirr of wheels against blacktop as Wes took a long arcing path around the still-growing memorial at the school's front door before disappearing around the side of the building to find his friends.

She stared at the building, wondering how someone that no one recognized managed to walk into the school, shoot four people, and then disappear through the tricky maze of the theater wing without being caught. It seemed unlikely that an adult, especially someone with no connection to the school, could pull that off.

She could press Chief Sterling for information with the tip from one loner at the school, but better to have a corroborating witness. Someone else who could confirm the shooter's escape path. Her eyes lingered on the building, sunlight glinting off the glass door as it opened.

Stella stepped forward with a friendly wave. "Excuse me—just a quick question?" She held her hand above her head, nearly pumping her fist when the woman gave her a jerky nod.

The woman was nervous, that much was obvious. She waited at the edge of the sidewalk, but when Stella got close, she walked toward the parking lot slowly, her head down, not making eye contact.

The woman's eyes darted around the parking lot and she clutched her chest when she saw the giant lens of Art's camera pointed her way. "Not on camera! We're not allowed to talk on camera. The principal made that clear."

Stella waved Art off and nodded reassuringly at the woman. "You're with the school?"

"Kathy Brimstone. I'm the head admin in the office."

"Kathy, I don't have a microphone, and my photographer's not recording. We won't put you on the news. You have my word." Then, to illustrate the message to the twitchy woman, she slowly drew a hand across her neck in the universal sign for "cut it." Art heaved the camera off his shoulder and headed toward his car.

That taken care of, Stella turned to look at the admin. She had collapsed against her car, her skin pale and drawn, almost gray around her eyes. Stella reached out and touched her sleeve. "Are you okay?"

The woman laughed humorlessly. "Hardly. Then again, I don't think any of us will ever be okay again."

Stella nodded understandingly. "I've never been through something like this, but I have interviewed many people who have. The ones who seem to get through it the best go to counseling. They talk through all their emotions. And I hear that at some point it's not the first thing you think about every day anymore. How long have you worked here, Kathy?"

The woman looked at Stella thoughtfully. "I've been the school secretary here for twenty-some-odd years."

"Bet you know everyone in the building *and* their families."

Kathy laughed, a little more warmly this time. "Flattery will get you nowhere, young lady." She shifted her salt-and-pepper hair away from her eyes with the back of her hand and smiled ruefully. "Actually, who am I kidding? Flattery will get you everywhere. But I was serious before." Her eyes shifted back to Art. "Nothing on camera. What do you need?"

"I heard the shooter escaped through the theater wing. Is that true?"

Kathy glanced guiltily over her shoulder at the building and motioned Stella closer. "That's the detectives' working theory. I heard them talking to the principal about it yesterday."

Stella pulled her hair away from her face and held it to the crown of her head while she tried to figure out how to phrase a follow-up question. She didn't want to accuse anyone of anything, but at the same time...

Kathy saved her the trouble. "They must've had inside help; you're right to think it." Stella must have looked as surprised as she felt, because Kathy smiled briefly before continuing. "The shooter knew the building well enough that they either had help or went to school here themself. It's possible," she added, at Stella's curious look. "I mostly know the standout kids, both good and bad. Sports stars, academic standouts, and the kids who are always in trouble. That means there are a good many that I don't know. All the kids who don't come into the office with any regularity."

Stella let her hair fall back down around her shoulders and dug into her briefcase for her notebook. "Are you saying that police believe the shooter had help from an existing student or staff member?"

Kathy held her gaze for several long seconds, then nodded slowly. "Don't quote me, but yes. The shooter either had knowledge of the school or had help from someone with knowledge of the school." She gave Stella a quick, tight smile, then climbed into her car and drove away without a backward glance.

Stella stared after the car until it disappeared around a turn, then patted her pockets, trying to find her phone. She needed to call the chief and ask about the theater situation.

"Stella!" Art called from the other side of the parking lot.

Her pockets were empty, which meant she must have left her phone in the car. She hurried over to check. "What?" She zipped past Art and reached into the car to scoop her phone off the seat. Five missed calls?

"Conrad says you're supposed to be at the Westin downtown. You've got an interview with Sophia Thomas that starts in fifteen minutes." Art scratched his chin pensively as Stella swore.

How could she have forgotten? "Crap. What's traffic like this time of day, Art?"

"Twenty, twenty-five minutes, no problem. Hey, he's not talking about *the* Sophia Thomas, is he? If so, can I come? I could run audio or something?"

"You have to get us there on time first."

She climbed into the car and he followed suit, muttering, "Challenge accepted."

Her stomach swooped as he gunned the gas. That last direction might have been a mistake. She grabbed the handle above the door and held on tight, glancing at the clock. She was no closer to having a confirmed update on the shooting for the evening news and about to spend the next two hours working on a different story altogether.

She grimaced, knowing what Kenny would think about the situation, then nearly screamed when they came within inches of another car.

"We're fine, jeez," Art said, irritation coming through clearly in his tone.

Stella unshrugged her shoulders. Well. Maybe they wouldn't make it anywhere. She considered whether the news of her and Art's death could be the first time her missing a breaking story actually made Kenny happy.

13

They needn't have rushed. Sophia Thomas was late. *Late*, late, which was fine by Stella. She had spent the last hour in the small hotel-room bathroom attempting to corral her hair and makeup into some semblance of style.

Conrad whistled low when she came out. "Looking good, Lala."

She squinted as a sudden flare of light burned into her pupils.

"Ha!" Art snorted, swiveling the light back around to the chair where Sophia would sit. "Wanted to give you a taste of the spotlight."

Stella swallowed a sigh, then dabbed at her watering eyes with the edge of a tissue and tried not to mess up the eyeliner and mascara that she'd just applied.

Conrad edged Art out of the way to reset the light and shot Stella a look that made it clear he wasn't any happier about Art's presence than she was.

Knock, knock.

Art moved faster than Stella thought possible to beat anyone else to the front of the room, wiping his hands on the seat of his pants. He pulled the door open so hard that it rebounded off the doorstop and smacked him right in the face. "Erff!"

Louise Barr, Sophia Thomas's assistant, stood in the open doorway. She threw both hands over her mouth and gasped. "Oh my God! Are you okay?"

"Who're you?" Art managed to say, before he snorted deeply, bringing up enough snot from his throat that Stella nearly gagged at the sound. He whipped a handkerchief out of his back pocket and loudly spit into it, then wadded it up and shoved it back into his pants.

Louise stared at him, mouth agape.

Stella cleared her own throat (much more delicately) and stepped in front of the cameraman.

"Louise, hello again. How are you?"

She steered Louise by the elbow into the room past Art, and Conrad smiled encouragingly at the beautiful woman.

"I'm fine. Really good, thanks." She shot a furtive glance behind her at Art, then seemed to shake herself as she turned back to Stella. "So, ah, Sophia is on her way. Should be here any minute."

Stella took the press packet that Louise handed over, and while Conrad walked Louise through the specifics of the interview, she took the free moment to page through the documents.

Only snippets of this interview would air during the fundraising gala this weekend, so Stella didn't have the weight of breaking any news today. She didn't have to worry about finding a never-before-heard story for air. The entire interview was going to focus on Lucky's charity and why Sophia Thomas supported it, with the goal of moving people to give money Saturday night.

And yet...

Her boss made it clear that if anything interesting popped up, she should let the producers know, and they might farm the clips out to entertainment programs at NBC.

Rumor had it that Sophia recently had a falling out with a major director, so Stella would have to ask about that. She wrinkled her nose, thinking that just once, wouldn't it be nice to just do a happy, fun interview? One with no controversy? Her musings were interrupted when the door rattled with a light knock.

Art lurched forward, then stopped and rubbed his jaw, apparently deciding that he might make a better impression if he stayed exactly where he was.

Louise and Conrad were still deep in conversation about the interview process, so Stella walked across the room and, carefully, opened the door.

"Stella Reynolds, so nice to finally meet you." Sophia Thomas's hands embraced Stella's own warmly. The woman radiated star quality; her dark brown hair fell effortlessly into an adorable pixie cut. Her manicure was glossy and unchipped. Even her smile was perfect.

"Thank you so much for agreeing to the interview," Stella said, welcoming the other woman into the room and giving quick introductions.

Art managed to grunt out a greeting but didn't move from his spot by the couch after the movie star smiled at him.

Louise handed Sophia the microphone, then expertly blocked her from the room as the star threaded the cord up under her shirt and clipped the end to her collar.

The assistant turned. "We've got thirty minutes set aside for the interview, hopefully enough time for the sit down and a walk-and-talk if you need it?" She looked questioningly at Stella.

"Yes, that sounds great."

Stella and Sophia took their seats and waited for Conrad to get the lights and audio volumes just right. Finally, it was time to get started.

Stella hadn't done many celebrity interviews, but she usually liked to start with some softball questions to make her interview subject relax a bit, and she'd planned the same thing for Sophia.

Sophia cleared her throat. "I suppose you need to ask me about the Chiblawsky situation?"

"Oh, um...yes." Stella was caught off guard, and shelved the rest of her softball questions. "Some media reports are saying the...that there was a...some kind of falling out. Can you tell me what happened?" Stella winced at the poor sentence construction.

"Martina Chiblawsky is such a gifted director; of course any actor considers themself lucky to be in her orbit. We are on very good terms, despite the recent reports to the contrary."

Stella inclined her head, noticing that Louise leaned forward nervously until that very rehearsed and canned answer of Sophia's was done.

"But what about the push heard 'round the world?" Stella asked, referring to a very public spat the two had had outside a Starbucks in LA, where Sophia used both hands to forcefully shove the director away—caught on camera by at least half of the dozen trailing crews of paparazzi.

Sophia nodded shortly. "Just a difference of opinion. Quickly sorted right out."

"So...you're on good terms with Chiblawsky?"

"That's right. Very good terms."

"And is she on good terms with you?"

Sophia's lips ticked up slightly before she tamped down her obvious amusement at Stella's question. "That's right. Excellent terms. As I said, she's a legendary director. Legendary. Now. Let's talk about Lucky's charity."

Stella smiled too, aware of the dismissal, and happy to take it. After all, she wasn't an entertainment reporter. She was here to get things ready for the gala. "Tell me how you got involved in Lucky's charity, Drive 4 Education."

Sophia smiled more genuinely and seemed to exhale at the same time. "I've been donating money for years to a local suicide prevention group, after a boy—a boy in my class took his life my senior year in high school. Mental health is so precarious for teens—maybe even more so today with cell phones and social media. But I also believe that education is the ticket out of nearly any situation you may find yourself in, whether you're poor, out of work, or unhappy in life. A good education is the foundation to make a change for the better, and when Lucky asked me to be an ambassador for the foundation, I jumped at the chance."

Stella asked a few questions about Sophia's other charity, and from there, the interview went smoothly, touching on Sophia's donation, how many kids the foundation would help this year, and their goals moving forward.

When Louise tapped her watch, indicating their time was almost over, Stella decided she already had plenty of great soundbites.

"Thank you so much, Sophia. You know, in the end it was a good thing we got our Monday schedule mixed up, because Conrad and I had to run out that morning to cover the shooting in Rivermoor. You grew up there, is that right?"

"Correct. Terrible business with the shooting this week. Just awful. What's the latest on all the kids' conditions?"

"Looks like everyone from the school will make a full recovery."

Sophia sighed. "Thank God."

"Would you care to make a comment about what happened Monday morning at your alma mater?"

"Me?" Sophia's expression closed up, her eyes shifting away from Stella, away from the camera. "It was a terrible thing, just awful, and senseless, and..." She glanced at her assistant, her expression oddly panicky, then she stood abruptly, beckoning Louise over with her hand. "I think our time must be up," Sophia said, already heading for the door.

"Yes, we'll need just a few more minutes for the walk and—" Stella started, but Sophia waved her off, sending a pointed look at Louise.

The assistant jumped, her mouth moving soundlessly for a moment before she recovered her wits. "Err, yes. We have something scheduled that I, uh...I completely forgot about. Sorry, Stella. I'm sure you can use other video of Sophia to fill out the story."

Sophia wrenched the door open, and Louise hurried after her, shooting an apologetic look over her shoulder.

The door closed with a thud, and no one inside the room spoke for a moment.

"Man. Movie stars are weird," Conrad finally said. He clicked off the lights and Stella breathed in a lungful of air through her nose, then blew it out loudly. What had Stella said that had set Sophia Thomas off? Her phone rang, and she absently answered the call. It was the Rivermoor police chief.

"I got your messages about the shooting. You better come in, Stella. I actually have some questions for you."

"Questions for me?" Thank God her voice didn't squeak on the last word, because her body temperature seemed to drop by fifteen degrees in an instant. She ran through her time since landing in Chicago as if on fast forward. Had she done anything illegal? She couldn't think of anything. She cleared her throat. "Do I need a lawyer?"

"Not that I'm aware of. But a lawyer would probably say yes," Sterling added, a hint of bitterness in her voice. "You're not under investigation, if that's what you're asking. I've spoken to Fran Miller. And I have...questions."

"Ah." Stella swallowed audibly. *Questions*. "I'll be there in thirty minutes, Chief." They disconnected, and she looked up to find Art still staring at the door through which Sophia had disappeared, a goofy grin on his face. "Art! Let's roll."

He snapped out of his reverie. "Yeah, boss? Where to?"

"The Rivermoor Police Department."

He looked at his watch, and then rubbed his chin. "I think if we take Lakeshore, we can cut over on Irving Park to Broadway and miss the usual backup at..."

She tuned out his traffic-beating plan, and by the time she clicked her seatbelt into place ten minutes later, she had earbuds in and a song blaring. The engine fired, and she closed her eyes and leaned back, hoping the music would distract her from the gut-clenching terror of Art's driving.

It didn't. The swerving and brake checks were all the worse for not being able to anticipate them.

"Of course," she muttered.

"What?"

"Nothing, Art." She gripped the dashboard with one hand and clutched at the seatbelt across her chest with the other. Of course you needed eyes wide open to know what was coming. Anything else was asking for disaster.

14

"I don't think I'll be long." Stella patted Art's arm, ignoring the disgruntled expression on his face. The photographer obviously didn't like acting as a driving service, but Stella wasn't about to invite him along for whatever the chief wanted to ask her about.

She felt his glare follow her as she disappeared into the building.

After just a few minutes in the small impersonal lobby, the chief's admin called her name. The older woman led her down a short brightly lit hallway with generic art on the walls and canned lights shining down from the ceiling every few feet.

"Wanda, thanks again for making copies of the police reports yesterday," Stella said to the woman's back. Was it a bad sign that Wanda—the same woman who'd requested Hank Smith's signed picture—would now hardly make eye contact?

Wanda raised a hand to knock on the last doorway in the hall but turned back abruptly, facing Stella. "She's been burned before, you know."

"Burned?"

"By a reporter. And it weighs on her. But if you treat her right, she'll do the same." Before Stella could ask her to explain, Wanda raised her fist and tapped on the door.

"Yes?" Chief Sterling's voice came from inside.

"Ms. Reynolds is here."

A chair scraped against the floor, and Chief Sterling emerged, her expression guarded.

The admin turned to leave, but first tossed a wink Stella's way. It was so fast she might have missed it, but she felt better as she stepped inside.

"Stella, this is Curtis Garrett."

A slim man with short sandy hair half-stood at the chief's introduction but didn't smile. Tension seemed to leap out of the air and permeate Stella's skin, and she suddenly felt like she'd walked into an ambush.

Outwardly, Stella only raised her eyebrows with polite interest as she took the only open seat.

"Mr. Garrett is the Dean of Students at St. Agnes, and he has some questions for you."

"Oh?" She looked over at the man again, this time taking in his wire-rimmed glasses, slim-cut business suit, and stern expression that must easily cow the teens and young adults with whom he usually dealt. Stella was disappointed to note her own stomach contracted guiltily, and she pointedly dropped her shoulders and met Garrett's gaze unflinchingly.

"We've had a complaint that you were on campus harassing our students this morning. I understand you're in town because of the shooting at the high school here in Rivermoor, and Chief Sterling has been trying to convince me that pressing charges will only complicate her case here."

"Pressing charges!" Stella's mind raced. Did he know where she'd been, or just that she'd been on campus? Campus itself was in the middle of downtown Rivermoor, making it perfectly legal for her to walk around without permission. She decided to see what he knew. "I was under the impression that public streets and sidewalks were fair game for anyone, including the press." She raised an eyebrow delicately at the police chief.

Sterling shifted in her seat, her expression neutral. She wasn't going to take sides, that much was clear. "That's certainly true."

Garrett blew out a loud breath through his nose, and Stella asked, "Was there a specific complaint against me?"

His frown deepened. "We received a call that you had unauthorized access to one of the buildings."

"I assure you, I did not." His eyes narrowed suspiciously. So did hers. "Who made the complaint?"

"We certainly cannot reveal a student's identity to the press."

"So a student complained?" Garrett flinched. Stella looked pointedly around the room. "Also, who's 'we'?"

A flush of color rose in his cheeks. "What I mean to say is that no one in the press is authorized in our buildings without prior written approval from the University President's office."

"What if a student invited me in?"

"Did one?"

"I'm speaking hypothetically right now." Stella's evasive answer was not appreciated.

"Well, I'm not!" Garrett was fast losing his grip on calm.

Stella felt her own temper rise. "Yes, I was on campus this morning, but not with any kind of camera or anything."

"No? Then why were you there?"

"I spoke to Fran Miller's roommate. The girl invited me up and we chatted." It was a bit of an overstatement, but Stella was in no mood to give out information just then.

"Lies! See?" Garrett looked triumphantly at the chief. "There is no roommate! You can't trust these media types. They're all the same!"

Stella opened her mouth to set this man straight, but the chief shook her head. The other woman's expression pulled Stella up short and she swallowed her defense, confused. It was almost like the chief knew something...something Curtis Garrett didn't. Sterling glanced at Stella, and when their eyes met, Sterling grimaced slightly.

"Curtis," Chief Sterling broke in. "I'll follow up with Ms. Reynolds and make sure she knows the rules moving forward. Thank you for your candor with regards to the other issue we discussed."

Sensing his dismissal, kind as it was, he stood abruptly, just as Wanda appeared at the door. "May I see you out, Mr. Garrett?"

"Good day, Chief." He looked down his nose and added, "Ms. Reynolds." He pivoted on his heel and left without another word.

When they were alone, Stella studied the chief for a moment as she chose her words with care. "What did Curtis Garrett have to say about Fran Miller being in your department's custody?"

Chief Sterling tented her fingertips in front of her chest and stared at Stella. "I think we need coffee. Wanda!"

The admin was back, hovering in the doorway to the small office, an inquisitive expression on her otherwise smooth face. Sterling issued orders for coffee service without taking her eyes off of Stella, then motioned with her hand as Wanda turned to leave. The admin raised an eyebrow, but dutifully closed the door behind her.

"The Dempster Stop N Shop ponied up video after you spoke to the owner. 'Lectured' him is how he phrased it. You convinced him to turn over a shot of the shooting suspect when my detectives only met a brick wall of silence."

Stella thought that "brick wall" was an apt description of the man she'd met behind the counter at the Stop N Shop. "I'm glad to have helped."

"And then Fran said she only came to us because you told her to." Sterling narrowed her eyes, her face still showing traces of the grimace from earlier.

"What?" Stella asked, when the chief continued to stare at her.

"I'm trying to decide if I can trust you."

"Which way are you leaning?"

Sterling allowed a small smile. "I'm leaning toward the fact that I might not have much of a choice."

"Because of Fran?"

Sterling nodded.

"Funny," Stella said, settling back into her seat with a smile of her own. "I was thinking the same thing."

15

Stella rolled the tension out of her shoulders as unobtrusively as possible. She and the chief sipped on terrible burnt coffee that was acidic enough to curdle her stomach. Stella coughed to cover her gag reflex and reached out for another tiny creamer. After Sterling took her own cautious sip, Stella asked, “What did the dean mean when he said Fran wasn’t assigned a roommate? I’ve met her. In fact, I was just in her dorm room earlier today.”

The chief swallowed and very carefully set her mug down on the desk. “Likely just a clerical error at the housing office. I’ve got a call into the University President’s office to help clear it up.” Sterling didn’t make eye contact, and Stella made a mental note to do some digging on that end. “Stella, I want to talk to you about Fran. Off the record,” she added when Stella pulled a notebook and pen out of her bag.

Stella narrowed her eyes at the chief. “Can I ask a few questions on the record first?”

The chief shook her head. “Not now. After.”

Stella reluctantly tucked the notebook back into the bag sitting at her feet.

Sterling let out a breath and leaned back in her chair. It was a monstrous black padded leather thing that hinged back like a La-

Z-Boy and looked just as comfortable. Stella shifted on her own metal chair with a spine-numbing lack of lumbar support and waited.

"Fran speaks very highly of you."

"That's nice to hear. I don't know her well, but our families go back quite a ways."

"She said that *you* suggested she come talk to us." Sterling fixed Stella with unblinking eyes, which Stella met.

"I guess I did, although I thought I was suggesting that she go to a counsellor on campus."

"Really?"

"Yes. From what she said, it sounded like she might need help processing some things, but she was very vague about what was going on."

"Hmm." Sterling looked down at her coffee cup and fell silent.

"She's not in police custody, though, is she?"

"What do you mean?" Sterling's head snapped up.

"I checked the jail records. No Fran Miller."

"She is not in jail, that's true. Putting her in protective custody allows us to hide her location from anyone with a computer and internet access, or the desire or knowledge to file a FOIA." At the mention of a Freedom of Information Act request, she looked disdainfully across the desk at Stella. "And we can keep her safe."

Stella's eyebrows shot up. "Does that mean she wasn't safe in her dorm room?"

"I didn't say that."

"But you're not denying it."

Sterling's lips smashed together in a tight line. A flush rose up from her collar; she'd said more than she meant to.

Stella pressed for more. "How did Malcolm McCoy get video of Fran in the back of the cruiser?"

"You're not the only one curious about that." The chief's nose wrinkled as if she'd smelled something foul. "I'll find out." Her voice held a ring of authority that made Stella glad she wasn't on staff at the Rivermoor PD.

"Incidentally, my mother would love to know too. She's been

friends with Fran's grandmother for decades, and frankly, they're both pretty ticked off with all media at the moment."

Sterling chuckled, a low throaty sound that made Stella's own lips quirk up. "What else did Fran tell you?" The question was casual, but Stella felt an undercurrent of curiosity that was as serious as the crime Chief Sterling was investigating.

Stella bit her lip. Not much, if she was being honest, but if she told the chief that, she might get shown the door without any information. "Let's make a deal. First, you confirm what I'm hearing on the ground about the high school shooter. Then I'll tell you what I know from Fran."

"Okay. You've got a deal."

Stella took out her notebook, pen poised over the page. "You know the identity of the shooter?"

"No."

"You believe someone from the school helped the shooter escape?"

Sterling set her cup down and leaned forward. "What if I promise you first access to my lead detective on the case if you sit on that information for a day? Maybe two."

"Why?" Stella hadn't expected confirmation so quickly. Her stomach fluttered. This was exactly the kind of news that would make Kenny stop riding her ass for a few days—maybe even a week.

"Because releasing that information now could compromise our case. And put Fran at risk. You wouldn't want to risk Fran's safety, would you?"

Instead of answering, Stella asked a follow-up question. "Tandy has something to do with the case here in Rivermoor?"

Sterling looked down her long straight nose at Stella with a dispassionate stare. "Sit on everything and I'll give you *exclusive* access to my lead detective."

Stella's head tilted to one side as she considered. "Exclusive for at least twenty-four hours?"

Sterling nodded without hesitation.

"Forty-eight hours?" Stella amended.

"Twenty-four. Anything else?"

Stella's eyes narrowed. "I need something for today that'll get me out of hot water over McCoy's story yesterday."

"You're in hot water over a libelous piece of incorrectly reported bad sensationalist garbage?" Stella nodded. The noise from Sterling's throat was something between a sigh and a groan. "You guys are just short of criminal. I'm almost certain you'd set your own house on fire if you could be the first to report on it."

Stella held her gaze, unperturbed by the description of the media. It certainly wasn't the worst she'd ever heard.

Sterling's stern expression broke. "Fine. I'm heading to meet with the principal and a select group of student leaders at Rivermoor High on how to move forward. I'll get you in."

"When?"

"I'm leaving in ten minutes. But first, I'm curious. What did Fran tell you yesterday?"

Stella thought back to the brief meeting she'd had with the girl just one day earlier. "She told me she was having trouble knowing whether to trust her gut, and that she was worried someone would get hurt. Or that maybe somebody had already gotten hurt. And I told her to meet the problem head on, not to wait." She shrugged. "To be honest, I thought she was talking about her own problems at school. Not anything to do with a school shooting."

"Would your advice have been the same if you'd known what she was talking about?"

"I would have driven her here myself, Chief."

Chief Sterling nodded without looking at Stella. "Meeting starts at four."

Stella stood. "Got it. And, Chief?"

Sterling's face tensed.

"Thanks."

"Thank *you* for sending Fran to us. She's in more danger than she thought."

"Is, or was?"

"Is. Remember that if you think about taking the story to press early."

Wanda materialized at the door and ushered Stella out.

In the lobby, she sent off a series of texts to her boss, who immediately gave her the go-ahead to cover the student meeting at the high school for the evening news, then texted Art to let him know they'd be rolling out soon.

Her stomach grumbled, and she dug around her bag, coming up with the last bite of a two-day-old granola bar. She popped it in her mouth and sucked on it to soften the stale edges before she chewed the stubborn bit of oats and processed sweeteners.

In spite of her hopefulness about a future exclusive, she didn't know how much she trusted Sterling yet—or what kind of highly placed source Malcolm had. After all, he'd broken the Fran story—incorrectly, yes, but also apparently without Sterling's knowledge or approval. Did he know the lead detective in the case? Would she even *get* the promised exclusive?

And did it really matter anyway? If Fran was in trouble, what did a one-day exclusive really get her? A few days without Kenny's wrath was hardly an equal trade to a girl's safety.

Suddenly, the wad of revived oats felt like lead in her mouth, and she couldn't muster the desire to swallow the blob down. Her eyes swept the lobby for a tissue or napkin, but nothing jumped out.

She looked guiltily over her shoulder, and satisfied the office was empty, she plucked her still-full coffee cup from where she'd set it on the side table and carefully spit out the glob of food with a disgusting *plop*.

"Did you want to take that with you, Ms. Reynolds?"

Stella started at the unexpected voice and barely avoided slopping the disgusting mixture of food, sugar, creamer, and coffee over the edge of the mug. Before she could answer, Wanda took the blue ceramic mug and tilted it over a disposable travel cup.

"What in—" The admin looked up at Stella, eyes wide, when the glob of food plunked into the new cup with an audible *ker-splosh*. She handed the cup to Stella, her lips puckered distastefully, then held out an arm toward the door, indicating it was time for Stella to go.

She hailed Art, and soon they were driving like bank robbers on the run, headed for the high school.

To distract herself from imminent death, Stella thought back to Sterling's final words. *Fran's life is in more danger than she thought.*

Her heart felt heavy as she considered her attitude over the last hour. Lucky thought she liked to see the bad guy held accountable. Lately the only pull she felt on her job was to beat the other reporters out there. But that wasn't why she'd started the job. The goal was—and always had been—to see that justice was served, not to get an exclusive. It was too easy to forget that when no one around her seemed to feel the same.

She would get through the meeting at the school tonight, but then she had to prioritize finding out more about Tandy. The girl wasn't who she seemed. So who was she?

16

Hours later, Stella stood in the darkened school hallway, one of the only people left in the building.

At Chief Sterling's urging, the principal had let Stella stay to do her live shot for the evening news inside.

She had merged the exclusive video and interviews with some student leaders with the information she'd gotten earlier in the day from her off-camera interview with Tandy Scarborough.

A thumbs up emoji hit her phone five minutes after the live shot ended, and that was as close to over-the-top praise from Ken as she'd ever seen.

Now the last remaining employee in the building, a janitor, was talking Art's ear off as he helped Conrad spool cables and repack gear into the satellite truck outside.

Stella eased down the main corridor until she stood alone in the semi-lit hallway that led to the theater wing; then, with a decisive nod as if to convince herself that she should, she followed the shooter's path according to Wes.

The only illumination came from thin strips of emergency lighting glowing from under the lockers that lined the space, and she moved slowly until she reached a hexagon-shaped lobby with three doors at the end. Stella shrugged off a sudden urge to mark her way with breadcrumbs as she pushed open the door farthest to the right.

A curving hallway with several glass-fronted doorways opened up into a cavernous space with an upright piano surrounded by chairs arranged on a three-level riser system. Individual practice rooms and the choir room, she thought, recalling her own high school building.

She stepped back, but kept the door propped open, then tried the middle door. Locked. A plaque on the wall labeled it a utility room.

Closer now, she noticed a thin beam of light shining from under the door on the left. Stella grasped the third door handle and pushed down. The latch easily gave way, and with a final look behind her, she walked through.

The tile floor of the hallway ended at the threshold, and as she crept into the room, her feet echoed on wide black wooden planks. She stopped to get her bearings. Dozens of huge canned lights hung from the ceiling; she was clearly in the theater—but hadn't expected to be on stage. Well—not on stage, exactly, but in the wings for sure.

She walked forward, following the lines of the floor. To her right, there was a gallery of seats that would put many professional theaters to shame. To her left, backstage, and all that went with it. High above the floor there were six—no, seven—hanging backdrop sleeves and a bridge of some sort. Plenty of places for a gunman to hide, if they knew how to get around a theater.

"Stage right," a voice called from the seats.

"Front of house!" Stella replied, suddenly remembering what those seats close to the stage were called.

A cackle of delighted laughter met that, and with a blinding flash, the lights around her came up full. The theater teacher who'd tripped on her way to the Dumpster yesterday was making her way from the audience seats up a set of stairs to join Stella on stage. On the last step, though, she grimaced and grabbed her hip.

"Ooh, arthritis. I'm trying to beat it into submission with yoga, but I don't think I'm winning. Have you heard of Raptor Yoga? The founder is a former student of mine," Madeline said with obvious pride. Her silvery hair was swept back into an elegant loose chignon. A few tendrils had escaped and wafted appealingly near her dark heavy brows as her expression turned curious. "What are you doing here?"

"I covered the meeting this afternoon in the gym. With the student leaders."

"Ah. Of course." Madeline folded her arms in front of her and shook her head. "Poor kids. No one knows what to do. What's the appropriate time to pause? How long should everyone put off their lives? Until there's an arrest? Until everyone's home from the hospital and back at school? There's really no rule book, is there?"

"No, I guess not," Stella agreed.

"Of course, I'm retiring at the end of the year, but I never expected to go out on a note like this! We're not sure we'll carry on with the spring play after everything that happened."

"Why? I mean, surely the students will crave some normalcy."

Madeline nodded sagely. "I agree, but it's up to the superintendent for now. So we'll see."

"What are you doing here?" Stella asked, looking around the empty room.

"Just thinking. Remembering. Being fatefully nostalgic, I'm afraid," Madeline said ruefully.

"I'm sure you've earned it." Stella took a few steps out to center stage and turned slowly, taking in the huge cavernous room. No doubt about it, there were a lot of places to hide. Huge beams ran across the backstage and wings; set pieces loomed large and ominous in the semi-darkness. In fact, by design, the entire room was full of dark, shadowy corners. If the shooter made their way here, they'd have been able to hide and escape at their leisure. She squinted through the darkness behind her but couldn't see past the layer of blackness to the rear of the stage lighting.

"I did a little research on you after our encounter yesterday," Madeline said, looking up at Stella through her eyelashes.

"Oh? What did you find?" Stella asked with a light smile.

"Many things, not all of them flattering, I'm afraid. But it appears that we're going to be at the same party this weekend."

Stella struggled not to grimace at the first part of Madeline's answer, choosing to focus instead on the latter. "You're going to the charity gala Saturday night?"

"Don't look so surprised, Ms. Reynolds. I may be a lowly theater teacher, but I have connections. Make no mistake."

"I'm not surprised at all," Stella said carefully, aware that Madeline's tone had shifted from friendly and nostalgic to condescending. "In fact, I met one of your connections earlier today. Sophia Thomas. Do you keep in touch?"

Madeline's lips smoothed into a smile. "Not as much as my current students might like, but yes, of course. We were very close when Sophia was a student. I directed her in four plays when she was here. You know she considered changing her name?"

"Really? To what?" Stella asked.

"Something less...common, I guess," Madeline shrugged delicately. "In the end, she decided to stick with what her parents chose." She shook her head. "And it doesn't seem to have caused her any trouble."

Stella grinned, wondering what Madeline thought of the name Stella, but she only said, "You're lucky to have such loyal alumni."

Madeline's eyes briefly narrowed, but she smiled and said, "Yes. Very lucky."

The door behind them opened with a bang that echoed across the stage, and Stella grimaced. Even though Art was backlit by the doorway, she could still make out his scowl. "There you are! I've been looking all over for you. Let's go."

Stella turned back to the theater teacher. "Well, so lovely to see you again, Madeline. I'm sure I'll see you Saturday night."

"Until then," Madeline replied.

It was only when she was sitting in the car next to Art on their way back to her hotel that she realized she didn't really look forward to seeing the theater teacher again. There was something unsettling about the woman's intensity that made Stella want to keep her distance.

She tried to shrug the feeling away, after all, she only had to see the woman for one more night, really, at the gala. Then Stella would leave Chicago and Madeline Mowery would slip into retirement, and their paths would likely never cross again.

That gave her some small comfort as Art narrowly avoided crashing into the back of a trash truck that had slowed in a line of traffic.

Keeping her eyes focused more firmly on the road ahead, Stella snorted softly to herself. She'd better worry about the threat in front of her right then, not an annoyance still several days away.

17

"Well, sure, Stella, I'd say it's the perfect place to hide. And escape." Ernie Bellars cleared his throat and bumped his glasses up his nose for the fifth time in as many minutes. He really needed a better-fitting pair, Stella thought absently.

She was video chatting with the house manager for a small theater company in Ohio with whom she'd done several stories earlier in her career.

"But only if you knew your way around a theater, right? I mean, I couldn't just walk in there and find the way up to the—what did you call it? The gangplank?"

Ernie's image distorted slightly with a wavering internet connection, but his snort came through loud and clear. "The catwalk. But I thought you said this is a high school theater? They probably wouldn't have the higher end—"

"Believe me, it's a very fancy theater. Rivals some main stages in large cities, at least as far as I could tell. Everything from the orchestra pit to a wall of those pulley things—for set pieces and backdrops?"

"The fly wall? Wow. I'm impressed. Who's the teacher, did you say?"

"I didn't." Stella frowned.

After a pause, Ernie bumped his glasses up again. "Well, you're not wrong. You couldn't just walk in off the street and find your way quickly to the catwalk. I mean, if they have hydraulic lifts to get up there, you'd have to know your way around the booth." She nodded. The control boards in a TV studio had the same kind of setup to control all the lighting and sound.

A shadow moved in her peripheral vision, and Stella glanced over to see Lucky framed in the doorway, tapping his wrist. He wasn't wearing a watch, but she got the idea that they were running late for dinner. She hastily thanked Ernie and ended the call.

"Reckon I'm the only guy who doesn't worry when he walks in on his girlfriend video chatting with another man at eight o'clock at night?" Lucky tried to wipe the scowl off his face, but only succeeded in turning it into a frown.

She looked him over from head to toe. "Long day, huh?"

Lucky had spent the last four hours with his business manager, going over the books for Haskins Racing Enterprises. The meetings always left him with tense shoulders and an uncharacteristic frown.

He stepped close and ran his fingers lightly down her arm from shoulder to wrist, then brought her hand to his lips and kissed her knuckles lightly. The frown disappeared. "Better now. Ready?"

She nodded and walked ahead of him out of the hotel room, leading the way to the elevator, but her mind was going over her conversation with Ernie. Something he'd said niggled at her. He'd said the lights were operated by a control panel in the booth...yet she could have sworn that Madeline had been sitting in the front row of the auditorium when the lights came up in the theater that night. If Madeline hadn't turned them on, who had?

"You okay?" Lucky asked, nudging her into the waiting elevator car.

She grinned wryly and shook her head. "Sorry. Just thinking about work." Then her eyes narrowed as she looked over at her beau and asked the question that had been on her mind since that afternoon. "How long have you known Sophia Thomas?" Sophia was gorgeous, young, and, if her last film was any indication, incredibly...

flexible. Her stormy thoughts must have been playing out on her face, because Lucky made a sound in the back of his throat and wove his fingers through her own.

"She's brunette." He shrugged, looking down his nose at his girlfriend. "I'm partial to redheads myself."

Stella's lips twitched and she leaned her head against his shoulder. "Hmm. Good answer."

~

IT WAS dark when she awoke with a start hours later. She could tell by the stillness of the hotel that it wasn't anywhere close to dawn. Even though she was lying in bed, her heart raced and she clutched the sheets on either side of her body so tightly that her right hand started to cramp. She concentrated on relaxing her fingers one by one, then swung her feet over the edge of the bed.

Lucky's strong and steady deep breathing calmed her, and when she was sure her legs could support her, she crept out of the bedroom into the sitting area of the hotel room.

She flicked a light on over the wet bar and grabbed a glass from the shelf, filling it with cold water from the tap. After the first gulp made its way soothingly down her throat, she pressed the glass to her forehead, trying to remember the dream that had startled her awake.

It had started out pleasantly calm. She'd been leaving a store along Chicago's Magnificent Mile, a bag in each hand, when she ran into Fran. The girl smiled, then turned, beckoning her to follow. But the faster Stella walked, the farther away Fran moved. Then the crowd around them grew restless, bumping into her from all sides until she lost her balance and was jostled from the sidewalk onto the street. She'd craned her neck to try and locate Fran, but then a horn blared. Another shove from someone behind her and she'd landed in the path of an oncoming delivery truck. She woke up right as the truck would have hit her.

She raised the glass to her lips again and drank, then set the crystal down carefully, her hand still shaky from the dream.

When she'd stopped trembling, one thought raced through her mind in a loop.

Madeline Mowery hadn't been alone in the theater last night. Someone had turned on the lights in the theater from the audio and light board, and Madeline had been sitting in the audience. Had Madeline hidden the other person's presence from Stella on purpose?

Lucky let out a loud snore, and the covers rustled as he changed position in bed. His slow, deep breathing started up again as she stood rigidly by the sink.

What did that mean, if anything?

She rubbed her face roughly and flopped onto the couch. Why was Fran in danger? How did it all fit together? And more importantly, how could she possibly find out, unless the chief decided to include her in the investigation? Stella snorted. Not likely.

But there had to be something...some way that she could do research on the school, on the students and staff. Her online searches hadn't been very helpful yet.

Stella's brow knit together, her brain clutching at seemingly disjointed strands of knowledge. She rubbed her forehead, willing the separate pieces of information she'd learned over the previous days to form together into something cohesive she could use, something solid.

Suddenly she sat up straight.

In the chaos of the last twenty-four hours, Stella had forgotten about the yearbook she'd swiped from Fran's room—that glittering, gaudy piece of school history that had been weighing down her bag like an anchor the entire day. It wasn't a smoking gun, but it was, at least, a place to start. Clutching the glass to her chest, she plucked her bag off of a chair by the door, and settled back onto the couch, wondering if this was the beginning of something, or just another dead end.

"Come out, come out," Stella muttered as she flipped open the front cover.

18

It was three in the morning, and Stella's brain felt fuzzy. She'd long since abandoned the glass of water and flipped haphazardly through the mysterious Rivermoor High School yearbook, hoping something incriminating would leap off the page.

No such luck.

After admiring the field hockey team and skipping past the wrestling team—she still couldn't look at a wrestling singlet without laughing—she flipped through the book, noticing for the first time that some pages had been torn out.

The book was missing pages thirteen through eighteen. She turned to the opening pages, but there wasn't a table of contents, so it was impossible to know what was missing.

God, she could use coffee, but it was too early...or too late. Stella wasn't prepared to admit that she'd be starting her day for good at this ridiculous hour. Instead, she took the book to the desk, flipped on the lamp, and rubbed her eyes. She ran a finger down the index at the back of the book slowly, looking with more focus, but after several minutes of searching, she groaned, flipped the yearbook to the first page, and began the tedious process of looking over all the class pictures, beginning with the freshmen.

Ten minutes later, her eyes watering with fatigue, she clapped the yearbook closed and moved to the file box that she'd saved from the Dumpster.

There were a seemingly random mix of essays, student evaluations, and blue book tests, and Stella tried to organize them, but couldn't come up with any kind of system.

She was too tired for this kind of work, and it was likely that she'd skim right past even a written confession without noticing. She flipped through papers by Francis Whitehall, Jarrah Jenkins, Raptor Garrett.

Wait.

She shuffled the papers until she got to the one by Raptor Garrett. That name sounded oddly familiar, but she couldn't figure out why. She puzzled over it for another few moments, but her brain couldn't come up with any connection.

She shuffled everything together and put the papers and yearbook back into the file box. She'd call Fran's grandmother in the morning and ask if the girl had any connections to Rivermoor High. She wanted to talk to Mrs. Miller anyway and confirm that Fran's roommate assignment was official. Something about the dean's proclamation that Fran didn't have a roommate and the chief's casual assurance that it was a clerical error just didn't sit right with her.

She crept back to bed and slid under the covers with a groan as her back flattened out one vertebra at a time.

Lucky opened one eye. "You all right, Bear?" he rasped, his voice gruff with sleep.

She reached out and ran a hand down his arm. "I'm fine." He trapped her fingers with his own and squeezed gently before his hand relaxed back into oblivion.

Eventually, Stella did the same.

She woke alone in bed, Lucky's spot cool to the touch. A note on the bathroom counter explained his absence. *Working out, then meetings. Dinner at 7:30?*

Timing would be tight—if Kenny wanted her live during the news, she wouldn't wrap until late, maybe close to 6:45. Then she'd have to make her way back across town. But she knew Lucky would wait for her. She wrote a note back letting him know. She zoned out brushing her teeth, only realizing that she'd been staring at herself in the mirror for some time when her toothbrush, suspended in mid-air, dripped foamy paste onto the counter below.

Stella's fingers tapped out an uneven beat against the counter. Kenny would be calling soon. What would she tell him? That she'd be investigating the roommate?

She shook her head. Ridiculous. She had work to do—and it wasn't the guess-what-might-be-going-on kind. She *hoped* that Chief Sterling planned to uphold her side of the bargain, but she had to be ready if she didn't. That meant paperwork. A small smile formed unconsciously on her lips and Stella jerked at her own reflection. Did she always look so evil, or was it just this particular mirror?

No matter, she thought, wrenching the shower nozzle over to hot. When a heavy white mist filled the room, her sense of foreboding rose as wisps of steam curled up around her head, almost like horns.

Stella eyed her clouded, fading reflection with rising humor. She wasn't going to do anything wrong. At least, not today.

An hour later, she cut the hair dryer off when her phone lit up.

"Reynolds," she answered in her usual bark.

"It's Sterling. Do you have a minute?"

Stella set the hair dryer down and picked up her phone, taking it off speaker. "What's up, Chief?"

"Well, if you're looking for a story today...I have an idea."

Stella hustled through the room to her briefcase, extracting her pen and notebook. "What's going on?"

"It's the school resource officer from the high school. She might be ready to talk to someone and wondered if I could hook her up with a trustworthy reporter. You came to mind."

"Thank you. Yes, we'd love to hear from her." She wrote down the information, and after they disconnected, she shook her head. She didn't know what McCoy had done to Sterling, but she needed to thank the unfriendly reporter. Because of him, Sterling was spoon feeding her exclusives in the case. Magic.

Before she got back to the hairdryer, though, she tapped another number into her phone to start the ball rolling in another direction with her boss.

"You want to file a FOIA? For what?" Stella heard a spark of interest in Kenny's voice. He loved paperwork, and creating a paper trail by filing a Freedom of Information Act form that authorities were required to consider made his day.

"I want the last day of security video that was recorded inside Rivermoor High, and I want the full, unredacted police reports from the school and the gas station shootings, with the names of everyone police spoke to. Cops aren't telling us everything, and it's a matter of public safety at this point."

"You'll never get it. Investigation is ongoing and all that. Plus, they're saying that the school video surveillance system was down the day of the shooting, right?"

"Yes, and I don't believe it. And furthermore, I want them to wonder why I'm asking for it."

"Well, that's obvious," Kenny said slowly, and she grinned. Was it? "Because you want better pictures of the shooter, and the names of the witnesses from the gas station."

"Yes, of course that. But I'm more interested in how the school shooter escaped the school building. How did he get out when dozens of cops were rushing in?"

"You got a line on her?"

"She might talk. I'll find out today."

"You let me know. That's who I want to hear from. Where's she been hiding?"

"Her mom's house. I'm heading there first thing."

"Well, don't let me stop you." Kenny hung up and Stella smiled. The fact that he hadn't had a snippy comment was almost as good as actual praise. She headed down to the lobby and texted Art, helping herself to the free coffee by the front desk.

"Oops, excuse me." A girl with light orange-red hair bumped into Stella and the freshly poured cup of coffee in her hand splashed over the rim onto the floor with an audible *plop*.

After a quick assessment, Stella smiled. Her suit was unspoiled. "Don't worry about it." She looked around for napkins, but the girl beat her to it, swooping down to the ground with a wad of paper towels in her fist. When the floor was dry again, the girl stood and stared at Stella.

Stella's eyebrows raised in question, but before she could ask anything, the girl hunched her shoulders and hurried across the bustling space, taking a seat in a plush armchair in the corner and burying her nose in a magazine.

Stella kept an eye on the stranger as she stirred a creamer and some sugar into her cup. The girl's expression had been unusual as she'd stared at Stella. Not unfriendly, exactly, but not just casual indifference either. It was almost like she was sizing Stella up. But for what?

Her phone buzzed—Art was outside waiting—and she blew out a cleansing breath, then took a long, slow sip before turning resolutely away from the girl.

Stella hadn't had a great night's sleep, and also hadn't had any coffee yet. The girl was just a girl. And her day had just begun.

19

"We're going where?" Art looked at her critically, and she felt a small sense of wonder at possibly stumping even *his* vast knowledge of city navigation.

"Mettawa." Stella tried out the pronunciation again, this time leaning hard on the "taw" instead of the "Met."

"Try Ma-tao-wa. I just—I just meant, why?" He fired up the engine and stroked his chin, clearly considering the best route to get them there.

"Lorna Vargas lives there."

"And who's that?"

"Billie Vargas's mother." Stella took Art's phone and plugged the address into his maps app. "Here. I'm sure you'll know a better shortcut, but this will get us started."

Art frowned but put the car into gear and pulled out into traffic, maneuvering a U-turn that made Stella clutch the door handle, her whole body taut from the utter certainty that they were about to get hit.

"And who exactly is Billie Vargas?"

The car swung just wide of a black Land Rover, and after the astonished woman driving it waved a decidedly unladylike finger at them, Stella unclenched her jaw to answer just as a text came into

Art's phone. She glanced at the screen instinctively. Art didn't notice —busy as he was squeezing his car between a semi-truck and a city bus in a lane that didn't exist.

She dismissed the text with a flick of her finger, then carefully set the phone in the cradle on the dash so Art could see the navigation instructions. "She's the school resource officer who was working at Rivermoor High when the shooter walked in."

Art made a noncommittal noise as he accelerated down the onramp, and Stella stared at him from under her eyelashes. The text had been short, something a wife might ask, yet there hadn't been a name entered into the contact information. So just a phone number came up with the words, *What are you working on today?*

Stella flexed her fingers and settled back into her seat. It could take anywhere from fifteen to sixty minutes to get through the city and head north to the Vargas residence. She forced her shoulders down away from her ears and rolled her head from side to side.

The text could be innocent. Or not. She narrowed her eyes as they barreled past the other cars on the highway. Was Art on her team? Unfortunately, she might not know until it was too late.

Around a half hour later, the photographer slowed the car and pulled to a stop along the curb in a lovely neighborhood on the east side of Mettawa. "Nice," he said.

Above the cedar roofline of the Vargas house, a cluster of pine trees towered over the neighborhood like spiky sentries, and if they hadn't driven past a Costco Warehouse just a mile earlier, it would be easy to forget they were so close to civilization.

"Why don't you wait here," Stella said over her shoulder as she climbed out of the car. "I'll come out and get you if they want to talk." She smoothed out her skirt and then headed up the front walk, turning back to see Art busily texting someone. He looked up guiltily. Or was that her imagination?

She blew out a sigh and set her mind on the task at hand: convincing Billie Vargas to talk about what happened inside Rivermoor High.

Knock-ock, knock-ock, knock-ock.

The sound of her fist echoed through the hollow door, and it wasn't long before Stella heard the tap of footsteps.

"Hello?" A woman with short feathered blond hair and a wary expression answered the door.

Stella hadn't even finished introducing herself before the woman shook her head.

"No, I'm sorry. We have no comment." There was a shuffling on the other side of the door, and a voice too low for Stella to make out spoke, but the woman holding it halfway closed didn't budge, just shook her head harder. "I think no comment is best." But there was a question in her voice.

Stella tried to press her advantage. "I think a lot of people are wondering how the shooter escaped. It seems to me like the school —or maybe police?—aren't releasing some key information. And I'm sure it's pretty terrifying to know that the person who shot Billie is still out there. Wouldn't it be nice if we could get the public's help to put the shooter away? Lock him up?"

"What makes you think it's a him?" A younger version of the woman moved around the half-open door, with the same short feathered blond hair, this time surrounding a face with no wrinkles. Stella thought she must be in her late twenties. "I'm Billie. Nothing on camera, please, but you can come in." She moved both of her crutches to one side so she could shake Stella's hand. "Thanks, Mom. I've got it." The older woman frowned but turned and walked back through the house, and Billie pulled the door all the way open. "She's furious. So am I, really.

"Come on back. The doctors told me I should get up and walk around as much as I can, but man, it hurts." At Stella's look she elaborated. "The bullet shattered my femur, and I messed up my knee when I fell to the ground. I've got a rod and six screws in there now, and damn if it doesn't ache like a rotten tooth." She hobbled across the room toward a chair and slowly pivoted around.

Stella winced as Billie sat in an armchair with a groan. Her right leg was in a blue brace from her hip to her ankle, Velcroed tight at regular intervals, and a wet stain spread out from the middle of her thigh, the rusty brown a sharp contrast to the white bandage wrapped around her leg. "We can't get the wound to stop seeping," she said with an apologetic shrug. She carefully set the crutches down on the floor and took a moment to get herself—and her thoughts—situated. "I don't really have anything to say about the school. I think they're handling things just fine. They're still in shock, I guess."

"You didn't recognize the shooter?"

"I didn't even get to see the shooter's face. I heard what sounded like a door slamming, and by the time I turned to see what it was, I was down. The bullet went straight through my femur and burst back out the front of my thigh. The bone shattered, and they're still not sure they got all the fragments out. Thank God I happened to have my radio in my hand so I could call for backup. I was worthless in every other way that day." Her face was like stone, but Stella could feel the anger and doubt battling for dominance behind her flat words.

"Have you given much thought to how the shooter managed to escape?"

Billie's eyes narrowed dangerously. "Have I given it much thought?" A short barking laugh escaped her lips. "It's about all I've been able to think about." She fiddled absently with one of the Velcro strap ends. "They knew the building. They knew it like they'd gone to school there for years. But no one knows them. Impossible, but there it is."

"What about the security cameras? What are the odds that the first shooting in the school's history would happen during the security company contract change?"

"Well, that hardly matters. There's a backup system in place during the switch."

"Not according to the principal and superintendent. They said there's nothing. Instead, police released a still shot from the second shooting—the one at the Dempster Stop N Shop."

"What?" Billie shifted in her seat and groaned again. "I haven't seen what they've released. I've been a bit busy." She motioned to her leg.

"Right. Of course." Stella dug into her bag and pulled out a copy she'd made of the picture released by police. "This shot is all we've got." The picture showed a blurry man, staring directly at the camera. Even through the fuzzy edges, you could see the anger in the set of his shoulders; in the intensity of his gaze.

Billie reached out for the picture and Stella handed it across the coffee table. "This is it?"

"Yes, just this. Nothing from the school."

Billie stared at the picture for another long moment without talking. She shook herself and looked up. "They've got fifteen cameras in the main hallways of the building. At least five more monitor some of the main congregation areas of the school: the cafeteria, student lounge, office. I can't believe they haven't released anything."

"Well, apparently the system was down completely."

Billie lifted the picture up to eye level again, looking at it with something like frustrated wonder. "This is the worst still shot I've ever seen." Billie dropped the picture down again, and an incredulous expression added a liveliness to her face that had been missing before. "I was standing just outside the office when I was shot, and that's by the main door. The shooter walked into the school and opened fire—they should have at least three different cameras on him from the moment he crossed through the door. And the system has a full backup hard drive, so that they'll *never* lose the feed. Something's not right here."

"If the school principal and superintendent don't know about it, who would?"

"It's the head of the math department. He's a computer guy, so he's been running the backup system for years."

"Billie, can we go on the record here?"

"Hell yes we can. I'm pissed off now. Here I am, doctors say it will take me six to eight months until I can be out of this cast, and I might never be pain free again." She stopped and shook her head. "Do you know how hearing that made me feel? That I might *never* not be in pain?" She blew out a slow breath. "And the school administration can't be bothered to access the backup security system? I mean, I couldn't identify this if it was a picture of my own son! What the hell is wrong with them?"

"Can I bring in my photographer?"

Billie nodded just as her mother walked into the room.

"I think that's enough, Billie."

"Mom, did you know about this? Have you seen this picture?"

"Yes, honey, and the last thing you need is to lose your job right now."

"Oh, I think—"

"This just came." Her mother shoved an envelope into her hands and she pressed her lips together.

"Damn bills." Billie leaned back and carefully shifted in her seat. She moved her gaze to the window and stared at the street outside for a long while without talking. "Mom's right. I won't go on camera, but you can use anything I said on the record. Does that help?"

Billie's mother crossed her arms and glared at the intruder in her home.

Stella stood. "You getting better is the most important thing here. Your mother's right. Thank you for your time, ladies."

The door closed behind her with more force than was strictly necessary. As Stella headed back to Art's car, he tucked his phone into his shirt pocket with a decidedly sheepish air. Stella wasn't imagining it this time. What was he doing that made him look so guilty?

"Struck out, huh?" Art fired up the engine as she climbed into the vehicle and gave her a look that made it clear he felt they'd wasted their morning driving to the middle of nowhere.

"Kind of."

"What does that mean?"

Stella leaned back in her seat and considered her next move carefully. "Let's head back to Rivermoor." She plucked her phone out of her bag and dialed the number for Chief Sterling.

"I don't know how you found out already, but fine. If you get out here before the end of the hour, I'll wait and give you a soundbite."

"Chief, I..." Stella stumbled, her mind racing. What was going on? "Can you just...ah...give me the address? We're in the car now and I'm not by my notes."

Art shot her a look and she shrugged, completely confused.

Chief Sterling rattled off a familiar-sounding street address and Stella rifled back through the pages in her notebook. "The Stop N Shop?"

"Where else? My detective is still questioning everyone, and I can't hold him here for much longer. But it's safe to say I'm relieved we've got something to go on. I mean, you know as well as anyone that with every passing day, our odds of catching him went down."

"Absolutely."

Stella disconnected and recited the address to Art.

"What's going on at the Stop N Shop?" he asked, stomping on the gas pedal with such force that they both lurched back against the velour cushioned seats.

"I have no idea."

20

Traffic slowed near the gas station, and as soon as they got close, Stella could see why. Police cruisers with flashing lights blocked both entrances, and drivers slowed to gawk on their way past. As Art pulled off to the side of the road and parked behind a third cruiser, Stella scanned the lot for Chief Sterling, spotting her on the other side of the police caution tape talking with two officers in uniform and her old friend Not Max.

The chief caught sight of Stella and headed over with a man in regular clothes who must be a cop, because she barked out orders to him about the case.

"Tell Suminaz to get the press release ready. Homicide will look over the phrasing before it's released to the media." The detective left with his marching orders and Sterling turned her attention to Stella. "How did you hear?"

Stella checked to see that Art was still gathering his gear at the car before confessing. "I really didn't. Called you about something else entirely."

Sterling swore. "My own damn fault. Well. You're here now." She checked her phone, distracted. "What'd you want?"

"I interviewed Billie Vargas today at her mother's house."

"How is Ms. Vargas? My detectives say the mother has hardly let them in to talk to her."

"She's a force, that's for sure." Stella smiled tightly. "Billie told me that even though the school was between security contracts, there's always a way to access a backup copy of the video."

"Not according to the principal or the superintendent. Off the record, Stella, they say we're flat out of luck."

Stella shrugged. "I know—I mean, I'd heard that too. But Billie says there's a way. There's a backup system that's there for regular system maintenance updates—something in place so they're never *not* covered." Sterling looked doubtful, so Stella pressed on. "Billie said the head of the math department knows all about it. Apparently, he used to run the entire security system before they hired an outside firm to deal with it." Sterling still looked doubtful, so Stella dropped the issue. She'd have to bring it up with the superintendent.

Art walked up and shouldered the camera and Stella flipped the microphone switch on. "So what's going on out here today, Chief?"

Sterling stared at her for a long moment, but much to Stella's relief answered the question. "Today, with the help of concerned citizens, detectives from the Rivermoor Police Department were able to identify a suspect in the recent shooting at the Dempster Stop N Shop. Ardale Jones is wanted by police, and we need the public's help to apprehend him. We consider him to be armed and dangerous."

"How did you identify him?"

Sterling hesitated. "An employee here recognized him from the surveillance photo we released on Tuesday."

Stella's eyes narrowed. That meant the suspect was likely known to the employee long before today. Why wait so long to publicly identify him? "What charges will he face if he's arrested?"

"Homicide."

Whoa. Stella bit her lip. Something had changed, all right. "Last I heard, the victim was in critical condition. When did that change?" she asked.

"Long-time Stop N Shop employee Dana Scott succumbed to her injuries earlier today."

"Does the suspect have any connection to Ms. Scott?"

Sterling clenched her jaw and sucked a hard breath in before answering. "They were married. He had been living with Ms. Scott until two weeks ago. She'd gotten a restraining order against Mr. Jones two days before the shooting."

Stella saw another news car in her peripheral vision pulling close to the scene. McCoy's hard stare passed over her and the chief as they stopped for a red light on the other side of the intersection.

"Does Mr. Jones have any connection to the shooting at Rivermoor High?"

"We aren't ruling anything out."

Stella frowned. That wasn't good enough. "Do you have any reason to suspect that Jones was involved in the shooting at Rivermoor High?"

Sterling frowned too. "Like I said, we can't rule anything out this early in the investigation. We had two shootings, geographically and logistically close enough together that one person might have been able to pull them both off. It is too early in this investigation to rule anything out."

Sterling was holding something back. Stella tried another tack. "Does Jones have any connection to the school?"

Sterling stepped back. "No comment. Sorry, Stella, that's all I have time for right now. Excuse me." Stella frowned as the chief pivoted and walked away, ignoring McCoy's shouted questions as he huffed his way up to the crime scene. She felt like Sterling wasn't telling her something about the suspect. But what?

"What's going on?" McCoy asked Art.

Stella shot her photographer a hard look, then smiled at the other reporter. "Hey, McCoy. Late again?"

McCoy growled in frustration as she and Art left him to wait for his photographer. They skirted along the police tape toward the second driveway of the business.

"Excuse me!" Stella called to the overlarge man chain-smoking as he chatted with a uniformed cop.

"No comment," the cop called.

"Not you—*you,*" Stella clarified, pointing to the store employee she'd met several days earlier. "Do you have a minute to talk?"

The cop melted into the background and the hulking employee walked over. "Stella, right?"

Stella nodded as she studied the man who'd been so unfriendly when they'd last spoken. His entire demeanor had changed since then. His expression was somber instead of confrontational. "I'm so sorry to hear about Dana. Had you known her long?"

"Years. There are only four of us, you know. I'd hired her five, maybe six years ago."

"Are you the manager?"

"Owner. Craig Bell." He reached out a hand. "Sorry I was so short with you the other day. We all knew right away that it was Ardale. But Dana begged us not to say anything. Didn't want her kids to lose their dad to jail, even if he was...well..." His jaw clenched and his folded arms flexed against his chest. "She always said he'd be the death of her. Just never knew it would literally be true."

Stella didn't say anything. Sometimes there were no words that made sense.

The man cleared his throat. "I was going to call you tomorrow, but we might as well do this now."

"Do what?"

"Were you serious? About sharing a GoFundMe page? Her family could sure use the help."

"Yes, of course. First, though, do you know if there's any connection between Jones and Rivermoor High?"

Craig Bell blew out a long, loud sigh. "His and Dana's girls go there. They were home the day of the shooting." At Stella's shocked expression he rubbed his forehead in defeat. "I know. It doesn't look good for him, not at all. Listen, I just gave the police a copy of the security footage from the morning of the shooting. You can have one too."

"You got the system up and running again, huh?" Stella asked, training her gaze on Craig's expression.

He shoved one hand into his pocket and rubbed the back of his neck with the other. "Dana's gone. She wouldn't want her killer raising her kids, no matter who he is." He shrugged. "So yeah. I got the system up and running again." He looked up, his eyes challenging Stella to question his motives.

She nodded. "Makes sense to me." Stella checked the time as she followed the overlarge man into the building. Just past one o'clock. Plenty of time to get a live shot together for the evening news. So much time, in fact, that she could go sniff around the high school and see what was going on with the backup security camera system there.

21

"Let me get this straight." Ken's words snapped like fresh laundry on the line. "You want to run a story about a gas station shooting on a national news program? Forgive me, Stella, were you missing *local* news so much?"

"Kenny, what we know right now is that the police just identified a man who shot and killed his estranged wife the same day that someone shot up the nearby high school—*to which he has a connection*. And both his kids were home from school on the day of the shooting. Coincidence? Who's to say? Is he responsible for both crimes? Police aren't ruling it out. Added all together, it's pretty compelling stuff."

She knew that Sterling hoped this one arrest would solve both cases, and Jones's link to the school made the pendulum of guilt swing his way. And if that meant that she could help two girls with mounting expenses who were still getting used to the reality of a murdered mom and a dad on the run—and soon to be in jail—then she was going to push for that with all her power.

"You'll lead the B block. Unless something better comes along."

Stella disconnected before Ken could. It was a very small victory. She'd take it.

She shouldn't have goaded McCoy outside the Stop N Shop. In

her heart she knew that. But it felt surprisingly good to see his face blanche when he realized that he'd missed the scoop. That he'd have to rely on Stella for the video from the convenience store, and that he'd have to wait for her story to air before he could use it. So was that his karma coming back at him, or had she just set a bad karmic phase in motion for herself?

She shook herself and focused on her story.

Hours later in the dark parking lot of the school, she stood in a ring of light with Art behind the camera, waiting for her live shot when her phone rang.

"Hello, this is Dan Kirkner from Tomorrow's Promise, calling you back about a, uh…a Sophia Thomas donation?" The man on the line sounded confused, which was never a good sign, in Stella's opinion.

"Mr. Kirkner, thanks so much for getting back to me. I'm working on a feature story and Sophia mentioned that she supports your charity. I was hoping to get a quote about what that's meant for your advocacy work in the suicide prevention area."

"Stand by, Stella. We're two minutes away." Art adjusted the light to her right and she squinted as the lightbulb swiveled into her line of sight.

"Mr. Kirkner?"

"Uh, sorry, Ms. Reynolds, I'm confused. Are you talking about the movie star?"

"Yes, Sophia Thomas."

"Wow, well, it would be great if she could get in touch. In fact, just what we need. We lost our major donor about four years ago and haven't been able to recover financially." Kirkner's cadence picked up with excitement. "In fact, I just told our board that we'll need to shut down at the end of the fiscal year if we can't find a new funding source. This could be a godsend. Is Sophia Thomas interested in working with us?"

"Uh…I think I'm confused now. I was under the impression that she'd been working with you for years. I'm so sorry. I must have written down the wrong…" Stella flipped back in her notebook. There was no way she wrote down the wrong charity. "Are you sure she's not a current donor? She gave me your name, said she likes to keep a low profile but has been donating money for years."

"I'm quite sure, Ms. Reynolds. We could use an infusion of cash, though, so again, let Ms. Thomas know to reach out if she wants to get involved. We're happy to keep it confidential."

Stella's brow scrunched together as she tucked her phone into her bag.

"Thirty away," Art said, and Stella pushed the confusing conversation out of her mind to focus on the live shot. She looked down at her notes one last time. "In five, four..."

She looked up at the camera in time to see Art finish the countdown silently with his fingers and then Hank Smith's voice filled her earpiece.

"New developments in an as-yet-unsolved school shooting in the Chicagoland area. Let's go straight to our reporter on the ground covering it all for us from Rivermoor, Illinois, Stella Reynolds. Stella, you have some exclusive video for us tonight?"

"That's right, Hank. We have just learned that the clerk who was shot here Monday morning, just minutes after the school shooting, died from her injuries earlier today. Investigators are turning up the heat as they try and figure out if the two shootings are connected, and whether one murder suspect is responsible for both shootings."

Ardale Jones's image soon took over the screen in the monitor at her feet, and she talked over the full-color video that Craig Bell had given her just hours earlier. "Police and the owner of this business tell me they are certain that the person you see here is Ardale Jones, the estranged husband of the victim. NBC News has exclusively learned that the couple's children attend Rivermoor High School, though they were not in the building Monday morning when shots rang out there."

The video clip ended, and Stella was back on live TV. "Right now, police are calling Jones a person of interest in the school shooting as they continue to investigate both crimes. Also, important to mention that with their mother dead and their father a suspect in her death, the couple's two teenage children are certainly looking at a new terrible reality. The owner of the store has started a GoFundMe page for the pair..." Stella rattled off the information on how to donate and signed off.

"Clear," Art said, then cut the lights, plunging the parking lot into semi-darkness. "Hey, Stella, you want me to send that video over to the local station now?"

"Yes. Make sure they have it by the top of their newscast," Stella said, biting back a grimace. It was her job to work with McCoy, and she'd stick to that plan, even if McCoy didn't like it. After all, she couldn't let his karma turn back on her, could she?

22

Alone in the hotel room later that night, Stella kicked off her shoes and laid back on the couch with an arm slung over her eyes. Lucky was out finding them something to eat for dinner, but her few minutes of silence were interrupted by the buzz of her cell phone against the coffee table. She sat up to see the screen.

The number wasn't familiar, but she answered anyway. No telling when a tip might come in.

"Stella? This is Carol Miller. Your mother gave me your number."

Stella's sluggish brain snapped to attention. Fran's grandmother. "Oh, hi, Mrs. Miller."

"We need to talk."

"Okay," Stella said cautiously. She hadn't spoken to Mrs. Miller since her college graduation party many years ago. Carol and Stu had given her a check for one hundred dollars and oven mitts, she suddenly recalled. Stella willed herself to focus. "Did you hear they identified a person of interest in the Rivermoor High shooting?"

"I heard, and that's why I'm calling. I need to know what's going on. Stella, please tell me what's going on with Fran."

Stella felt her forehead wrinkle. "Mrs. Miller, I think you spoke to her more recently than I did."

"I hope that's not true. She called and left us a message right before she went to the police, but we haven't actually spoken to her since last week. And we don't even know where she is!"

"What do you mean? She's not returning your calls?" Stella pressed her fingers into her temple. That didn't make sense. "Have you tried calling the police chief?"

"Of course, but she won't tell us anything about Fran, other than assuring us that she's safe. Which I guess is nice to know, but it sure doesn't feel accurate when we're seeing stories on the news linking her to a shooting!"

"I understand how frustrating that story must have been. But surely you've seen the correction the station was forced to issue. Fran is not a person of interest in the case."

"Well, of course she's not, but then why isn't she back in school? Why did she go to police in the first place?" Mrs. Miller's breath stuttered in and out twice before she continued. "Stella, I just don't understand why Fran isn't answering her phone or calling us back."

Stella frowned. She had to agree with Mrs. Miller, it was odd behavior. "I don't know, Mrs. Miller. I'd assumed that she was in contact with you."

"Well, she's not, and Stu and I are worried."

"I'm sure you are," Stella said. "I spoke to the chief today, and she told me that...well, not much, actually. Just that Fran is safe, and that they're working on solving the shooting." Stella dug her notebook out of her bag and flipped through the pages until she got to the one from earlier that day. "I checked the jail log, and Fran was never booked in. Chief Sterling told me that Fran is in protective custody."

"Where?"

"I don't know." Stella set the notebook down and pinched the bridge of her nose. "Mrs. Miller, what can you tell me about Fran's roommate?"

"Tandy? Why do you want to know about her?"

"It's just..." Stella thought back to the dean of students' assertion that Fran didn't even have a roommate, and how the chief seemed to discourage Stella from confronting the dean about Tandy, but then brushed it off as a clerical error. Something about the whole conversation had felt off, and Stella had put off looking into the situation. That had been a mistake.

"Mrs. Miller, did Fran mention having an argument with her roommate the day she decided to go to the police? Or anything else about her dorm life that might be concerning?" Stella rubbed the heel of her hand into her eye socket as the beginnings of a headache pulsed. What was she missing? And would Fran's grandparents know anything helpful from two states away?

"No, nothing! Her roommate is lovely. Tandy seems like a girl with great drive. Comes from nothing, and you can tell she's the type to work hard. No safety net, that one."

"What do you mean?" Stella thought back to the girl's well-worn clothes and unstylish shoes, surprised to hear it was more than just a fashion choice.

"Oh, poor thing came right out and told us during dinner that she was living on Cream of Wheat and Ramen. She lost her mother years ago, and her father didn't have time for her. It's why we thought she and Fran would become close friends, because they'd both suffered such loss." Carol sniffed. "Tattered clothes, hardly any possessions. And she had some kind of voucher for a free meal plan card, according to Fran."

"Huh. Mrs. Miller, one more thing. Did Fran grow up in Rivermoor? I mean, before..." She delivered bad news to people all the time, but somehow couldn't bring up Mrs. Miller's son's car accident just then.

"No, honey. Brenwich Square. About a half hour from Rivermoor."

"Huh," Stella said again. Had Fran found a copy of the Rivermoor High yearbook for some reason? If so, why?

They disconnected, Stella promising to do her best to find out more information.

She tossed the phone on the couch and barely noticed as it bounced off the hard cushion and landed with a thump on the carpet.

She rolled her shoulders away from her ears and tried to slow her heart, which was pumping blood through her brain so loudly she could scarcely hear anything else.

It was too late tonight to expect anyone to answer the phone, but Stella knew just where she would start in the morning. With the president of St. Agnes College.

23

"I think you're being dramatic." The president of St. Agnes College stared at her over an immaculate desk in an airy open office. They were surrounded by ten-foot-tall windows, and Stella wondered how much tuition money went to keeping them so sparklingly streak free.

"Dr. Kleinman, I met Tandy. I know for a fact that Fran's parents took the girl out to dinner. We all thought that she was Fran's roommate. If she wasn't, if Fran wasn't even assigned a roommate, then who is Tandy?"

Dr. Kleinman spread his arms out wide with a tired sigh. "I could fill one of your newscasts with the antics that college kids get up to these days. I had a student tell his parents he made the basketball team just so they'd send extra money for food. He lied about it all the way up to the first home game, and not until the parents stepped into the gym for the season opener did he confess to the ruse. And don't get me started on the parents; they're just as bad—maybe worse!" He dropped his arms and pounded the desk for emphasis. "If another girl was in the room, any number of things might have happened." He ticked off the possibilities on his fingers. "Maybe Fran had a girlfriend and didn't want her parents to know." Tick. "Maybe this girl didn't like the room she was assigned to and decided to bunk with Fran off the books, so to speak." Tick. "And, yes, maybe there was an administrative error, and they were assigned together, and that fact didn't make it into our system, but I assure you, that's the least likely of the scenarios I just listed out."

"It seems like it should be easy to get to the bottom of things, though. Just search the room."

Dr. Kleinman nodded somberly. "Yes, of course. That's the first thing we did after the police contacted us."

"And?" Stella prompted after he fell silent.

"And there was no evidence of anyone else living there."

The word "what?" died on her lips as she remembered walking in on Tandy packing up her bags the last time she'd been to campus. The girl had seemed rushed, nervous. Had she known that she had to leave? Had she known that she wasn't supposed to be there?

"None," the university president said for emphasis. He sat back and surveyed Stella benignly. "The second bed was empty, the closet was full of Fran's stuff, even the other desk in the room had Fran's classwork spread evenly throughout the drawers."

"Well...that's just—what about the TV?" Stella asked. Kleinman raised his eyebrows and she rushed ahead. "I was in the room earlier this week. Tandy and her boyfriend were glued to a TV in the corner of the room—with a gaming system!"

Kleinman flipped open a folder on the desk and ran his finger down the page. "Nope, nothing about a TV or gaming system here. Just clothes, toiletries, and the like, consistent with Fran Miller being the only occupant of the room."

Stella sat back. How did you prove that someone *had* been living there when they were already gone? "What about other people in the hall? Surely I'm not the only one who met Tandy!"

"We will, of course, launch our own investigation into matters, and to that end, I have something for you." Kleinman looked up.

Relief flooded her veins. Finally. Some answers! She leaned forward and took the paper he held out across the desk. But when she read the first line, her body went rigid. "A temporary restraining order? What?"

"Our dean of students said that you've been harassing members of our student body. Now you've come in with a far-fetched theory tying a completely fabricated student to a shooting at the high school in town? Our lawyers decided we don't want trash tabloid press operating within our boundaries."

"But this—this is outrageous!" Stella's head felt like it might explode. She'd come here with serious questions, major concerns, and instead of getting answers, she was getting railroaded. "I'm not harassing anyone. You might have paired Fran Miller with a dangerous person, but at this point, no one knows, because you have no idea who was in that room with her. And your solution to this massive situation—this huge, pulsating, ready-to-explode PR problem—is to kick the person asking important questions off your campus?"

A sharp knock on the door interrupted Stella's monologue, and she stood, her heart pounding, wondering if she was about to be arrested.

"You wanted to see me?" A round-faced but lean bald man stepped across the threshold and studied Stella with interest.

"Jim, thanks. Can you please escort Ms. Reynolds to the exit?"

Jim's brows creased, but he stood by, waiting while Stella turned back to stare at Kleinman with an open mouth.

"I'm not the only one asking questions, you know. Fran's parents want answers. They're going to ask the same questions as me, and believe me, they're not going to go away quietly. Their granddaughter is in danger until you figure out what was going on in her dorm room. And they're going to talk to me. And I'm going to talk to everyone."

Kleinman looked down at his desk through his steepled fingers and didn't respond. Stella turned on her heel and swept out of the room, past a surprised admin and into the main hallway of the building. She only knew Jim had followed her when she made a wrong turn and he cleared his throat.

"Exit's that way." He pointed behind Stella, and she pivoted with an irritated huff.

"Who are you?" She shrugged into her jacket and slung her bag over one shoulder as they snaked their way through the building.

"I'm the Communications Director. And you're not wrong."

She stopped in her tracks and assessed her escort. He wore a thoughtful frown and avoided eye contact. She chose her words carefully. "He can't run away from this. There's a gunman on the loose and one of your students is in police custody. This won't just disappear."

Jim sucked in a breath through his teeth. "I don't agree with the president, or with Dean Garrett. I mean, listen, you can't just go traipsing around the dorm rooms with cameras. That's not fair to our students. But we shouldn't lock you out. Colleges are known for moving glacially slow. The media, of course, is just the opposite. Seems like we could help each other here, doesn't it?"

Stella cocked her head to the side. "Can you help me, Jim?" He started walking again, and she was quick to follow. "I just need access to the dorm for an hour. If I met Tandy, and Fran's grandparents knew her, so did everyone on that floor. They can surely fill in some gaps for us."

He shook his head. "I'm sorry. I didn't mean to get your hopes up. I can't go against the president's decision, but I wanted you to know that I disagree with it."

They'd made their way to the grand entrance, and Stella snorted as she reached for the door, feeling more frustrated than she had in the president's office. "Well, that's just great, Jim. I'm sure your silent thoughts on the matter will help everyone involved."

Jim flinched, either at Stella's caustic tone, or because of the arctic blast of cold that hit them.

"I'm sorry." Stella pressed her lips together, then forced the rest of an apology through. "That wasn't fair. But this is bullshit and you know it. Here." She shoved a business card into his hand. "Call me if you decide to take a stand for what's right."

She stalked outside, still clutching the restraining order in her hand. How could she possibly continue covering the story if she was no longer allowed on campus? How could she tell her boss what happened and not be pulled from the story—pulled from the state, completely?

She stopped at the curb, unable to keep walking.

What was she going to do?

She looked down at the paper in her hand and started to rip it down the middle. She just wouldn't tell Ken about it.

As if summoned by her thoughts, her phone rang, his name showing on the caller ID.

"Reynolds, I've got an email here from a law firm in Chicago. Says you're not allowed on campus."

"Listen, Kenny. This thing at the college is going to blow over—"

"Not that campus. The high school campus. Rivermoor. It's a temporary restraining order. What did you do?"

24

Stella brooded as the car lumbered down Michigan Avenue, barely seeing the shops and crowds of people they passed. She'd had Ken read the new restraining order, and it matched the one in her hand from St. Agnes word for word. This was clearly a coordinated effort by the principal at Rivermoor High and the college president to get her off the story...but why? *Someone* was going to cover the shooting. What difference could it make which reporter did the job?

"Hey." Lucky's shoulder nudged hers. "You with me?"

"Sorry." She looked up and found Lucky assessing her from the driver's seat. She'd called him for a ride back to the hotel from the college campus. "What did you say?"

His lopsided smile was full of understanding. "I said, even if they do pull you from this story, it's not the end of the world. Like you always say, news never stops. You'll be off covering something else by Monday anyway."

Her lips tugged down into a frown. "But that's not the point. Why is this happening now? What are they trying to hide?"

Lucky nodded slowly and she looked out the window, feeling frustrated. He wasn't trying to minimize anything—she knew that deep down—but it felt like a slap in the face for him to dismiss her situation so casually.

"What?"

His tone rubbed her the wrong way again, and she snapped, "Nothing. Just my job, my whole career on the line. But you're right. I'll just move onto the next crisis. No big deal."

Lucky rubbed his jaw and replied in a measured tone, "That's not what I said, and certainly not what I meant."

"Sure." She stared out the window. "What time is this happening?"

Lucky blew out a nearly silent sigh, but before he could answer, her phone trilled him to silence. With a resigned shake of his head, he flapped his hand toward her phone. "Go ahead."

"Reynolds," she barked into the phone.

"Hank and I spoke, and we're pulling you from the story."

"Kenny, you can't be serious!"

"You're not allowed to be on either campus where the news is happening. Why don't you tell me how you're supposed to continue covering this story?" Her executive producer always snapped out his words, but this time, he sounded like he was truly asking Stella for a way forward.

"You're going to get in touch with the superintendent of the school district, and then Hank's going to call the Board of Regents for the college. And you're going to pressure both organizations to lift the bullshit restraining orders by five o'clock tonight. And I'm going to continue working this story until it's over. That's what's going to happen. This is my story—" Lucky flinched in the seat next to her, and she lowered her voice, but the venom was still there. "This is my story," she repeated. "And I'm not giving it up. And you and Hank need to be asking yourselves why they want me off this story so badly. It's because it's bigger than a school shooting. Something is making them all nervous, and we'll miss it if you pull me."

She concentrated on quieting her breathing in the silence that followed.

"Stella..." Kenny trailed off, uncharacteristically uncertain.

"I've got an exclusive with Fran Miller's guardians set up. They're angry. She's not involved in the shooting at the high school, but she's got knowledge of someone who is. Give me until the weekend, Kenny. I just need more time."

"Fine. We'll make some calls. Stay away from the campuses until you hear back from me, you hear?"

"Done. Thanks, Kenny. You won't—" But the rest of the words died on her lips. He'd already hung up. She grinned, feeling victorious.

"The story lives?" Lucky offered.

"For another day, at least. Now, it looks like I'm free until five, and you were about to tell me what time they booked you for the hospital visit." Lucky was going to Lurie Children's Hospital to visit with some of the long-term care patients.

"Soon. About an hour." Lucky pulled up to the valet parking at the curb by their hotel and when they were both on the sidewalk, he pulled her close, taking both of her hands in his and rubbing his thumb across her knuckles. "Stella...can I say something without you biting my head off?"

She stiffened, but he tightened his hold on her hands, raised them up to his mouth, and planted a gentle kiss on each.

"Okay."

His lips lifted in a rueful smile. "Work isn't life. And life isn't just work. Don't let the two meld together, or there'll be nothing good left some days. And those days turn into weeks, and then it's all shit."

She freed her hands and rubbed them uncertainly. "Easy for you to say. You won your last—what? Six races? Do you even know how it feels to lose anymore?"

He tucked her hand into the crook of his elbow and led the way down the sidewalk. She didn't think he was going to answer; in fact, he slowed at the window of a tiny jewelry store tucked into the lobby of their hotel and paused to glance at the diamond rings in the display window. She averted her gaze and he laughed, a wholly unhappy sound, and towed her forward again. "Yes. I know what it's like to lose."

Stella's irritation melted away at his tone. She didn't know why she was giving him such a hard time. He'd certainly lived through difficult times; his mother had died years ago and his brother had been murdered shortly after Lucky and Stella had first met. She turned to him, but his eyes were locked straight ahead. She leaned into him, gripping his arm tighter. "Well, you don't have to anymore."

He looked at her sideways and smiled, and something inside her chest loosened at the sight.

"We've got a little over an hour until I have to go." Lucky raised his eyebrows as they reached the hotel. "What *shall* we do?"

Stella walked ahead of him into the lobby, glad they were back to their normal casual banter. "I can think of a few things."

"I can think of a few more."

"Ms. Reynolds?"

Stella turned at the thin wavering voice that came from her left. "Yes?"

The same pale girl who'd spilled her coffee the day before stood nearby, her eyes shadowed with exhaustion, her carrot-red hair pulled back into a tight ponytail at the crown of her head. "Do you have a minute?" The girl looked at Lucky suspiciously, and Stella swallowed a smile.

"Lucky, I'll—"

"See you upstairs," Lucky finished, shooting the girl a curious look before he walked to the bank of elevators at the back of the lobby.

When he was out of earshot, the girl cleared her throat nervously.

"My name is Penelope Triblay, and I wanted to ask you about a local student that I think you met recently."

It sounded like a rehearsed speech. Penelope's lip twitched and she took a deep breath. A pair of businessmen pushed past them, and the girl nearly lost her balance at the slight contact. Stella grabbed her elbow to steady her, realizing at the same moment that the poor thing was near collapsing.

"Penelope, let's talk over here." Stella led the girl to a set of chairs by the restaurant entrance and positioned herself so that they were in adjacent seats, knees almost touching. She dug into her bag and asked, "What's wrong?"

The girl's eyes flooded with tears at the sight of the pen poised over Stella's notebook. "I—I haven't seen my roommate in days. I, uh...I go to the University of Chicago. A-and I'm not sure what to do about it, because no one seems to care at my college, and I can't even get a hold of her parents, and my parents think I'm going nuts, but it's really all because I think something's wrong with her."

Stella dutifully wrote down the student's name, Sandy Bowen, but it wasn't anyone she'd ever heard of before. "And how long has she been missing?"

"I haven't *seen* her since Monday morning, but—"

"Did you file a missing persons report with the police?"

Penelope's eyes opened wide. "It never even occurred to me."

"There's not much I can do until she's officially missing, and even then, my hands are a bit tied." Stella laid a hand gently on Penelope's, unsure how to tell the poor girl that thousands of girls go missing every year, and only a few ever make it onto national TV. And unless Penelope's missing roommate was a pregnant young mother, chances were pretty slim that anyone at network would care.

"So I should file a report with CPD?"

"If she's missing, that's where I would start. Or even your campus police department," Stella added, thinking they might be more likely to take Penelope's concerns seriously. She repacked the tools of her trade and extracted a business card and handed it across to the girl. "If anyone launches an investigation, keep in touch. My email address is right there."

"Wait! Ms. Reynolds." Penelope still held Stella's card up in front of her, then plucked a twin business card from her pocket and held them next to each other. "I already have your card."

Stella's eyebrows raised, waiting for an explanation.

"Sandy must have come back to our room while I was out yesterday. She cleared out her desk, and her closet's empty. She..." Penelope bit her lip, looking uncertain for a moment before plowing straight into what sounded like another rehearsed speech. "She's been gone for weeks at a time before and always said she was visiting her family and just going straight from their house to classes, but this time it feels different. She's never packed everything up before without a word. She's always checked in, or we've talked on the phone...sometimes even had lunch or dinner together in the dining hall."

"And my card?" Stella asked, plucking both copies of her business card from Penelope's hands.

"I found it in the trashcan in our dorm room. I thought you might have been the last person to see her. I'm just...I'm worried about her."

Stella sighed and gave both business cards back to Penelope. She handed her card out like candy on Halloween, usually going through twenty or thirty a week. You never knew when someone you met would email months later with a great story idea. So, this Sandy girl: Stella might have met her this week at a fast food joint or a year ago in another city. There was no way to tell. "How long have you known your roommate?"

"Since we moved in this past September."

Stella took pity on the girl. "Listen, go ahead and email me her picture, and all the information you know about her—her height, hobbies, heck, even her parents' information if you have it. That way I'll have everything I need to know right out of the gate if we can move forward." She glanced around the lobby and saw Lucky leaning against the wall by the elevators, waiting for her. "But I'm afraid I wasn't on UC's campus at all this week." Penelope's face fell, and Stella repeated, "Send me what you can, and I'll make some calls."

Penelope nodded slowly, but didn't rise, and Stella left her sitting in the lobby.

She looked back while she and Lucky waited for the elevator. The girl held her phone up and nodded, then seemed to be waiting for Stella to do something.

She looked at her own screen and tapped the icon to open her email. Sure enough, a new message was there from Penelope Triblay. Her finger hesitated over the download, wondering if she was about to open some kind of malicious software, then chiding herself, she tapped the jpeg file and waited.

As soon as the picture started to load, she looked up and found Penelope staring at her from across the room. She gave the girl a thumbs-up, letting her know that she got the image, and Penelope nodded, then turned and made her way through the lobby with a crushing tide of middle school soccer players and their parents, clearly headed out for a game, matching uniforms making the space briefly feel like a stadium.

"Ready?"

Stella smiled at her boyfriend and turned toward the bank of elevators, then froze when her eyes caught the now-fully loaded image on her screen. The girl staring back at her was *Fran's* roommate. The roommate that everyone at St. Agnes insisted didn't exist.

Tandy, with an arm slung around Penelope's neck, smiled up at Stella. A choked sound must have escaped her lips, because Lucky looked over in concern. But before he could ask what was wrong, she was striding across the lobby, frantically scanning the crowded room for the girl.

The soccer team was gone, along with Penelope. Stella ran out the revolving door, nearly getting her bag stuck in the rotation, and burst out onto the sidewalk, only to find a line of soccer players and their parents waiting for valet parking and taxis.

"Did anyone see a redheaded girl just now? Anywhere?" Stella asked the closest group as she scanned the sidewalk and street for Penelope.

"I'm looking at one right now," a man drawled, making his wife and daughter laugh.

Stella ignored him, still searching the area, but only seeing taxis and Uber drivers, soccer players and businesspeople hurrying by.

A gust of wind sliced through her thin button-down and she shivered, staring at her phone screen once again.

Penelope Triblay knew who Tandy was. And Stella had let her slip through her fingers.

25

Back in the warmth of her hotel room, Stella sent a short email to Penelope, asking her to call, and then another, with her phone number, Lucky's, and even Art's. She wanted to make sure Penelope could get through to her, no matter what she was doing.

Now that she'd had a moment to collect herself, she berated herself for blowing the girl off in the first place.

Tandy Scarborough was also going by the name Sandy Bowen. For some reason, the girl that Stella had met as Fran's roommate was also Penelope's roommate.

Why was she operating under a dual identity?

And what about her had made Fran go to the police? Did the University of Chicago have a record of the girl, or was she a ghost at both places? Were *either* of the names she went by her real name?

Penelope might have some of the answers; after all, she knew how to get in touch with the girl's parents. Stella couldn't believe that she'd let the girl walk away.

"Where's the nearest police station?"

Lucky shrugged. "Let's see..." He pulled his phone out and did a search. "Looks like four blocks away."

"Okay." Stella nodded, her mind still racing. "Okay...I'm going to go there now. I told Penelope to file a police report; maybe that's just what she did."

"Do you want me to come with you?"

That was one of the things she loved about Lucky. He was ready to roll with the changes to their day without complaint. And though it was tempting to have him along for the ride, Lucky's fame wouldn't help her in this situation. "Thanks, but I'll be okay. And I'll probably be back soon."

She shrugged back into her jacket, tossed carelessly onto a chair near the door, and grabbed her briefcase.

"Bear?" Lucky called from the couch. "Good luck."

Her phone rang as soon as she hit the pavement outside, and the number wasn't familiar to her—might it be Penelope?

"Stella, it's Stu Miller, Fran's grandfather."

"Mr. Miller, how are you?"

"Not good. I just had the most frustrating conversation with the people at St. Agnes. The president is pretty sure he's a big deal."

"What happened?"

"He's telling me there is no Tandy Scarborough. That my daughter wasn't assigned a roommate."

"He told me the same thing, but we know that's not true."

"Exactly what I said. 'So who did my wife and I take out to dinner?' I asked. And that smug jerk had the audacity to tell me that my daughter must have 'taken in a stray.' Like Tandy was nothing more than a pet project of Fran's! A stranger to save."

"Is that possible?" Stella stepped around a grate in the sidewalk.

"No!" Stu roared. "We got the roommate assignment in the mail in July! From the college! Now they're telling us it didn't happen? Then who sent us the letter?"

"Can you find the letter? Email a picture of it to me?"

"I can't imagine we still have it."

"Please check. It's important."

"I'll ask Carol to search the house. We sent our girl to St. Agnes for an education, and it feels like we're getting a lesson in mismanagement and breach of contract instead."

"Have you been able to talk to Fran? What does she say?"

"Fran says she and Tandy left for classes at the same time most mornings. She told Fran that she was a liberal arts major, for crying out loud! She went to class along with everyone else in that dorm."

"So who was she?" Stella wondered out loud, meaning more than just the girl's name. Whichever name was true, Tandy Scarborough or Sandy Bowen, the girl posing as Fran and Penelope's roommate was involved in something either illegal or close to it, and Stella wanted to know why.

"They don't know," Stu said, answering Stella's question. "They don't have anyone named Tandy Scarborough listed as Fran's roommate—not even registered at the school! So, if she wasn't supposed to be in that dorm room with Frannie, then I want to know where the hell she was supposed to be."

"Me too," Stella muttered. The police station was across the street, and she unconsciously looked for Penelope as she spoke. "Mr. Miller, I've got to go. I might have a line on Tandy, but I've got to do some digging."

"You and me both, Stella. Keep me posted, please."

"You, too."

Stella slipped her phone into her pocket and took a deep breath before she entered the police station.

She shouldn't have bothered. She was back on the street fifteen minutes later with no information on Penelope and a now-suspicious sergeant with her name and phone number asking why she was looking for a college student when she'd had two restraining orders placed against her by organizations full of students in the last twenty-four hours.

She checked her email, but there wasn't anything new from Penelope. She spotted an empty park bench and sat, rubbing her palms against her thighs as she thought. Tandy was as elusive as a thief in the night, and just as sneaky. But she'd been in contact with so many people that she wasn't going to be able to stay out of the spotlight for long.

After all, Stella knew her roommate at St. Agnes College *and* the University of Chicago. And she was going to track Penelope down and get as much information as she could. Tandy was the key. Stella was certain.

The University of Chicago was eight miles away, straight down Michigan Avenue. And now she had a picture of Tandy/Sandy to show around.

She shifted forward on the bench and heard the torn pieces of the restraining order crinkle in her pocket, reminding her that she wasn't allowed on two campuses at all, and because of the restraining orders currently in her possession, she'd have a hard time convincing anyone that she didn't know that she needed to get permission to walk into campus buildings at UC's campus, too.

With a grimace, she made a split-second decision to ignore the rules. The University of Chicago campus was a huge bustling area in the middle of a busy section of Chicago! And she was alone, no photographer trailing her, causing a scene. No one would notice a lone woman walking around asking questions. She should be able to fly under the radar and might even get some answers about Tandy.

Four blocks later, she'd convinced herself that she was right. She texted Art to let him know he might get a call, and asked him to immediately conference Stella in should Penelope reach out to him first. She also asked him to head her way, in case she found someone who knew Tandy. She wanted to get everything on camera. She hopped in a taxi, stepping onto campus just fifteen minutes later.

Stella hesitated by the main entrance to the dorm building Penelope had identified as hers in the email, waiting for someone to walk out. It didn't take long, and soon she caught the door after a group of students left and slipped in, then stopped short when she nearly walked into a campus police officer.

"Stella Reynolds?"

She thought about lying, running, and grandstanding in quick succession, and ruled them out just as fast. "Yes."

"Please come with me. Non-students are not allowed on private school property."

"Shit."

A few students walking by stopped and raised their cell phones.

Their cameras followed her progress as the guard escorted her out of the building.

26

When Chief Sterling's number came up on her phone just a few minutes after the campus officer had dumped her at the edge of campus, Stella turned in a slow circle, looking for the camera. It felt like her every move was being recorded.

"Chief, what's going on?" Stella asked, trying to keep her suspicious tone at bay.

A Chicago police officer walked by and she put her head down and scurried in the opposite direction, looking for a cab.

"I just wanted to let you know that we've made an arrest."

"Who? Where?" she asked, barely swallowing a swear word when she jammed her finger into the point of a pen as she searched her bag for a notebook.

"Ardale Jones is now in custody, charged with intentional homicide in the death of Dana Scott."

"And...?" Stella asked, sucking on her finger quickly before jotting down the information.

"And that's it." Sterling blew out a slow breath. "He has an alibi for the school shooting."

"Oh." Stella stopped in her tracks, chewing on her lip for a moment before she remembered that she was wearing lipstick. "A good one?"

"Airtight. With surveillance video to back it up."

"So he's not your guy for Rivermoor High."

Sterling sighed. "Afraid not. Our detectives continue to investigate. Just wanted to let you know."

"Thanks, Chief." Before Sterling could hang up, though, Stella asked a final question. "Chief, I've learned something about Fran's roommate."

"Stella, I don't have time right now. Can we talk later?"

"Sure, it's just—"

"I'm sorry, Stella. I've got to get this press release out before the TV stations all blow their lids. I've got two minutes. Is it fast?"

"Not really."

"Then call me tomorrow, okay? Or maybe Monday. If I'm available, I'll pick up."

"But, Chief—" She stopped talking when she heard the unmistakable click of the line going dead. She texted Ken to let him know about the arrest, but it was no longer a story for national news now that it wasn't connected to the school shooting.

However, Stella's job was far from over. She opened the rideshare app on her phone and ordered a car. She had work to do.

TECHNICALLY SPEAKING, Stella was not allowed on the Rivermoor High campus at all. But even before the restraining order had been filed, she was supposed to get permission from the school principal to go onto campus and ask questions.

But following rules like that never led to getting any real answers, and more often than not, tipped officials off enough that they could circle the wagons and prevent her from getting any information at all.

So Stella asked Art to drive her to Rivermoor High School.

"How long are we going to wait here, anyway?" he complained after about five minutes of sitting in the quiet car.

Stella bit back a snarky retort. "I'm not sure. I'm looking for someone."

"Who?"

"I don't know."

Art grumbled and then put in some earbuds, cranked up the music on his phone, and leaned back with his eyes closed.

When she was sure he was totally zoned out, she took out her phone and dialed. The school secretary picked up on the second ring.

"Rivermoor High School. How may I direct your call?"

"Is this Kathy Brimstone?"

"Yes?" came the cautious reply.

After Stella introduced herself, she said, "They made an arrest in the gas station shooting, did you hear?"

"Oh—no. No, I didn't hear. Is it someone...I mean, do they think they've solved our shooting too?"

"No. In fact, they know the shootings are unrelated now."

"Oh. Oh my."

"Do you have a minute? I have some questions about the backup security system at the school."

There was a long pause, then speaking low and fast, Kathy said, "I'm on break in ten minutes. If you can get here, I'll be around back, by the soccer fields."

Kathy hung up and Stella stared at the school for a long moment. The fact that Kathy didn't shut her down immediately meant something. But would the woman know enough to make a difference? Would she go on the record with whatever it was she did know?

She shook Art. "I'm going to walk around the building. Stretch my legs. Be back in a bit."

"Suit yourself," Art said, then muttered something about if Stella wanted to freeze, that was her own business.

She buttoned her coat up as she climbed out of the car. It was cold, but not bitterly so, with a ceiling of low-hanging clouds keeping in some of the day's warmth. Looking at the building, she remembered the chaos of Monday morning. Could the gunman have slipped out with thousands of other students and simply melted away? Or did he wait, holed up safely inside until someone gave him the all-clear?

There was one way to know for sure. To see security video from that day.

Stella walked around the far edge of the parking lot, not wanting to get too close to the front windows—and administrators—of the school. As she followed the road that ran alongside the building, though, she paused as the vastness of the athletic fields became clear. Six soccer fields lined the road that led behind the school. Then to the north of the structure, six tennis courts, a second large parking lot, and beyond that, the football stadium backed right up to the interstate.

Stella stayed near the fence across the parking lot from the school and her eyes swept the structure, wondering from where Kathy would emerge. She leaned against the fence to wait, slipping her gloves on as the chill seeped through her coat.

After a few minutes, Kathy came out of a door by the boxy gymnasium and scanned the area, nodding briskly when they made eye contact.

She stepped off the sidewalk onto the asphalt and set off at an angle across the parking lot. Stella started walking, and they intersected paths by the sidewalk that led past the football stadium fence.

"What do you want to know?" Kathy asked, keeping her pace brisk.

"I spoke to the school resource officer yesterday. She said there's a backup to the security system that should have been recording Monday during the shooting."

Kathy licked her lips. "Yes, she's right. But the department chair who oversees the system says it wasn't running. He doesn't know why."

"Who's the department chair?"

"Man by the name of Charlie Hartman. He's been with us for nearly twenty years."

"What does he say went wrong?"

Kathy flipped her collar up against the cold. "He doesn't know what happened. He'd set it up to be automatic. It runs off an algorithm. When the main system shuts off, it flips on. Automatically."

Stella walked in lockstep with the school admin for a few steps, thinking. "Is it possible for someone to override the system?"

Kathy grimaced, either against the cold or Stella's questions. "Yes, of course. It's not a bank vault, it's a high school. Other people could have access, no doubt."

"Who?"

"Well, any teacher, really. We all have master keys to get into most of the rooms in the building. But really, why would anyone want to override it? What could anyone gain?"

They reached the far end of the football field and Stella turned to look at the school administrator.

"Kathy, if someone inside the building helped the shooter escape, is it really so hard to imagine they helped plan the attack in the first place?" Kathy flinched, as if the thought pained her, but Stella pressed on. "And if someone who works in the building helped plan the attack, they'd want to make sure there wasn't any video evidence of the crime."

Kathy's eyes looked troubled as she surveyed the end of the field and the interstate beyond.

"Kathy, talk to me. You can't tell me that *every* teacher in the building could access the computer systems that record the security video. That can't be true. There must be passwords, usernames, security questions that only the administrators of the program could access. Who had access, besides Charlie Hartman?"

"I don't know everyone who has access!" Kathy said, her voice plaintive.

"But you know *some* of the people. Start there."

Kathy chewed on her fingernail, distraught. "But I don't want to point a finger at someone who might be innocent."

"I'm not the police, Kathy. No one will get in trouble. But your information might just make a difference in identifying the shooter."

Kathy's head dropped. She rubbed her forehead and then pulled her hair back, holding it at the crown of her head as she looked back up at Stella.

"The school principal, of course, Chris Evers. I remember the gym teacher, Joanna Rillers, was granted access after the volleyball team she coaches needed extra floor space. She asked the team captains to run drills in the hallway and wanted to keep an eye on things from her office."

"Anyone else?"

Kathy sighed. "The theater teacher. Madeline Mowery. She has an account from a production they did in the fall. She needed overhead shots of her cast dancing in the hallway, and Charlie gave her access to the whole program. I never heard of anyone else with access, but that doesn't mean no one else did."

"But as far as you know...?"

Kathy blew out a resigned huff. "Yes. As far as I know, that's it."

"Anyone in the school administration talking about when the system went down?"

Kathy slid a sideways glance at Stella. "Yes."

Stella's eyebrows shot up as she waited for Kathy to continue, but the other woman didn't. "Well?" Stella prompted.

"I overheard the principal tell the superintendent that it was all working fine until Sunday night."

"The system 'went down' right before the shooting? More likely someone shut it down, don't you think?"

Kathy's head dropped, but she didn't have to say anything. The answer was obvious.

"How do you access it? Can you log in from any computer, or is there a specific system you have to use?"

"It's a separate system. Charlie said you've got to access it from the main hub."

"And where's that?"

"It's..." Kathy shook her head, uncomfortable in her role as informant.

"I'll find out eventually, Kathy. You're just saving me a few hours and phone calls."

Kathy sighed. "The hub is in the fine arts wing. In a small supply closet between the theater and choir room."

Red and blue lights flashed across Stella's vision. A police car rolled past the fields on the closest road, a hundred yards away. Stella turned away instinctively. The restraining order. She wasn't supposed to be here.

"I've got to go. Anything else I should know?"

"Nothing I can think of. But Stella? Be careful."

"You, too."

Stella walked back to the car, her head down against both the wind and recognition. She ducked into Art's car just as the cruiser pulled into the school parking lot.

"Go," she said, the urgency in her voice making Art's eyebrows shoot up.

"We on the run?"

"No. Of course not. Just running late." Stella hunched low in her seat and kept an eye on the officer as he climbed out of his cruiser and glanced back at their car. She held her breath until he turned back to the school building and Art pulled through their spot and spun the wheel, driving out of the parking lot.

Art hummed tunelessly along with an Elvis song, and Stella's lips puckered.

She was just being paranoid. There was no way the officer knew that Stella was there and breaking the restraining order. Then again, it had felt like the campus security officer had been waiting for her down at UC's campus earlier that morning. And that seemed like more than just bad luck.

27

Stella heard Lucky open the hotel door but didn't roll over to face him. She just wasn't ready. He came into the bedroom with a gust of cool air that followed him from the hallway and sat down in the "c" of her curled body.

"Bear. I brought you news."

She opened her eyes. "News of what?"

"Just news." He smacked her hip with a rolled-up newspaper and then leaned down to plant a searing kiss on her lips.

"How was the hospital? How were the kids?"

"Great." Lucky ran his hand through his hair. "And awful. You know how it is."

Stella nodded. She knew exactly what it was like to visit with children fighting cancer. The kids were amazing. Their situation was just awful. It was hard not to let it wedge into your heart.

"I ordered us a late lunch," he said, motioning to the table by the door. "Remember when Friday afternoons were for leaving work early and getting a head start on the weekends?"

"Barely," Stella said.

A light smile brushed his lips and he tossed the paper down on the tray of food between two covered dishes. "Best get a move on before that phone of yours starts up again."

He glided out of the room and Stella sat up, knowing he was right. She'd been wallowing in despair at the way her day had played out, but at any minute, Ken might call with an update on the restraining order court fight. She might as well enjoy the small uncomplicated part of her day that was left before that happened.

She climbed out of bed and smoothed her suit, wrinkled just slightly from her time horizontal. Then she unfurled the paper, pressing down against the middle fold, and uncovered the nearest dish. Scrambled eggs and some kind of roasted potatoes. But before she could take a bite, Lucky made a strange sound from the other room.

"Lucky? You okay?" she called. When he didn't answer, she went to investigate, still holding the newspaper in her hand.

"Bear. How're those eggs, huh? You save any for me?" He met her at the door and tried to push her back into the bedroom. She might have let him, if she hadn't heard her own name coming from the television set.

"...Stella Reynolds, a lovelorn network reporter, was just arrested for trespassing in downtown Chicago."

"What?" she said, and Lucky let her push past him. She approached the TV like it was a wild animal, her stomach clenched as tightly as her fists. On screen, the entertainment reporter was replaced by cell phone video of Stella being escorted from campus. Those shots then melted into video of her from different charity events and speaking engagements from the past two years as the story continued.

"Twenty-seven-year-old Stella Reynolds, an NBC national news correspondent, was ejected from the University of Chicago campus just hours ago and served with a notice to appear in court for violating a restraining order recently filed by the university."

Stella stood stiffly in front of the TV, one hand covering her mouth. "What...That's not even true. I...they..."

Lucky moved next to her in time to hear the next absurd line.

"Insiders tell this reporter that the network correspondent was despondent over former flame John Stevenson's recent engagement to Victoria's Secret model Jarissa Headley. Had she been holding out hope that she would someday reunite with her former lover? Maybe Reynolds is tired of the fast lane with NASCAR star Lucky Haskins and wishes she could settle down with Stevenson. Other sources confirm that the nearly over-the-hill redhead's bosses aren't happy with the overhyped star, and are close to pulling her assignments and placing her on leave."

Stella quenched the ridiculous urge to laugh.

Lucky remained irritatingly calm while Stella flopped into a chair in the corner, abandoning the newspaper on her lap and pressing her fists into her eyes as the gossipy reporter came back on screen to take a question from the gossip anchor. There was more? What else could they make up about her day? Her life?

She hadn't even told her boss about being escorted off campus that morning. It frankly didn't even warrant mentioning. Reporters were asked to leave places they weren't supposed to be all the time.

Lucky moved across the room and crouched down in front of her, his hands on the arms of her chair. "Stella?"

"Yes?" Stella didn't move her fists from her eyes, preferring to see the blank black backs of her eyelids to cell phone video of her being escorted from campus. Not arrested—escorted!

"I said the clown who just did that slam job's name is Gail McCoy. Do you know her?"

"McCoy?" Stella's head flopped back, but she didn't open her eyes. She felt unaccountably tired. How could she continue to work on a story when her every move would now be assessed under the false narrative of this dubious report? She finally looked up to answer Lucky, when something lurking in the depths of his eyes made her grab his hands. "I don't, you know." She wasn't talking about Gail McCoy, and Lucky knew it.

"Are you sure?"

"God, Lucky! I swear. I haven't seen him—haven't even thought of him—in a long time. You have to know that."

He squeezed her hand reassuringly. "I believe you, Bear. But you've got to wonder why Gail McCoy is saying so."

Stella stood and started pacing again, slapping the folded paper against her palm as she spoke. "I've never even heard of Gail McCoy.

There's a TV reporter in town, *Malcolm* McCoy. I mean, it's not a last name like Smith, but McCoy isn't so unusual that there couldn't be more than one in a town the size of Chicago. It might be a coincidence."

"Looks like they're siblings," Lucky said, reading from his phone screen. "According to Wikipedia, anyway. Both have been in the news business in Chicago for years. And she's the city's premier gossip reporter."

She groaned and peered over Lucky's shoulder to read his screen. The words on the page blurred in front of her eyes—not from tears, but because she was so angry, she could hardly see straight. She stepped back and then threw the newspaper across the room, watching with satisfaction as the pages scattered to the ground.

"Stella..." Lucky looked down to hide a ghost of a smile. "I know better than to tell you what to do, and I know you well enough to know that you've got this. That clip means nothing, and it won't matter more than your history of excellent work for NBC." Lucky stood without speaking for a moment, and Stella flashed him a smile of thanks, but was still too angry to speak.

He nodded to himself and then headed for the door, turning back at the last moment to say, "And you're not even close to over the hill."

She snorted as he left, then slowly sank to her knees, the fit of rage leaving just as suddenly as she'd been overcome. *Arrested, my foot.* Gail McCoy was trying to railroad her in some strange, misguided show of loyalty to her brother.

The paper crinkled under her knee, and she pushed herself up to collect the pages and put them back into order. The TV set was still on, and a commercial for the upcoming newscast cut in. "A student from the University of Chicago has been found dead, and officers suspect foul play." Stella gasped as the anchor continued, "Our reporters are on the scene in Rivermoor and we'll have the latest, tonight at five." By the time the weather anchor was predicting snow flurries for the evening, Stella had grabbed her coat and was out the door.

28

"You're where?" Ken's characteristic biting tone was gone. Instead, he sounded confused.

Stella hopped out of the Uber and waved to the driver. "I'm just out getting some air." Her eyes watered with a gust of icy wind that swept through the intersection, and she blinked rapidly, looking for police cars. She followed their flashing lights around to the back of a strip-mall parking lot located at the far west side of Rivermoor and tried to focus on her boss's words.

"I've got good news, Stella. One of the regents at St. Agnes is an advertising exec that Hank knows. Frankly, the guy couldn't find anyone to explain why the restraining order was filed in the first place, so he's convinced the college to drop it. And get this: the high school doesn't know anything about a restraining order. The superintendent says it didn't come from his office. Looks like someone's playing a trick on us."

"How?" Stella asked.

"Exactly," Ken said. "I told him that he'd better look into his own shop and see who's sending faxes full of fraudulent and fake legal filings to NBC News. That should be someone getting fired right there."

"Agree, and surely whoever sent the fax knew the risk they were taking." She slowed her pace. "Interesting that someone wants me away from campus that much, don't you think?"

"Not sure it even matters, Stella. If they don't make an arrest soon, we're pulling you anyway. Time to move on." He disconnected.

Stella slipped her press badge out of her briefcase and held it up as she approached the outside ring of the crime scene. The officer guarding the road let her pass, and she hurried toward a cluster of cameras and reporters gathered at the back edge of the parking lot behind the strip mall.

"What's going on?" Stella asked a print reporter she recognized from the press conferences at the Rivermoor police station.

"They're about to move the victim," he said, scratching his chin with the edge of his notebook. "Then RPD will send the Sarge over to talk."

"Chief Sterling's not here?"

"Haven't seen her yet. What are you doing here, anyway? NBC sending you back to local news?"

"I was just..." Stella shook her head, suddenly unable to speak. A line of cruisers and an ambulance blocked the view of the back of the building. A group of cops and medics stood together half a block away near a Dumpster.

"Coming through!" A horn blasted two short beeps from the opening of the road between two sections of the strip mall, and a uniformed police officer rushed over to push the crime scene tape up so a nondescript minivan could drive closer. It maneuvered around so that the headlights faced the reporters and the back doors banged open toward a bank of Dumpsters by the building.

Two people wearing shirts with the local coroner's office logo on the chest trundled a gurney out and disappeared from view.

"You got someone on the other side, by the storefronts?" Stella asked the local CBS photographer, who looked just as frustrated as she felt by their inability to see what was happening.

"Nah. They're not bringing the body through the store, that's for sure."

And so they did what reporters everywhere spent half of their working hours doing. They waited.

Stella silenced her phone, not interested in taking calls from her boss or Lucky, or God forbid, her mother, who had a knack for calling at the worst possible time. She simply stared at the minivan, hoping that the dead student on the other side wasn't Penelope. That she hadn't turned away a desperate girl who'd decided Stella was her last hope. That someone one step removed from Fran Miller hadn't met her death in a cold alley. Alone.

"Hup, hup!" one of the photographers called, some twenty minutes later.

The gurney made its journey in reverse, slower this time, as the people from the coroner's office moved the victim to the waiting minivan. One of the cruisers had left, giving the assembled press a good view of the scene.

When they were just a few feet away, the gurney hit a particularly large divot in the asphalt and the victim's arm flopped off the board.

The closest attendant lifted the sheet to tuck the arm back in, and all the blood drained from Stella's face. A flash of carrot-red hair confirmed that Penelope was dead.

An officer approached as the gurney disappeared into the back of the minivan.

"Just a few comments, guys. Just a few." A Sergeant walked over, holding out her hand for microphone packs and a couple of the photographers gratefully handed them over. She deftly clipped them on and got down to business. "I am Sergeant Wendy O'Neal with the Rivermoor Police Department's homicide unit. We were called out to the Moorings Strip Mall just after ten o'clock today on reports of a body. Responding officers were directed to this alley, where they found a white female, unresponsive. After further investigation, it was determined that the victim was deceased."

The officer paused for a breath and Stella jumped in. "Cause of death?"

O'Neal was unfazed by the interruption. "She was a student at the University of Chicago, and while we're not releasing the cause of death, we do suspect foul play. Certainly, we want to locate her next of kin before releasing her identity. It will be important for us to reconstruct her final hours, though, so we're asking her roommate at the University of Chicago to come forward and meet with detectives." O'Neal continued giving non-answers and "no comments" until she ended the interview. "We'll send out any new information as it's available, guys, thanks. Oh, one more thing. The yoga studio is cooperating fully with our investigation and wants the community to know that they'll help us solve this crime any way they can."

"What yoga studio?" Stella asked the photographer next to her.

He motioned to the back of the strip of shops. "The body was found behind their Dumpster."

She moved to the side of the alley to intercept O'Neal as she headed back toward the crime scene. "Sergeant O'Neal? Stella Reynolds, NBC News. Off the record, I wanted to know if you've identified the victim yet?"

She sighed, but stopped walking to answer. "No comment."

"I work for network; believe me, I'm not here to report on a local case."

"Then why are you here?" O'Neal glanced away, and making eye contact with a colleague past Stella, she rolled her eyes as if to say, "The media, right?"

Stella's mind raced, trying to come up with something on the spot that would convince the sergeant to share some intel. "Just working on a long-format piece that might run sometime next year, on...on runaway teens and, um..." Her brain blanked, and she felt the unwavering stare from the officer.

"And?"

A flash of inspiration struck. "And how they get lost in the system." It was true; not that she was doing a story on it, but that it happened with heartbreaking regularity.

Sergeant O'Neal's brow furrowed, but she finally shrugged. "A lot of cases go nowhere, and let me tell you, there ain't usually anybody asking any questions after the morgue releases the bodies."

Stella made a mental note to actually dig into that statement for a future story, but just then, she cleared her expression, waiting for O'Neal to finish.

"But I don't think this is one of those cases. Off the record—and

I'm serious, the chief will bust my ass if she gets wind that I released this without clearance—but her student ID says her name is Penelope Triblay. Detectives should have already let her family and the school know. We're probably about thirty minutes away from sending out a press release with her name."

"Damn." Stella's stomach dropped as if she'd missed a step—no, missed the whole staircase.

"Yeah. You'll be hearing about this one on the local news, mark my words."

Stella tried to school her features into something that resembled impassive. She backed away from a group of officers, suddenly sure they could sense her guilty feelings from across the blacktop.

"Is Chief Sterling available?" Stella's throat was dry and scratchy, and she couldn't seem to swallow. She wanted—no, needed—to tell Sterling what she knew; the chief would understand the layers to the case that would take hours to explain to a sergeant who didn't know Fran—didn't know about the missing roommate.

"She's off today, but you can be certain that our department can operate without her having to be at every crime scene." O'Neal was irritated. Stella didn't blame her.

"Can you have Sterling call me? She has my number."

O'Neal's eyes narrowed. "She's strictly DND today." At Stella's blank look the officer frowned. "Do not disturb. A family issue."

"Of course." Stella's stomach plummeted again. This time like she'd stepped off the roof of a building. She backed away from the police cruisers and headed toward the street, pulling out her phone with shaky hands.

After finding a bench to sit on, she opened her email and tapped the message that Penelope had sent just the day before.

Penelope had been looking for her roommate yesterday, and now she was dead. Fran was supposedly in protective police custody. That left one person unaccounted for. Sandy Bowen.

There it was in black and white in the email. Sandy Bowen's home phone number. Stella tapped the digits on her screen and then heard the line ring as the call went through. It was answered midway through the first ring.

"Hello?"

"I'm looking for Sandy Bowen," Stella said, glad her voice was steady.

"This is Rebecca, her mother. Stepmother," she corrected. "But I'm afraid she's not here."

"When should I call back?" Stella asked.

There was a long pause, and when Rebecca answered, her voice was guarded. "I don't know."

Stella introduced herself, then cut Rebecca off when she tried to politely disconnect. "I need to speak to you about Sandy. I think she's in trouble."

Rebecca cleared her throat once, then again when her voice broke on the first word. "I think you're right."

29

Call waiting beeped in, but Stella ignored it. She had Fran's elusive roommate's stepmother on the phone—and there were a lot of questions that needed answers.

She jerked her briefcase open and dug a notebook and pen out of the bag, but before she could ask the first question, Rebecca cleared her throat.

"Ms. Reynolds, why do you want to talk to Sandy?"

It seemed like a good time to gauge the other woman's reaction to what Stella knew. "Do you know how I met your stepdaughter?"

"No." The single word sounded strained.

"I was talking to an old family friend and happened to meet her roommate. Tandy."

"I'm sorry, the connection must be bad, but oh dear, you knew Penelope, then? We just got word about what happened to her, and I'm so—"

"Not Penelope." She paused to let Rebecca process her words. "Mrs. Bowen, I met your stepdaughter in the dorm room she shared with another student at St. Agnes College in Rivermoor. She introduced herself to me as Tandy Scarborough."

"Scar—" Rebecca sucked in a loud gasp, then, her voice wobbly, said, "What are you—that's, that's not—it's not...Oh, God." The name Scarborough clearly meant something to her, but what, Stella had no idea.

"Then, a girl named Penelope Triblay tracked me down at my hotel and asked me to help her find *her* missing roommate at the University of Chicago, Sandy Bowen. Penelope emailed me a picture, and when I opened the file, I saw Tandy Scarborough staring back at me." Stella turned away from a couple walking slowly by with a shiny-haired Golden Retriever and moved the phone closer to her lips, lowering her voice. "I'm in Rivermoor now, where I just watched the coroner's office arrive to take Penelope's body to the morgue, and now I'm trying to find out why Sandy and Tandy are the same person, and why that person is living a double life."

A muffled conversation followed, as Bowen spoke to someone in the room with her. A rumbling, deep voice answered, though Stella couldn't make out any of the words. Stella waited, though her pen now lay across the notebook. There wouldn't be any notes to take in this conversation. They were clearly, all of them, trying to catch up to the facts, not share any.

"Sandy's in hiding. She says it's not safe here—not safe anywhere! Her father thought she was being dramatic, and then we just got a call from the university about Penelope. S-s-sweet g-girl." Her voice caught again, and she took several loud breaths before continuing. "If we can protect Sandy, we will. But at this point, I don't even know who we're protecting her from."

Stella processed that for a moment. "So...is she there with you?"

"No!" Rebecca snapped the word out like it hurt to say, then let out a choppy laugh that ended with a hiccup. "No, she's not here."

Stella perched at the edge of her seat, cradling the phone between her ear and shoulder. "What's going on, Mrs. Bowen? Why isn't Sandy safe?"

"It has to do with the teacher. That damn teacher, I'm sure of it."

"Is this a teacher at St. Agnes University, or at the University of Chicago?"

"I've never even *heard* of St. Agnes."

Stella let that slide for the moment. "So it's a teacher at U of C who is doing...what?" She had no idea what Rebecca was going to say and didn't want to put words into her mouth.

"No, not at U of C. I—it's hard to explain." Rebecca fell silent, as if she were groping for words. "I obviously don't know half of what's going on, but I do know this: Sandy has been acting strange and distant since her senior year in high school. That's when she met a theater teacher from Rivermoor High."

"Madeline Mowery?" Stella asked, confused by the sudden turn of the conversation.

"Exactly."

"Did Sandy go to Rivermoor?" Stella could feel her eyes grow wider at this admission. To have Sandy's stepmother link her to Rivermoor High, the school currently investigating an escaped shooter that put several students in the hospital, wasn't good—not good at all for Sandy.

"No," Rebecca said, her voice catching again. There was an extra layer of meaning behind the word that Stella noted but didn't understand. "No, they met during a community theater production, and Madeline seemed to take Sandy under her wing. We thought it was marvelous, of course. At first, anyway. But since Sandy went off to college, it feels like this teacher has too much influence over our girl. And everything that's happening now makes me think it's even worse than we suspected." Rebecca took a deep breath and pushed on. "Sandy is a young, impressionable girl of nineteen. She told us this summer that she and Madeline were working on something—but it was all very mysterious. She wouldn't really describe what the project entailed."

"Couldn't you ask Madeline?" Stella asked.

"Have you met her?"

"Yes."

"Then you know you get nothing out of Madeline that she doesn't want to give you."

Stella nodded, though Rebecca couldn't see her. That had certainly been her own assessment of Madeline Mowery over the last week.

Rebecca cleared her throat and pressed on. "Sandy...She's in over her head. We can't figure out what's going on, but maybe you can."

Stella leaned forward, weighing her words carefully. "Mrs. Bowen, I'm happy to hear your story, look into whatever threat you think exists, but Sandy needs to go to the police. She needs *their* protection if she thinks she's in danger. The power of the pen is often strongest after the violence, not before."

"I'm sure that's not—"

"Mrs. Bowen, three kids were shot at Rivermoor High, and Sandy's been leading some sort of double life that you didn't even know about until I called today. Now one of her roommates is dead, and the other roommate, the one you knew nothing about, is in protective police custody, and it has something to do with the violence at the high school. I hate to say this, but...are you sure that Sandy's the one who needs protecting?"

Rebecca Bowen's breathing was loud and erratic over the phone, and when she finally spoke, her voice was small. Broken. "I have to think that you'll be able to find out more than I ever could. Ask questions. Do your job."

And with those final parting words, Mrs. Bowen disconnected the call. Stella stared at the sidewalk, hardly feeling the cold wind that lifted her hair into a wild halo around her head.

The theater teacher from Rivermoor High School was retiring; what kind of pull could she possibly have over Sandy Bowen?

She walked backward through everything she'd learned over the last several days, after talking to the esteemed high school theater director herself. She did lay claim to at least one famous alumna. But what could that have to do with Penelope's death, the current school shooting, Fran, and the girl living a double life?

She needed corroboration. Someone else to talk to her about the theater teacher. Someone not currently connected to the school.

She jumped up from the bench and hailed a passing taxi. She could think of one person who probably wouldn't answer *her* call but might just answer someone else's.

After giving the driver the address for her hotel, she picked up her phone and tapped the name at the top of her favorites list. He answered on the first ring.

"Lucky? I need your help."

30

By the next morning, Stella felt like she'd been waiting for the upcoming meeting Lucky had helped her set up for days. Years, even. She paced in front of the TV in the hotel room, looking at her watch and the wall clock in regular intervals.

"Go!" Lucky said, softening his words with a smile. "Just go. Wait there. You're going nuts, and you're about to push me over the edge with you."

She held up her hands, defeated. "This was my version of 'waiting patiently.' You're telling me I didn't exactly nail it?"

"You're wearing a path in that carpet, darlin', so no, I'd say your patience routine needs some work."

"I won't be long," Stella said, already reaching for her bag. "Maybe an hour and a half?"

"And by then, I'll be off and running. Just some last-minute items to check off before tonight's gala. You do have your dress, right?"

"Of course," Stella said, wondering where she could find a dress at this late stage.

Lucky's eyes narrowed, easily catching her in the lie. "Bethany picked out two dresses for you and said she'll leave them in the closet by lunchtime."

Bethany was Lucky's assistant; she took care of everything from his dry cleaning to his calendar, and that meant occasionally taking care of Stella's needs too.

Stella grinned. "Your idea?"

"No, hers. She doesn't want another Austin on her hands." Lucky smiled back and they both laughed. Months ago, there had been a black-tie event for which Stella had been wildly unprepared, sending her and Lucky to a department store at the mall on their way to the dinner.

"The airline lost my luggage! That was definitely not my fault."

"And tonight?" Lucky challenged, his eyebrows raised.

"And tonight, I'm thankful for Bethany's help," Stella said, planting a kiss on Lucky's cheek.

A half hour later, inside the smoothie shop where they'd arranged to meet, Stella ordered an energy shake called "Milky Whey" while she waited for her interview subject to arrive. The drink, which tasted not even remotely like a delicious chocolate bar, had cost nearly ten dollars, tasted like grass, and looked like dead leaves.

The door opened, and Stella set the beverage down with relief when she recognized the woman entering the shop.

Sophia Thomas swept into the store like she'd walked onto a movie set, and even though people said that movie stars were just regular people, this one practically shone from the inside.

She pulled her designer hat off and looked around, running a hand through her hair. Every movement radiated confidence.

Her eyes landed on Stella and lit up. "Stella!" Her warm voice was like hot cocoa on a cold day, and she grabbed Stella's hands in her own, her eyebrows drawn together with concern. "Lucky said there's an emergency?"

Stella gulped. "Thanks so much for agreeing to see me on such short notice."

"Anything for Lucky. Ooh, do you like it?" she asked, looking at Stella's drink.

"Ummm, it's very healthy," Stella said, trying to be judicious in her review. Sophia had glowed effusively about the store, saying it had been a favorite treat back in her younger years.

Sophia bit her lip, and her cheeks dimpled adorably. "Well, you can't have taste and good nutrition all at the same time, I guess."

She placed an order, then motioned to the back of the store toward a booth in the corner. "Let's sit. I forgot how much I love this city! So bustling, and everyone's too busy to care about anyone else walking by. Fabulous."

A cluster of girls walked noisily into the shop and Sophia took a large swallow of her beverage, stoically avoiding the grimace that curled Stella's lips inward when she sampled her own drink.

The girls fussed around with their cell phones, taking pictures of each other and the menu board in the shop.

Stella turned back to find Sophia staring wistfully at the girls. "You don't know how great that age is until you're well past it."

Stella smiled. "I think everyone's too busy looking ahead to appreciate being seventeen." She pushed her drink over to the side and leaned forward. "Do you get back much to visit?"

"No." The word was loaded, and Stella looked up to find Sophia's gaze shifting restlessly around the room. "I'm...busy, I guess. No. I don't come back often. Not since I graduated, actually. But I do donate to a local charity, so part of me will always be here."

Stella looked up, curious. "I wanted to ask you about that charity, Sophia. I must have written down the wrong name during our conversation on Wednesday."

"Tomorrow's Promise. It's a fantastic group, Stella. They do really great work."

"Hmm. Well, I spoke to the director a couple of nights ago—and forgive me, but he'd never heard of you."

"What?" Sophia's gaze flew from the girls still mugging in the front of the shop to Stella.

"Well, correction. He's *heard* of you, of course, but has no knowledge of you supporting their charity."

"There must be a clerical error, then. I've been sending money to them since I signed my first contract in Hollywood. Oh!" She sat back and laughed lightly. "But not in my own name, of course. It's through a trusted advisor, so they wouldn't know me personally. But they do really great work in the community."

"Well, that's just it. The director told me they're going to have to close down at the end of the year. They apparently lost a major donor about four years ago and haven't been able to recover."

"No. Four years ago? Are you sure?"

"Sure enough that the director was pretty excited to hear you might be interested in supporting their mission. Do you want his information?"

Sophia stared right through Stella.

"Sophia? Do you want the information for the organization?"

"Yes," she answered slowly. "Please send it on to my assistant, if you can."

"Of course."

"Is that all, Stella? I've got to rest up before the gala tonight."

"Actually, Sophia, the main reason I asked you to meet me here was to ask you about Madeline Mowery. From Rivermoor High."

Sophia's face blanched for a flash, before an ill-timed visit from the mixologist interrupted them.

"I wanted to offer you both a sample of our most popular drink, the 'Walk This Whey.' Ms. Thomas? I'm a huge fan, by the way! I forgot to mention that I gave you a free upgrade to organic locally sourced honey."

"Thank you, but I'm all set. Stella?"

The girl couldn't tear her eyes away from the movie star to acknowledge Stella's murmured "no."

"Okay, well. I'll just be behind the counter if you think of anything."

Sophia smiled charmingly at the young girl and took her time before returning her gaze to Stella.

"Some things are better left undisturbed. And I'd put my time with Madeline Mowery in that category. I don't know you well, Stella, but take my advice: stay away from that woman."

"I can't. Just yesterday, I spoke with the mother of a former student of Madeline's. She's worried that the teacher is taking advantage of her daughter."

"You have to want it bad enough to get through the hard times."

Sophia's voice was as cold as a steel beam in the winter, and as unforgiving. "Not everyone wants it bad enough."

Stella's brow furrowed, not sure that Sophia was in the same conversation that Stella was trying to have. "That's just it, Sophia. Now the hard times have roped in a friend of the family."

Sophia shifted restlessly in her seat, and Stella leaned forward, reaching out but stopping just short of putting her hand on Sophia's arm.

"Here's what I know: there was a shooting at your high school alma mater. A family friend who attends St. Agnes is now in protective police custody, somehow related to the shooting. We now know that her roommate, a girl named Tandy, was never even enrolled at St. Agnes—certainly not assigned to live with anyone on campus.

"Then another girl—who attends the University of Chicago—searches me out yesterday to ask if I know where her *missing* roommate is. But I brushed her off—God, why didn't I just let her talk to me?" Stella raked her hands through her hair, her frustration boiling over. "But no! I brushed her off, and by the time I realized that her missing roommate was the same girl who'd been living with my family friend—she was dead. *Dead!* Killed and abandoned in an alleyway behind a yoga studio! And this girl with two identities is now in hiding —and her stepmother says it all has to do with Madeline Mowery!"

Forgetting about the vile taste, Stella sipped from her smoothie and nearly choked when the thick sludgy mouthful made its way down her throat. When she'd wiped her streaming eyes with a napkin, she looked up at Sophia. "So, forgive me if I can't just *walk away*. There's too much at stake."

The gaggle of girls stood as if on cue and started making their way across the small shop, phones out, giggling. "Oh my God, it *is* her!"

"Told you so."

They jostled each other as they walked, and just before they reached the table, Sophia leaned in, her voice low and throaty. "I don't care who's involved. You should walk away. Or you'll wish you had." She turned, and in an instant, her pinched, worried eyes opened wide; a vivid, sunny smile replaced the drawn brows as she welcomed the strangers with a hearty, "Hello, girls! How lovely to meet you!"

"I'll see you tonight, Sophia," Stella said, excusing herself, knowing she wasn't going to get anything else out of Sophia just then. But as she walked out of the shop and onto the nearly deserted street, heading toward her hotel, she couldn't help but remember the brief but certain look of panic—no, unadulterated dread—on Sophia's face when Stella had recounted what she knew about Sandy Bowen and her theater teacher. Sophia knew something that might help Stella put the pieces together. The movie star just wasn't ready to share it. Yet.

There were dots to connect, but Stella's mind couldn't find the path yet.

As she walked, she took out her phone and searched the strip mall where Penelope's body had been found, spending some time on Google Earth, looking at the five stores that made up the particular strip behind which Penelope was found. It was your typical string of shops, including a martial arts studio, a health-food store, a physical-therapy business, a dentist, and the yoga studio.

Raptor Yoga.

Something about that name rang a distant bell in the back of her mind. She refined her search a bit, and several articles from the local papers popped up, explaining how a kid from Rivermoor High, Raptor Garrett, made it big with his YouTube fitness channel.

Rivermoor High!

Stella's heart beat faster; she ripped her glove off to operate her screen better. Raptor Garrett had apparently hit some kind of search-algorithm lottery and gained so many subscribers that he dropped out of Northeastern Illinois University and opened a yoga studio six months ago.

She scrolled further down the search page and gasped. A still shot from the *Rivermoor Weekly Herald* of Raptor Garrett onstage, starring in the high school's production of *A Midsummer Night's Dream*.

Stella called the number for the business.

"Raptor Yoga, how can I help you today?"

"I'm looking for Raptor Garrett."

"He's not in right now; can I take a message?"

"Tell him that Stella Reynolds from NBC called. And I have questions about Madeline Mowery at Rivermoor High School."

31

By the time Stella had finished dressing for the gala, she was close to being late. Lucky had texted several times to check her progress—a situation that only served to *add* to the time it was taking her to get ready, she finally reminded him after his fourth text.

"Thumbs up emoji?" she muttered to herself after his terse response. "Everyone knows that's like a giant fu—"

"Can I call you a ride, Ms. Reynolds?" The concierge loomed over her; by his tone, she'd missed his first attempt at getting her attention. "Do you need a taxi or car service for the night?"

She tucked her phone into her pocket and carefully tottered forward. She'd traded her sensible work heels for taller stilettos for the evening's black-tie event.

"No, thank you. I'm just crossing the street."

She exited the hotel and waited at the busy intersection to cross E Delaware Place, heading straight for the Hancock. The giant skyscraper was technically known as 875 North Michigan Avenue now, but everyone still called it the Hancock.

The day was warmer than it had been in months, according to the local weatherman. "False spring," he'd called it, and with a smile, Stella thought it was the perfect phrase. It was thirty degrees warmer than it had been the day before, and the setting sun was shining without a single cloud in the sky.

She would probably regret not bringing a proper coat later, but it was altogether too nice to worry about it yet, and the bolero she wore over her outfit was the perfect, light-weight jacket for now.

Stella hurried from the sidewalk down the steps to the courtyard entrance of the building. Lucky's charity had rented out the entire ninety-fourth floor, and she passed signs warning that 360 Chicago, usually full of tourists, was closed for a private event.

She wound her way through the lobby and gift shop, then through a narrow maze of hallways designed to explain how and when the building was constructed before finally finding the elevator.

An attendant operated the door, pushing two buttons to get the elevator moving. Ascending ninety-three floors took less than a minute, and Stella's ears popped three times before the car stopped. When the doors opened, Lucky was waiting for her on the other side. He whistled low as she stepped off the elevator. "I'd say you clean up real nice, but the truth is, you look this good every day. Tonight, you're just sparkly too."

Stella glanced down at her outfit. She didn't know how Bethany had done it, but the long skirt and strapless sweetheart neckline top fit like it had been made for her alone. From far away, the silky dark blue sparkly material looked like a dress, but the two pieces would make it easier to clip on a microphone when her emcee duties called. She grinned up at Lucky. "You're looking very dapper yourself. And I can say with certainty that you clean up real nice, since half the time you're at work, you're covered in motor oil and grease from the garage."

Lucky's dimpled face broke into a full-on gleaming smile, and she nearly swooned at the sight. He leaned in and rubbed his freshly shaved cheek against hers, then planted a soft kiss on her lips before tucking her hand into the crook of his elbow and towing her forward.

"They want to mic you up early. After mic checks you'll just turn yours off until it's time to present the awards."

"Mmmhmm," Stella answered, but in truth, she'd barely heard Lucky, captivated instead by the view outside. As they approached the east window wall, the enormity of Lake Michigan stretched long and unfathomable, disappearing into the horizon like the very lines of traffic she'd complained about earlier.

But as they came to a stop right by the glass pane, the city revealed itself below. Suddenly, the minute-long elevator ride seemed impossibly fast. Looking down at even the tallest skyscrapers around them, Stella marveled at the sheer size of the city. As she glanced to the south, the city stretched and disappeared endlessly into the horizon. Far below, Lake Shore Drive snaked around the footprint of Chicago, so close to the water that it was a wonder the road hadn't been swallowed up long ago.

Lucky gently pulled her past the band toward a set of doors. "I'll be by the bar when you're done."

Stella watched him walk away, then ducked into the room, immediately finding Conrad by the tech table, sifting through a pile of microphones and cords in the tiny windowless room.

He squinted down at the lower half of Stella's outfit.

"I'd like to have you wear a clip-on lavalier tonight, but wasn't sure what color dress you'd have on. In fact, I'm still not."

Stella plucked the end of her full skirt up and held it out. "It's called midnight cerulean."

Conrad looked blank.

"So, it's like a dark midnight blue."

"Ah. Perfect." He held out a clear plastic microphone clip. "Lucky said black, but I figured men don't always pay attention to the little details."

"Truth," Stella said with a smile. She held the device in her hand for a moment, considering, then clipped the battery pack to the back of the skirt waistband and snaked the microphone cord around the inside of her top.

She turned away from Conrad, then plunged one hand down the front of her top and passed the microphone itself from her belly button up to her other hand, then finally clipped the clear plastic end to the top of her dress. She adjusted the tension around her belly and tucked the extra cord into her waistband, then turned back to the photographer. "What do you think?"

Conrad motioned to the jacket, and she shrugged it back on, then shifted back and forth.

"Let's move it slightly so it's not so in your face." Conrad stepped closer, his eyebrows raised. Stella nodded, giving permission, and with a delicate touch, he moved the clip over a few inches so that it rested just at the point where her top met her collarbone.

"Nearly invisible!" Conrad crowed. "I'll tell you what, Lala, it was nice working with you in news this week, but I'm glad to be back to special events. No more grand, emotional outbursts over murder, natural disasters, or terrible crimes waiting for me anymore." He rubbed his hands together, then turned back to the counter to wind up an extra wire and put the spare black lavalier microphone back in its box. "Hey, I just put brand-new batteries in there, and I'll be standing behind the stage to remind you to turn that baby on when it's your turn to speak."

Back out in the main room, Stella stopped again to appreciate the view.

Attendants manned the "Tilt" feature, where windows tilted out over the city like an amusement park ride along the south windows. Stella shook her head, silently acknowledging her fear of heights as she continued around the space in search of the bar.

"You all set?" Lucky asked, soundlessly gliding up from behind her.

She leaned into him briefly. "Can you feel it?"

"What?"

She stepped back and surveyed the room, buzzing with waiters, audio and camera techs strapping bulky cables to the floor with wide strips of tape, and the band, their opening strains of music warbling from the speakers like a welcoming call. "Something's going to happen tonight. I feel it in my gut."

Lucky's hand slapped against his lapel, almost as if he was covering his heart. "Something good?" His question was unexpectedly intense, and Stella turned to focus on him.

"I don't know." Her brow furrowed as she looked inward. Her

chest felt tight, and not just because the one-inch-wide battery pack made the fabric of her already-snug top even more strained. Maybe it was because the situation with Penelope, Fran, and Sandy was unresolved, but for a moment, she had trouble catching her breath. She forced a smile, though, and looked up at Lucky, surprised to see her own jumbled emotions reflected on his face. "Are you okay?" she asked.

His lips lifted in a lopsided smile. "We'll see, huh, Bear? We'll see." With that enigmatic remark, his gaze shifted across the room, and he lifted his hand in greeting. "Come meet the mayor. She's been a big supporter of the charity." Instead of making her feel better, his unreadable eyes knocked her back a step. Lucky turned around, unsmiling. "Big night all around, huh?"

She straightened her shoulders and smiled again as the mayor approached, tamping down her feelings of unease. She'd been surrounded by bad news all week, but tonight was a big night for Lucky. She'd make sure to remember that.

32

After an hour of schmoozing with various bigwigs from both the city of Chicago and the arts community, Stella found herself alone at the bar. "Can I get a refill, please?"

"Lord, please tell me that's vodka."

Stella looked over to find Sophia standing at her elbow. She smiled ruefully. "Straight-up water, I'm afraid. I'm emceeing tonight and vodka would not help the show go on."

"Are you speaking from experience?"

Stella shuddered. "Thankfully, no."

Sophia deposited her empty glass on the counter and the bartender filled a new rocks glass with ice and vodka, slipping two lime wedges onto the rim. Sophia dimpled her thanks, then added a twenty-dollar bill to the gleaming crystal tip container, perched unobtrusively at the corner. "You take care of Mama, Mama takes care of you." She pushed the two small cocktail straws together, took a long sip of the beverage, and then added, almost as an afterthought, "At least that's how I thought it was supposed to go." She didn't wait for a response; instead, she looped her arm through Stella's and towed her to a relatively quiet corner of the room.

"I've been thinking."

Stella rattled the ice cubes in her water and looked at Sophia. "Oh?"

Irritated with the straws, Sophia held them against the far edge of her drink and took a proper sip, wincing only slightly as the nearly straight vodka slid down her throat "About our conversation at the smoothie shop this morning. There are some things...I don't know if it's appropriate...But it seems like..." She struggled to find the right words, but Stella didn't interrupt. Sophia cleared her throat and tried again. "Madeline Mowery has an unusual teaching method. Very unique." Sophia looked past Stella out the window. The Chicago skyline resembled a faraway carnival from the ninety-fourth floor, with lights blinking invitingly down below as if they were rides beckoning. "She really put me through the paces years ago. It's not something I ever want to do again, but I honestly think it prepared me for this life in a way nothing else could have." Sophia's beautiful brow was furrowed and in the dim lighting of the room, tiny crow's feet wrinkled just under her eyes. Sophia wasn't old by any normal person's definition, but that hardly mattered in Hollywood.

"She had promised me..." Sophia cleared her throat again, drawing her focus from the window to Stella's own face. "I had heard that her methods had relaxed since I had her..." Sophia seemed to be searching for the right words. A quick smile and apologetic shrug meant she couldn't. "Well, I'd been assured she had been taking a lighter approach. But all I've been able to think about since you and I spoke this morning is that her methods were crazy enough when I went through them. And if there's a chance that she might have known someone involved in the shooting, even one or two connections away from the school shooter, well—"

Sophia's words cut off with a *yip* and she and Stella both jumped when surprisingly strong, athletic arms wrapped around them from the side. So engrossed in their own conversation, neither had noticed the very drama teacher in question arrive.

"Look at this!" Madeline Mowery's eyes danced as she looked between the two women. "What are you two lovely ladies over here whispering about?"

Stella heard an underlying note of accusation in Mowery's words that made the hairs on the back of her neck prickle uncomfortably, but aloud she said, "Just some last-minute notes for our onstage interview."

Mowery didn't take her eyes off of Sophia, whose smile had tightened to the point of looking uncomfortably grim.

"Oh, the stories we could tell, Stella. They'd make your toes curl," Mowery said. "Stories from back before Sophia was anything. Before she could even dream of having a major career, huh?"

Sophia, as if in a trance, lifted her drink to her lips and drained it. Eyes watering, she excused herself for the bar, a slight wobble in her step sending a nearby waiter shuffling sideways to keep his tray balanced.

Stella and Madeline stared at each other for a beat, and maybe Stella read too much into the look, but when the teacher turned and walked away, she felt as if she'd been warned. About what, she didn't know.

Her eyes followed Mowery's progress through the room, and only when a burly tuxedoed man had enveloped the teacher in a hug and dragged her to a group of people did Stella snap out of her own trance and turn to find Sophia. She wanted—no, needed—to hear what Sophia had been about to say, and now, several drinks in, her barriers lowered, was likely the only time she'd be able to get the information out of the movie star.

She found Sophia at the bar, getting another double, maybe triple shot of vodka laced with lime juice. Stella swiped the drink out from under her fingers and took a quick step back when Sophia tried to grab it back and the drink sloshed up and over the rim.

"Oh. S'you."

Stella blew out a sigh. She might already be too late to get any good information out of this wobbly, tottering, less-than-sober actor. And the drink she'd just downed in front of Stella and Madeline Mowery wasn't even really in her bloodstream yet.

"Sophia. I need you to tell me what you know about Madeline. It's important."

Sophia looked owlishly around the room, trying to spot her old theater teacher. Stella cut in, "Someone just asked her to dance—they're around the corner over by the band. We have a moment."

Sophia shook her head slowly. "There's no break. You never *have* a break. There's no chance to escape." She pressed her fingers against her temple and closed her eyes, swaying dangerously toward the bar counter. Stella dropped the drink onto the nearest tray and gripped Sophia under the elbow to steady her.

"I did some research after I left the smoothie shop this morning. You said in an interview in *Vogue* last year that you haven't been back to Chicago since you graduated high school. Is that true?"

Sophia nodded.

"What kept you away?" After watching the way Sophia and Madeline interacted, it wasn't hard to imagine that the theater teacher had something to do with it.

Sophia shuddered. "It was all my fault, but *she* should have known better. She should have known something would happen. She pushed me too far. I was so young..." A sob split her last word into two jarring syllables, and Stella looked around nervously. A passing waiter slowed, curiosity drawing his eyebrows up. Was that a cell phone in his hand? Did he just look away guiltily?

Hastily, Stella moved Sophia back to their original corner and pressed her own ice water into the actor's hand. Her voice was low and urgent when she spoke again.

"What happened back then? What happened to you, Sophia?"

"She called it a character study, and I didn't know any better. She was my world back then, my ticket to the big leagues." She snorted, but then her eyes bored into Stella's, suddenly clear. "She said it would be the best way to get into another person's skin. But it wasn't. All it was...well, it was lying. And when he found out..." Her eyes pooled with unshed tears, and Stella couldn't turn away.

Sophia blinked rapidly, trying to collect herself. She stared above Stella's head and her voice dropped several decibels until she was practically whispering. In the noisy chaos of the cocktail party, Stella had to lean close to hear, but when she made sense of Sophia's final words, it was almost like everyone in the room had stopped talking at the same time.

"It was my fault Ryan died. Madeline said it was God's plan, and I tried to believe it back then, but I'm an adult now and I know. God had nothing to do with it. It was all me. All my fault."

"Sophia, where were you Monday? We were supposed to meet for our interview, but you didn't show up." Stella was almost thinking out loud, but now that she'd said it, she looked at Sophia with renewed interest. Was it possible Sophia had been at Rivermoor High, planning to even some score from her high school days? Had she been there when the shooting started? Had she had something to do with it?

But Sophia didn't answer. She couldn't. She collapsed into a chair and slid back, her jaw slack. The actor had just passed out.

33

Stella turned when she felt eyes on the back of her head. Lucky was across the room, but she could feel his concern from twenty feet away.

She tried to smile to let him know she was okay, but she must not have been convincing, because he started moving toward her.

Stella stood helplessly by Sophia, now slumped in a chair by the window, her face pale and slack, her gorgeous peacock green dress collecting wrinkles like old women collect secrets.

Sophia's young assistant appeared out of nowhere, sighing only slightly when she saw the state of her employer.

"Can you...?" She motioned to Sophia's other side, and together they lifted the tiny slip of a woman up from the chair and headed toward the ladies' room.

"Does this happen often?" Stella asked curiously, trying to calm her own beating heart more than anything.

"Ever since we got to Chicago...Uh..." Louise Barr's cheeks flushed as she realized what she'd said. "It's got to be some kind of bug—germs. She's just not feeling well lately is all."

They awkwardly bumped their way to the ladies' room and gently set Sophia down on the divan in the sitting room.

"Thank you. I've got it from here," Louise said, standing between Stella and Sophia.

"I see that you do." She turned to leave, but then added, "Be careful." As she left the room she couldn't decide if she was talking about getting puked on or watching out for Madeline Mowery.

Lucky was waiting for her in the hallway.

"Everything okay?"

"I don't know," Stella admitted. "Something's not right with Sophia. And Madeline Mowery."

"Who?"

She looked up at Lucky, about to tell him her suspicions about the theater teacher and how she might be connected in some bizarre way to the school shooting, but his lips were set in a grim line, and she realized with a jolt that this was his night. Not hers.

She forced a bright smile onto her lips and shook her head. "Sophia's had a bit too much to drink, but she'll be fine. I gave her my water."

Lucky tilted his head to the side, his eyes narrowed. "That's going to change the tenor of the evening. 'Movie Star Pukes Onstage' isn't quite the headline I was going for."

"I think her assistant can fill in for her if Sophia doesn't sober up in time."

Lucky grimaced. He knew there was more to the story, but he didn't press her.

"Is it time to get started?"

"Almost. Conrad was looking for you. The band will play two more songs, then it's go time." They walked side by side through the crowded room. "It's going to be a big night. An exciting night. Are you ready?"

"Of course! Piece of cake." She waved to a familiar-looking woman who was smiling brightly at them. "Who's that?"

Lucky's eyes swept the crowd. "Oh, that's Liz Fendon. She's the principal for an investment firm that's been a big supporter of the charity. Hey." He turned to Stella, started to say something, but then pressed his fingers against his lips. He met her eyes with a searching look. "Is everything okay, Bear?"

Stella's gut clenched. The run-in between Sophia and Madeline made her uneasy, but out loud, she only said, "Yeah. Everything's fine."

She knew he didn't buy it, that he was disappointed she'd brushed off his question. But she also knew that the biggest night of the year for his charity was not just underway, but about to crescendo. So instead of pressing the matter, he smiled. It was only later that she realized that smile didn't reach his eyes. That smile that flashed on and off like a faulty lightbulb didn't mean he was happy.

He squeezed her hand and left her wondering if she should have asked him the same question. But she'd missed her chance. The mayor was leading over a group of kids, the recipients of Lucky's charity's grants, and she didn't want to ruin the moment for him.

She was still debating whether to call Lucky back over when a harried waiter approached Stella, her tray of hors d'oeuvres held out rigidly.

"Oh, no thanks." Stella's preemptive response was met with an embarrassed smile.

"Actually, Ms. Reynolds, there's someone here to see you at the staff stairwell. She said it's urgent. Her name is Sandy Bowen."

Stella jolted at the name of the very woman she'd been trying to locate for several days now. Lucky shot her a look from across the room. *Are you okay? Do you need me?* She shook her head with a small smile, and he relaxed back into his conversation with a trio of housewives. Stella briefly considered whether she should ask him the same question when one of the middle-aged women laughed a little too loudly while reaching out to touch his arm.

Her face must have twisted into a frown, because Lucky grinned suddenly, catching her eye again, and then winked.

She pivoted to face the waiter. "Lead the way."

They wound their way between strategically placed cocktail tables, back toward the south-facing windows and the ladies' room. Conrad looked up from the tech table tucked into a small alcove between the bar and kitchen entrance where he was fiddling with a video camera. "All well?"

Stella nodded but hardly slowed down. "I hope so." Her face felt flushed. If what Sandy's stepmother had said was true, Sandy was likely feeling hunted, possibly in danger. One roommate was in police custody, another was dead. She was somehow connected to a school shooting and didn't feel like she could trust authorities. So why did she feel like she could trust Stella?

The waitress slowed to a stop and motioned to a door tucked into an alcove by the freight elevator. "She said she was going to wait in there."

"How did she get there?" Stella wondered aloud.

The waitress shrugged, shifting her tray of prosciutto-wrapped persimmons with goat cheese to her other hand. Stella dismissed her with a smile, then squared her shoulders and reached for the door handle.

But her hand stopped just shy of the cold metal lever. Sandy could be dangerous. Fran certainly thought so. So did Rivermoor Police, who'd put out a BOLO for Sandy after Penelope was murdered. Be On the Look Out for Sandy...with her official roommate murdered, police surely thought that Sandy, supposedly missing from the U of C campus all week, might be in danger too. But Stella realized with heart-thudding certainty that she'd asked the wrong question a moment ago. It wasn't whether Sandy could trust Stella. The question was, could Stella trust Sandy? Alone in a concrete stairwell, with a party going on so loudly in the background that it would mask the sound of any struggle?

With a resigned sigh—of course she had to know why Sandy was there; she had to know what the girl knew about the school shooting, Penelope's death, and yes, the theater teacher, like she had to breathe—she reached out and pushed the door open.

34

Stella squinted against the relentless fluorescent lights in the stairwell as she stared at Fran and Penelope's roommate. The girl looked different than before. Paler, yes, obviously from the stress, but also more...put together. Gone were the tattered sweatshirts and ill-fitting jeans. Now the girl wore stylish athleisure wear.

Stella sized her up, making an effort not to cross her arms protectively in front of her chest. It was just a girl, after all.

A throat cleared from behind her, and Stella's head whipped around.

It was not just a girl.

"Stella?"

"Yes."

"I'm Rebecca Bowen. We spoke yesterday." Stella looked expectantly at Rebecca, who nervously cleared her throat again. "Ms. Reynolds, I guess I'm not sure where to begin."

"Let's start with her real name." Stella shot a quick glance through the narrow window in the door behind her. Feeling confident that no one yet knew she was missing, she turned back to the two women in front of her. "Are you Sandy Bowen or Tandy Scarborough?"

"I'm Sandy Bowen."

"But when I met you, you introduced yourself as Tandy Scarborough. Why?"

"It's...complicated."

"I bet."

Sandy had the grace to blush. She stared down at the toes of her Chuck Taylors.

Stella looked at the girl standing in front of her. Was she the shooter? Could those scrawny arms have wielded a gun? And if so, why? "If Sandy is involved in the shooting at the high school..." She held Rebecca's eyes for a moment, then both women looked at Sandy, who continued staring at her toes. "Then I think you need to go to the police right away."

"It's not quite that simple, unfortunately." Rebecca worked her lips soundlessly for a moment, then sighed. "It's not simple at all."

Stella waved her hand impatiently. "If you know who the shooter is, it *is* that simple. And if Sandy is that shooter, there are even more reasons to count your blessings that nobody died. At the high school," Stella added, picturing the glossy locks of Penelope's hair as the medics moved her body into the ambulance.

Sandy flinched, finally raising her eyes to meet Stella's. "I didn't shoot anyone, but I might as well have." Her voice broke on the last word and Rebecca moved toward her stepdaughter and drew her close.

"Tell this woman what you know. She might be able to help us figure out what to do."

Stella resisted glancing at her watch. It was almost time for her to take the stage, but she could hardly leave what might be a massive confession for later.

What if Sandy lost her nerve, or whoever had hunted down Penelope tracked her down as well? She quickly crossed back to the door and pushed, searching for Conrad. They made eye contact, and she held up five fingers indicating she needed some minutes. Conrad hesitated, a video camera perched on his shoulder, then lowered his headset microphone. Seconds later the band struck up another song.

Ducking back into the stairwell, she stepped close to Rebecca and Sandy. "Talk now and talk fast. I don't know if there's anything I can do to help, but if there is, I'll do it."

Rebecca nodded and Sandy took a deep breath.

"I think she was just trying to help, but I don't know where things went wrong. And when things felt like they were going wrong, she told me to keep going, and I felt like if I could just do what she asked me to do, everything would be okay in the end. I was so wrong."

"Are you talking about Fran?"

Sandy looked up, eyes wide. "No. Ms. Mowery."

"Remember, we don't have much time, Sandy, but you'll need to start at the beginning."

Sandy twisted a ring on her finger, uncertain where to start. "Every year Ms. Mowery takes a student under her wing. I never thought it would be me! I didn't even go to Rivermoor High. We live one town over. But she was impressed with a community theater production I was in."

"Ms. Mowery was always looking for fresh talent in the surrounding communities," Rebecca Bowen broke in, her pride at Sandy's past accomplishments sounding wildly out of place to Stella's ears.

Sandy continued as if she hadn't been interrupted. "I—I felt so lucky that she had such confidence in me. She said I could do great things if I was prepared to work hard enough. And I was! I was ready to work hard. I just didn't understand what I was signing up for."

Rebecca tapped her foot impatiently. "That woman has been manipulating Sandy for months, asking her to do things she couldn't possibly understand the ramifications of. And the fact that she required Sandy to keep the information from us, from her own family, tells me that she knew what she was asking Sandy to do was wrong! And that's all you need to know!"

"Not even close, Mrs. Bowen. Sandy, what did Ms. Mowery ask you to do?"

"She said it was an acting exercise, one that would take me to the big leagues. The same acting exercise that propelled Sophia Thomas to the top. I would enroll in college at the University of Chicago as I had planned, but at the same time, Mrs. Mowery got me a spot in a dorm room at St. Agnes. But I wouldn't be Sandy Bowen there. I would be someone else entirely. I would have a full year to pretend to be someone else, to *act* like someone else. She said the only way to get to the next level was to commit to this project. To the process."

Stella's eyes narrowed. "There's obviously more to it than that."

Sandy swallowed audibly, then nodded. "Right. Well, if I was going to learn to be an actor and live in someone else's shoes, Ms. Mowery said that I had to do it as another person entirely, but we had to use bits of my real life or else I'd never be able to hold up the persona for so long. I became Tandy Scarborough. The name had to be close enough that if someone were to call me either name, no one would be suspicious. My mother remarried. Her new last name is Scarborough."

Rebecca cut in. "Ms. Mowery told Sandy she would be working on the Cinderella complex."

"What's that?" Stella asked.

Sandy's cheeks colored under Stella's intense stare. "Instead of having a great life, the character I would be playing at St. Agnes had had a terrible upbringing. A mother who died, a stepmother who was mean and treated her poorly, and a father who wasn't engaged in her life. And as a result of all that...history, Tandy made bad choices, had bad luck. She chose the wrong friends, the wrong boyfriend. That was the part I had to play in order to really learn how to be that person, you know? To get into their skin."

"So that's what you did?" Stella asked incredulously. "You became unlucky, Cinderella-complex Tandy Scarborough?"

"Exactly. And it was hard, and Penelope was confused about why I was gone so much. My parents knew I was stressed out but didn't know why. But it was working. I could see *exactly* what Ms. Mowery meant. The stakes were so high! I didn't want to be found out. And because of that, I really was able to feel the emotions of the character in ways that I never had before."

"What went wrong? Why are we here talking about a school shooting? A dead roommate?"

Sandy sucked on her bottom lip and her eyes darted toward

Rebecca. "That's when I feel like Ms. Mowery abandoned me. I made weird friends and tried to understand what the friendships were based on, because it wasn't having anything in common, I'll tell you that. I even found an odd, socially awkward boyfriend...I mean, you know, someone I would never pick in real life—"

"Just how far did you take this?" Stella asked, wondering how close she let the boy get.

"I know what you're thinking, and it wasn't like that. At least it wasn't like that for me." Sandy shuddered. "I mean, God! The things he said! The way he acted." Her face twisted in disgust, and so did Stella's.

"You led this boy on, then? For—what? For months? Kept him close, but didn't let him get too close?"

Rebecca shifted uncomfortably, but Sandy didn't seem to understand Stella's disquiet.

"I never made him any promises! But I needed him to think we had a chance. That's how I was going to get better as an actor."

All three women looked over the railing of the stairwell when a door slammed below, but whoever it was shuffled down several flights and another door slammed, leaving them alone once more.

But the interruption knocked Rebecca out of her trance, and she cleared her throat.

"Sandy."

Sandy flinched at her stepmother's tone and nodded slowly. "Right. So...I mean, Dominic...he didn't understand why I was keeping some distance between us. And he kept trying to do things to win me over completely, at least that's what he said...and, I mean, of course he'd heard about my awful stepmother." Sandy looked up at Rebecca through her eyelashes. Her shoulders rounded in on themselves. One tear leaked from the corner of her eye. "And I made up really terrible stories about things that she'd done to me and he said he wished he could make it all go away for me and I said I wished he could too, but I didn't know...I had no idea what he was planning..."

"What are you talking about?" Stella turned toward Rebecca. "Did Dominic try to hurt you?"

"That's exactly it, Ms. Reynolds. I'm the art teacher at Rivermoor High. Dominic came to my classroom on Monday with a gun."

"What?" Stella couldn't believe that she'd missed such a huge piece of information. But days ago, Anna Matykiewicz had told her that a substitute teacher had tied a tourniquet around her arm after she'd been shot. Stella had never once investigated who was supposed to have been in the classroom that day. But Rebecca wasn't done talking, and Stella refocused on Sandy's stepmother.

"Apparently Dominic decided on his own that getting rid of me would curry him favor with my daughter, so he decided to come into the school with a gun. I was out sick the day of the shooting." The guilt in her eyes was unmistakable. Even though she'd had nothing to do with the planning of the shooting, it happened because she was supposed to have been there.

Bam, bam.

Sandy yelped as a deafening knock on the door behind Stella interrupted them. Conrad poked his head in. "There you are! We're live in five, okay?"

Stella nodded mutely, and Conrad pivoted and headed back into the party room, muttering under his breath about battery levels and lighting gels.

But Stella stared at the door for a long moment after it was closed. Because Conrad had handed her a folder of papers, but also unnecessarily brushed firmly against her side. Had he flipped on her microphone pack? Did Conrad know what was going on?

She turned back to face the two women in the stairwell, her mind racing. It was time to find out everything that Sandy knew.

Stella's eyes narrowed as she considered things. "There's only one problem, Sandy. If it was Dominic who fired the gun inside the school—how did he escape? How did he know how to get out of the building? Where to hide in the theater department, and where to wait until the building was cleared? How did he know all of that, Sandy? Did you help him plan the shooting?"

Rebecca put a reassuring hand on Sandy's arm. "She's a child, Ms. Reynolds. She didn't know what she was doing."

"Didn't know what she was doing? Sandy's nineteen years old, not a child." Stella turned to the teenager in question. "I found a Rivermoor High yearbook in your room, Sandy. You told me that it belonged to Fran. But how could it? She didn't go there. She has no connection to that school." Stella shifted her focus back to Rebecca. "And you just happened to take a sick day on Monday? You look okay now. What was wrong with you?"

Rebecca blanched, and her chin trembled when she looked at Sandy.

"Sandy wasn't feeling well. She asked me to stay home with her, and I did." Rebecca wouldn't—couldn't—make eye contact with anyone as she uttered the unbelieveable words.

"You understand this isn't something a detention will address, don't you, Rebecca?" Stella's incredulous expression froze when Rebecca straightened her shoulders and lifted her chin. "You don't care?"

"I care. But I care about making sure the right person is held accountable."

"It seems like there's enough accountability to go around in this case, Rebecca."

"But this will not fall only on Sandy's shoulders! She would have never hatched this plan on her own. And then Ms. Mowery left her with no oversight! Like an internship feeding lions, only to have the door slammed at your back as soon as you enter the enclosure!"

"I—" But Stella's head cocked to the side, because beyond the steel door, the simmering sound of the party had changed. No more clinks of glass and silverware; instead, a buzz of conversation that reminded her of a presidential debate after one side landed a particularly low blow.

She reached out for the door, but it flung open before she touched it.

Conrad stood at the threshold, his face ruddy with exertion. "I need you." He thrust a stick mic into Stella's hands. "Sophia Thomas is about to explode."

Stella grabbed the microphone, calling over her shoulder, "Don't go anywhere!" before she hurried after the photographer.

35

As Stella hurried after Conrad, she realized how many unanswered questions she still had for Sandy. What had happened to Penelope? Where was Dominic now? She opened her mouth to tell Conrad that she was going back—that she couldn't possibly leave, when Conrad stopped short and snaked his arm around Stella's midsection to the battery pack of her lavalier microphone clipped at the waistband of her skirt.

Click.

"Your mic has been hot for the last ten minutes. It's off now."

"I knew it!"

"The local NBC picked up the feed."

"What feed?" Stella asked blankly.

"The gala feed! It was being broadcast on the local access channel, but with everything that's going on, confessions, A-list movie star meltdowns, NBC just cut to us five minutes ago." He reached out to flip the stick microphone on, then, seeing the confusion on Stella's face, he added, "I was one floor below in the stairwell. I heard the girl confess to her bizarre part in the school shooting, and I...Well, I decided it sounded a hell of a lot more interesting than a fundraiser. So I made your mic hot, and piped it into the speaker here when the band wrapped."

"You—you what?" Stella's first thought was of Lucky. He must think that she'd planned this! That she was purposely sabotaging his biggest fundraiser of the year.

"As soon as the older woman said the name Mowery, Sophia Thomas went nuts. She's still at it." Conrad motioned to the main floor. "Get in there."

"This is—I can't do that! Lucky has a—there's got to be a way to—"

Conrad's camera was up and recording, and he strode toward the corner of the room, leaving Stella spluttering behind. But not for long. A crash of glass and splintering wood ended Stella's soul searching.

Brushing past a gawking server, she entered the space. A beautiful crystal centerpiece sat in splinters on the ground, and the wooden risers that led to the stage had been knocked over; at least one was in pieces, shiny bits from the exposed nails glinting in the light from the overhead chandeliers.

But it was the two women in the center of the room that drew her attention.

"Lies!" Sophia bellowed, and she looked nothing like the glamorous movie star Stella had chatted with earlier in the evening. "You said it was over. Done. You lied!"

Madeline Mowery's eyes darted around the room, looking for safe harbor. But the only thing she saw in the fascinated stares around the room was grim curiosity. Like witnesses at a car crash suddenly realizing they smelled gasoline, everyone stepped back, but no one looked away.

Mowery refocused on Sophia, a large phony smile on her face. "Soph, listen—"

"Don't call me that!"

"Fine, Sophia—just let me explain!"

"Explain? Explain how you nearly ruined my life, and even though you promised no one else would have to go through what I did—now I find out that you're doing it right up to the bitter end? When does it stop, Madeline? When?"

"It's not like that—not at all."

Sophia glanced wildly around the room and her eyes landed on Stella. "Come here," she demanded.

Stella walked into the center of hell without a wobble, but instead of having her microphone extended, she wrapped an arm around Sophia. The woman was shaking from her core. "Sophia—this is not the time. Come with me. We can all talk this out, but not like this—not in front of all these people."

"That's what she wants," Sophia said, but she looked uncertain—or perhaps aware for the first time of the scene she was making.

"What's going on?" Sandy's voice warbled from the edge of the room. She flinched when all eyes in the room turned to her but soldiered on bravely. "Ms. Mowery, why is Sophia yelling at you? I thought you—" Her voice faltered. "You told me that you were close. That Sophia would help me out when the year was over. Is that...Is that still the plan?" Her voice, thin and nervous to begin with, almost disappeared on the last word.

Out of the corner of her eye, Stella saw Conrad motioning wildly for Stella to move the microphone closer. She shook her head.

Sophia stared at Sandy, though her shaking slowed to a stop during the girl's questions.

"What's going on is that this woman used you, just like she used me. And none of it is your fault."

"I'm not so sure about that," Stella muttered.

"You need to know—" Sophia's voice cut off and she grabbed Stella's hand, pulling the microphone close, raising it to her lips. "You all need to know what this woman is capable of. And I'm going to tell you."

"This is ridiculous. I won't stand for this." Madeline turned unsteadily, tripping on her heels as she walked away from the stage, away from Sophia and Stella. The shimmering fabric of her dress caught the light, reflecting a rainbow of color on the dance floor. Conrad popped up in front of her, the camera like a huge glaring insect on his shoulder, and she froze at the edge of the dance floor.

Stella's hand gripped the microphone, not because she wanted to, but because Sophia's fist still enclosed hers, trapping them both. Loud breaths punctured the silence of the room.

"This woman used me twelve years ago and someone died because of it. She swore to me that it was over. That no one else would be subjected to her teaching methods. And now someone else is dead." Sophia raised her voice for her last words. "And it's your fault again, Madeline."

A hush that had fallen over the room extended, sparked, and Stella was certain that someone dimmed the overhead lights and turned on a spotlight.

Stella's training and instinct overtook her better judgement, and she leaned toward Sophia, ready to question her, to pull the information out slowly and succinctly. "Are you talking about the death at Rivermoor High your senior year?"

Sophia's lower lip trembled, but she gripped the microphone—and Stella's hand—harder. "It has everything to do with Ryan's death. And I'll never forgive myself. Or you, Madeline."

Madeline's chest heaved as she turned back and stalked toward her former star pupil. "You are where you are today *because* of me. And don't you forget it. Don't you forget anything about that night." The drama instructor's finger poked Sophia in the chest to make her point. "We're in this together. Always."

"Not anymore. Not since I found out that my monthly donations in Ryan's name stopped going to the charity years ago. Oh, that's right." She raised her eyebrows and looked at Madeline imperiously. "Surprised I know about your duplicity? All that money, just lining your pockets, Madeline. You don't regret anything that happened that night. And that means I don't owe you a damn thing."

Suddenly, without warning, Sophia dropped Stella's hand and pushed past Madeline. "Stella, come with me." She looked around the room. "Where's the camera? I'm going to do what I should have done that night. And then everyone will know. Everyone."

She stood in front of Conrad. "What do you want to know, Stella? Ask me anything."

36

Stella felt like she was in a dream. Or a nightmare. She had one of Hollywood's hottest stars giving her an exclusive—the only problem was, she didn't know on what.

She made her way across the ballroom floor, noting peripherally that the sun had set completely, the lake outside was completely void of light. She knew the feeling.

"A student died your senior year. You were close with him," Stella guessed, and was rewarded with a nod. "And you've felt responsible for years; that's why you've never come back to Chicago."

"I am responsible. But I'm not the only one."

"Who else?"

"Madeline Mowery and I had it all planned out by the end of my junior year. I was going to go to Hollywood right after graduation. She'd set me up with one of her contacts at the soap opera. It wasn't my dream—but it was certainly an in. But that summer, she said I needed to up my game."

A sheen of sweat broke out across Stella's forehead. The hot light from Conrad's camera felt like an open oven. She blew out a breath and tried to focus on Sophia. "She had you pretend to be someone you weren't?"

"Yes," Sophia hissed.

"But where? You were still in high school."

"There. At Rivermoor. I ditched my friends, my boyfriend, everyone. Joined a different social group. I played a part for the whole year. Lived in someone else's skin."

"And Ryan..." Stella had no idea where Sophia's story was going to go, but knew she had to keep her focused; otherwise her obvious rage would make headlines, but wouldn't solve crimes.

"Ryan was devastated when I broke up with him. He loved me—I loved him. He didn't understand any of it, and I—I couldn't explain it. Madeline was adamant that I make a clean break! He...he killed himself just before graduation. His mother found him. I...I'll never forgive myself.

"And I didn't go to the police, because I knew it was my fault, and you *promised* you'd never do it with another student!" She pointed a finger at Madeline. "That you wouldn't encourage that kind of training—that method of teaching—for anyone else."

"But look where it got you!" Madeline said, her voice low and steely. Enraged and enthralled, she stood a scant three feet away from Sophia, but Stella would bet that the whole room could hear her every word. "Don't fool yourself. It's *because* Ryan died that you can reach into your soul and put on such true and inspired performances today. Do you think for a moment that you would have understood true loss, fear, or betrayal without my lessons? No!

"You have everything! *Everything* an actor could want! And it's *still* not enough for you. You're greedy—and you always have been. That's your problem. You were successful because of what you learned that year. Because of what I was able to teach you. And now you can't stand the thought of anyone else having that same success. You didn't want anyone else to go through my program, because you knew they'd be taking your roles down the line. You have nobody to blame but yourself." She spit the final words out in disgust.

"N-nobody to blame? Nobody—" Sophia couldn't get the words out. "Y-y-you were the last one to see him. Ryan's mother told me. He came to you for answers. And whatever you told him was the end of him!"

Madeline's lips worked furiously, but nothing came out.

Stella's mind had split in half. One side listening to the story unfold, the other trying to work out something Sophia said that had tripped a silent alarm in her brain. It came to her like a sudden tornado—without warning and just as deadly. "Madeline. What did you do to Penelope Triblay?"

Madeline's lips finally snapped shut. A red flush worked up from the neck of her evening gown, painting the woman guilty before she could even speak.

"Did she come to you for help, like she came to me? With concerns about your protégé, Sandy?"

Madeline threw her hands up in the air, and Stella realized if they were indeed on live TV, she had some backstory to fill the viewers in on.

Stella motioned Sandy forward. "Yesterday morning, a girl approached me in the lobby of my hotel. She had some concerns about her missing roommate and had reason to suspect that I had met her recently. I didn't know it at the time, but this girl, Penelope Triblay, was talking about you, Sandy. By the time I made the connection, Penelope was gone; I couldn't track her down. Now she's dead. Murdered."

"What did you do?" Sophia said to Mowery, her voice a deadly whisper. "What did you do to her?"

"Ms. Mowery—tell them it wasn't you!" Sandy wrung her hands in front of her chest, her face frozen in horror. "Tell them it wasn't—it couldn't have been—" Her voice choked off and she fell silent.

Madeline finally recovered herself enough to speak. "I love students, and I have spent my life and career working to shape them into exceptional people. That you would sit here and smear my reputation—"

"Your *reputation!*" Sophia roared. "That's all you've ever cared about! Ryan is dead. This girl—what is her name?" She locked eyes with Sandy, who whispered her roommate's name. "Penelope is dead! Nobody *cares* about your reputation, but believe me, with everything that's happened, it's set in stone."

"Nobody cares, nobody cares. That's all I've heard for decades.

It's why I'm retiring. Well, I cared." Mowery hit her chest with a fist. "I cared too much. I cared more than anybody. Certainly more than you!" She turned an accusing eye toward Sophia. "I made you—and what's the thanks I got? You refused to return my calls, you shunned me in public, and you acted like you rose to fame and prominence on your own. You're as much of a fraud as I am."

Sophia's mouth snapped shut. She lowered herself slowly to a nearby seat and finally nodded. "You're right."

Stella turned from Sophia to Mowery. "But it's not just about those two deaths. Did you know there was going to be a shooting at the school on Monday? Madeline, did you help the gunman get away with the crime?"

Mowery leaned heavily against the nearest table, her glamorous makeup at odds with the crestfallen expression on her face.

"I had no part in Monday's violence. None! But I admit, I made a mistake."

Sophia snorted angrily, but Stella stayed her with a hand. It was important that Madeline talk now.

"The day of the shooting, I heard the chaos out in the hallway, but I didn't know—I couldn't know that Dominic was there with a gun! I walked out of my room just as the overhead lockdown announcement came. We—we made eye contact. I saw the gun. And I said to him, 'What have you done? I knew if I didn't help him escape, the whole story would come out. And after decades of helping kids, of making sure they reached their full potential, that's all I'd be remembered for! A terrible shooting perpetrated by a disillusioned kid high on video-game violence! I couldn't stand the thought!" She looked up at Stella, her eyes begging to be understood. "It was a mistake—I know that now. But in the heat of the moment, I just wanted him out of the building. Away from my students."

"That's an interesting story, Madeline," Stella said. "But how did you know the boy? Had Sandy introduced you?"

"What?"

Stella cleared her throat. "And why was he in the theater hallway to begin with?"

Mowery flinched, and Stella walked slowly toward her. "He headed straight to the art room, looking for Sandy's stepmother. He shot three people. Then he walked clear across the school to the theater wing, without shooting anyone else. And you just happened to walk out of your room in the middle of a lockdown and make a split-second decision to help him?" Stella's eyes narrowed. "Because it sounds like a man you knew, went looking for help after he'd finished his job. And the security cameras!"

"What?" Mowery said weakly, but Stella saw the fear in her eyes.

"You made sure to disarm the school's backup security cameras that morning, didn't you? But why, Madeline? Why would you help him?"

Mowery's eyes twitched toward Sandy, and Rebecca must have seen it too, because she gasped.

"No!"

"Sandy?" Stella asked. "What did you know about Dominic's plan? No—*when* did you know about his plan to go to the school? The pages missing from the Rivermoor High yearbook. What was in them? A map of the school? How long had the two of you been planning the shooting?"

Sandy cringed from the sudden attention and wouldn't raise her eyes from the floor. "I—I..."

Rebecca's face crumpled. "Oh, Sandy. No."

"Rebecca..." But Sandy had nothing else to say. No way to defend herself against the truth.

"Why, honey? Why?"

"I—I didn't think he'd actually shoot anybody, and I made sure that you weren't there that day, just to keep you safe! I thought he'd scare some people and then leave the school when he didn't find you. And then I would end things with him. I'd end things with Ms. Mowery, too, and just go back to my life.

"And—and then I'd have firsthand knowledge of all *kinds* of emotions that I could draw on for my career as an actor. You can't pretend your way through that, right, Ms. Mowery?" She looked at the theater teacher, but Mowery continued to stare at the floor. The certainty in her voice faded and she said, much quieter, "You need to know how it all feels."

Rebecca shook her head violently. "No. This was not Sandy's fault. That woman is responsible. And she left Sandy to navigate the minefield left behind all on her own. She *abandoned* her."

"Did she? Or have you been in contact the whole time, Sandy? When I came into the theater for the first time, Madeline was there, but someone else turned the lights on. It was you, wasn't it, Sandy?"

Sandy's gaze dropped to her feet and after a long silence, she looked up at her stepmother and mumbled, "I just want to say that I love you."

The words sounded like a confession, but before Stella could process it, a bang rent the silence and a sudden flurry of confetti and balloons fell from the ceiling.

"No!" Lucky moaned. Stella hadn't even seen him off to the side, but when she glanced over, it was clear he'd positioned himself close enough to jump in and help her if things got out of control. The knowledge that he was there—even as she was responsible for ruining his charity event—was a shot of moral support she hadn't known that she'd needed.

However, his expression melted into horror as he glanced from the ceiling to the double doors, and Stella wondered what fresh hell he was expecting. He lurched forward, arms extended, but it was too late. The doors flung open, and a quartet of singers burst into the room singing "Goin' to the Chapel" in four-part harmony.

Stella's jaw dropped, and Lucky strode across the floor, taking a bouquet of roses from each performer as they held them out toward her.

"Change of plans—Jesus, God! That wasn't the right signal!" His face flamed red as he looked over his shoulder at Stella. She suddenly understood that he'd had a performance of his own planned for the evening. One that she'd completely ruined.

He looked at her helplessly, and she stared, speechless, right back.

On the cusp of a massive confession in the high school shooting, with an unasked yet life-changing question ringing in her ears,

Stella stared, gaping at Conrad. The red light on top of the camera had never seemed so large and bright. Where did she go from here?

Before she could come up with anything, another voice rang out across the otherwise silent room.

"Chicago police. Everyone stay right where you are. We're taking you all in."

37

Stella's phone hadn't stopped vibrating for hours. The executive producer at the network, along with the main anchor, wanted immediate callbacks; the local NBC station had a number of questions for clarity about the story; Fran's mother, *Stella's* mother—they all wanted to hear from her.

Lucky? She'd not heard a peep from him since she left the Hancock. To be fair, he'd had a long night, with a gala to continue, a program to go through without an emcee or celebrity guest, and a pair of scholarships to give out.

And the engagement—the engagement! She wouldn't even allow herself to think about what Lucky'd been planning, how she'd messed it up, or the look on his face when it was all swirling down the toilet.

"Ms. Reynolds?"

"Huh?" Stella jerked her mind back to the small interview room she'd been deposited into several hours earlier. "I'm sorry. What was that, Detective?" She shifted in her seat and tried to smooth her unspeakably wrinkled evening gown with her hands.

The bear of a man flashed a paternal smile her way. "Long night, huh?" She nodded. "I just said that Chief Sterling is on her way in. Need any coffee?"

"Sure." Stella watched him leave, marveling at the cooperation between law-enforcement agencies. Apparently Chief Sterling's niece had alerted the chief to the live feed from the gala, which must have initially seemed like nothing more than a paparazzo's dream, until Sandy started talking. The chief had called a friend in the Chicago Police force, and they'd brought all the players to the nearest station.

Sterling had driven downtown with her detectives to get to the bottom of things in her cases, and clearly Stella was a low priority at the moment.

She wondered where Sandy and her stepmother were. And Sophia. Was the movie star also being offered stale coffee, or had she already been released? Her phone buzzed with yet another incoming text, and she shot off a quick response to Ken's question about new details. *Waiting on Chief.*

Ken's text back caught her by surprise. *Mandatory time off begins Friday. You'll get us through the week with updates on the case, then take two weeks off. Mental health break. It's been decided.*

Before Stella could figure out if this was good news or not, Chief Sterling walked through the door. She sat down in the chair opposite from Stella and passed a cup of coffee to her across the table. "I'm not sure whether to thank you or charge you."

"For what?" Stella figured it was the right question for either part of Sterling's query.

"Thank you for identifying all the players and bringing them together...or charge you for getting in the way of my investigation."

"Well...I guess I'll go with 'thank you,' but, honestly, after everything that's happened, it's close for me too."

Sterling chuckled. "Tough night, huh?"

"And nowhere near finished yet." Stella pushed her chair back a few inches and leaned forward, resting her elbows on her knees. "Do you have the shooter?"

"Off the record?"

Stella nodded. "For now."

Sterling nodded. "Fair enough. My detectives arrested him about an hour ago in his dorm room at St. Agnes College. Sandy gave us his information." Sterling sat back and studied Stella. "How long have you known?"

Stella shook her head. "I've known some of it for too long. I've been kicking myself that I couldn't put it together until it was too late."

"Not too late."

"Too late for Penelope." Stella had to concentrate on her breathing. She stared over Sterling's head, avoiding eye contact. The emotions of the night had started to worm their way into her heart, but she refused to break down. Not here.

"We've managed to piece together Penelope's last few hours from interviews with Mowery and Penelope's Residence Hall Advisor at the University of Chicago. Sandy hadn't been to her dorm room in days, and Penelope was worried. We now know that Penelope called in a missing persons report with campus police Friday afternoon—"

"I told her to do that, but I should have done more."

"—but they dropped the ball. Apparently the lead detective there was trying to leave early for a wedding this weekend, and he put it in the file for Monday," Sterling went on as if Stella hadn't interrupted. "But Penelope was tenacious. According to her Advisor, she'd found a Rivermoor High sweatshirt that had been stashed between Sandy's mattress and box spring. After she left your hotel, she went to Rivermoor High School to ask some questions."

"Penelope was at Rivermoor High Friday afternoon?" Stella's voice faltered, and she barely got the last word out.

Stella had been at the school on Friday afternoon, too, trying to get information out of the school admin.

Sterling's coffee cup was frozen halfway to her mouth, and she stared at Stella with obvious curiosity when she continued. "A lady who works there..." She looked down at her notes, "...ahh, let's see, here it is. A lady named Kathy Brimstone connected her to the one person in the building who knew Sandy the best."

"Madeline Mowery?" Stella asked, stunned.

"The admin had no idea that Mowery was working hard to cover up her part in the shooting at the high school. How could she?"

Stella looked down at her hands, shaking now that she knew

how close she'd come to finding Penelope; to possibly *saving* Penelope. She cleared her throat and tried to tell Sterling, but she couldn't do it. She couldn't face the fact that Penelope had been so physically close to her, and she'd blown it. Instead, she focused on her misstep at the hotel earlier that day.

"She came to me for help. I—I..." Stella blew out a sigh. "I really messed up there. She came to me and I blew her off. I think if I'd taken her seriously, she might still be alive."

"I don't know if that's true, Stella. I suspect if you'd have gotten involved earlier, you might be dead too."

"What do you mean?"

"We have a full confession from Mowery. When Penelope started asking questions at the high school, Mowery told Penelope that she knew where Sandy was. Instead, she drove her to the alley behind Raptor Yoga and killed her."

"In broad daylight?" Stella dropped her head into her hands after Sterling nodded.

"That woman has no real emotions. Everything's an act with her. She didn't know that Penelope had already gone to you. She thought killing her would be the end of anyone knowing about Sandy's duplicitous life."

They sat in silence for a few minutes. Sterling finally reached out and patted Stella consolingly on her arm. "It's not your fault. Don't you dare feel guilty for anyone else's actions this week."

Stella looked up and wiped her eyes. Sterling was right, but it was going to take some time until she got herself to believe it. She cleared her throat. "Do you have enough to charge her?"

"Not yet, but we will. The labs will come back with evidence from the crime scene. Fingerprints. Hair fibers. Mowery said people only remember the last thing you do. And she wanted people to remember her as someone who accepted her part in a sad story."

"Wow. Acting up to the very end, huh? What about Sandy? Her stepmother? Will they face charges?"

"Ah, yes. Sandy," Sterling sighed. "That's more complicated, I'm afraid. Her parents are pulling out all the stops to get her off, of course. It's going to be hard to pin down what was her idea and what was Madeline's."

"So she might get off without criminal charges?"

"Too early to say." The chief studied her hands for a moment, then looked up at Stella, her eyes hard. "I want a full account of your reporting."

"Network is sending a lawyer. My boss says I can't talk until she gets here. But I do have some questions for you."

Sterling frowned. "This is why no one likes reporters, you know. It's always, 'What's in it for me?' and not 'How can I help?'"

"Well...what's in it for me?"

Sterling blew out a disgusted sigh. "Exclusive interview for the morning news. First video of the shooter when we move him for his initial appearance in court."

Stella glanced over her shoulder, as if Ken might jump out from behind a plant and berate her for talking to Sterling without an attorney. "Done. What do you want to know?"

"How did you know about Madeline Mowery?"

"I really didn't have anything more than suspicions until I got caught up in the drama at the gala. However, I do have some new information."

"What now?"

She held up her phone. "I just had a chat with Raptor Garrett."

"The owner of the yoga studio?" Sterling asked, her expression halfway between irritated and intrigued.

"Yes, he's the owner of Raptor Yoga, but he's also a former student of Madeline's and the son of Curtis Garrett."

"Curtis Garrett? The dean of students at St. Agnes?"

"One and the same. Raptor was apparently in the Rivermoor High theater program up until last year. He showed a lot of promise on stage, but his real passion was fitness. After he graduated, his YouTube channel exploded with over one million followers. Enough to skip college and open his own yoga studio in Rivermoor.

"When I realized that Penelope was murdered behind his studio, I made a call. Raptor shared some disturbing things about Madeline Mowery. He believes that Mowery killed Penelope outside his studio as a warning to his father to keep his mouth shut about what he'd done."

"And what did *he* do? What are you suggesting?" Sterling looked down at her empty coffee, but Stella didn't miss the chief's obvious frustration. Apparently Madeline had left out quite a few details in their interview earlier that evening.

"Raptor and Sandy did some community theater together over the years. Madeline asked Raptor's father to get Sandy into a room on campus for her little acting experiment. But after Fran disappeared from St. Agnes in a cloud of suspicion, he told Madeline that he was going to go to the police and explain the whole charade—including Madeline's involvement. She wanted to make sure that never happened."

Sterling frowned. "Curtis Garrett didn't break any laws by squeezing Sandy into a private room on a private campus, though. What was he worried about?"

"It might not have been illegal, but surely he knew that if it became public that he stuck a random person in a dorm room with a legitimate student that his job—no, his entire career—would be over." Stella leaned forward, stretching out unconsciously toward Sterling. "But what about Fran? She came to you on Tuesday! Didn't she tell you her suspicions?"

"Fran is...complicated. I sent a deputy to pick her up Tuesday. She told me that she thought Tandy was somehow involved in something illegal, but I was up to my ears with the shootings. By the time I tried to find out more about Tandy, the girl was gone." Sterling opened her mouth to say something else, but her phone rang first. She tapped the screen and had a brief hushed conversation before disconnecting and looking back at Stella. "I've got to go. Still a lot to do tonight. Thanks for your help, Stella. I'll let the college leadership know about Curtis Garrett."

"Sure. But I already did."

Sterling looked at Stella with mounting respect.

Stella didn't tell her that she suspected Garrett of working with Madeline to file bogus restraining orders against her. It hardly mattered anymore, now that one was lifted and the other was revealed to be fake. But she did have one last thing to say. "I just want you to make sure that Fran's okay. She's been through a lot, and she's so young. It kind of breaks my heart."

Sterling smiled as she stood up, pushing away from the table. "Maybe I like you after all." She held the door for Stella and followed her down the hall toward the exit. "We'll have more questions, of course. We'll be in touch with your lawyer. But first, someone wants a few minutes alone with you before the real madness begins."

38

Fran stood up from a comfy chair in a corner office, looking tired but relieved. “Hey, Chief.” She turned and nodded. “Stella.”

Stella looked between the two women and Sterling smiled faintly. “I’ll leave you to it, Fran.” The chief backed out of the room. The door closed with a light click.

Fran bit her lip and dug her hands into the middle pocket of her St. Agnes hoodie, looking anywhere but at Stella.

Stella sat, wishing for the hundredth time in as many minutes that she was in sweats instead of silk.

“I feel like I have a lot to explain,” Fran began, and Stella could see that she was wringing her hands inside her pocket.

“Fran, you don’t owe me anything. Of course, I’m all ears if you *want* to tell me what happened. And it can be off the record too. Totally up to you.”

The girl looked startled, but relaxed into her seat and almost smiled. “My gram always said you were a tough nut, but I think I like you.”

Stella snorted, taking the jab and compliment in stride. “What have you been doing for the last week?”

"Jana Sterling was my best friend before...before my parents died."

"Chief Sterling's...?

"Niece."

"Ah." Stella hadn't known about the connection, but there was obviously more to the story, so she waited for Fran to organize her thoughts.

"I called Jana after you and I spoke and she hooked me up with the chief. I thought I should take your advice and tell her what I suspected about Tandy."

"And what *did* you suspect?" Stella asked, leaning forward. She was dying to know why Fran had become suspicious of her roommate in the first place.

"It was little things that had been happening since Fall semester started, really." Fran took her hands out of her pocket and rubbed them together. "She had a really dramatic story about her mother dying, but it didn't really ring true, you know? I mean, I do have some experience in the area." Fran frowned, her eyes far away. "But it just felt like she spent a lot of time pumping me for information about my feelings. To be honest, it was exhausting. Who wants to relive all that...anguish, all that sadness all the time?"

Stella nodded slowly, her own feelings shifting from guilt over Penelope to sorrow for this girl in front of her who had already lived through so much trauma in her short life.

"And then she'd be gone for class, like, all the time, but St. Agnes is small, you know? And she never knew any of my professors, or any of the professors of the other girls in our hall. But the really weird thing was that she was gone all the time. She said her dad lived in the city, and so I just figured she went home a lot to be with him, but even that didn't add up in the end."

"She was actually enrolled at the University of Chicago, taking classes downtown. She had a roommate there and everything."

"Chief Sterling told me about Penelope." Fran studied her hands for a long moment. "Dominic started coming around almost from the beginning, and their relationship never made sense. They met at freshman orientation, and he was always in our room, even though he seemed to annoy the crap out of Tandy. He certainly annoyed me. And she was always shooting me these long-suffering looks when he'd say something odd, and I never understood why they were together.

"But they had a big fight the night before the shooting at Rivermoor High. I was on my way into the room, but stood out in the hall to listen. I mean—" She looked up guiltily. "I didn't intend to eavesdrop, but I didn't want to walk into them having a huge fight, you know? So anyway, she was telling him if he loved her, he had to prove it. And he was saying that he was tired of proving things to her, and she had to believe in him." She shook her head. "It didn't really make sense, but then again, they never did. By the next day, all anyone was talking about was the high school shooting, and Dominic was amped up like I've never seen. Tandy was too. I probably would have written the whole thing off as just them being super weird as usual, except that I saw the Rivermoor High School yearbook open on Tandy's bed, and it had drawings all over it, like arrows and labels, and it was like a map? And Tandy saw me see it, and she just...stared at me. Like she was daring me to say something."

"Did you?" Stella asked, wondering what must have been going through Tandy's head. Did she know that Fran had suspected her?

"No, I...I mean, what was I going to say? Did you go shoot up that school? Because there were drawings on the yearbook? No, I just left. I spent the night with the girls down the hall, and I thought that would be the end of it. But the next day, Tandy wouldn't let it be. She was following me around the room, picking at me, just trying to get into an argument. Then she accused me of not confronting my feelings about my parents' death, and I...I lost it. Just started throwing things at her, yelling. It was intense."

"Was she right?"

"No! God, no. I mean, Gram and Pop had me in therapy from the minute my parents died. I've dealt with the emotions. I think—honest to God, I think she was trying to learn how someone who'd lost their parents would behave."

"And that's when I walked in?"

Fran's face reddened, and she looked down at her hands again and nodded. "And I left with you and never went back to our room. I called Jana on my way to my next class, and the chief sent a car to pick me up."

"And then McCoy got video of you in the back of the cruiser—"

"And called me a *suspect*. I've never seen the chief so angry." Fran looked up, her eyes wide.

Stella shifted in her seat to alleviate the pressure of the tight shapewear she had on under her outfit. "And did you tell the chief what you suspected? Did you ask her to investigate Dominic? Or Tandy?"

Fran dropped her head into her hands and sighed. "I did. But at the time, the chief thought the two shootings were related, and she was looking for someone who had a connection to both the high school and the Stop N Shop. I don't think it was until after it was clear the shootings had nothing to do with each other that the chief thought I might be onto something."

"And by then it was too late. Wow." Stella slumped back into her seat and felt exhaustion settle in. It was two in the morning. She was tired, uncomfortable, and emotionally drained. Fran looked the same. "You going to be okay?"

"Yeah. Sure. What other way is there to be, really?"

Stella reached out and clasped the girl's hand. "My mom always said you were a delightful kid, and I think she was right."

Fran's lips quirked up and she squeezed Stella's hand and then stood. The two women walked out of the office and made their way through the hallway to the lobby, where Sterling sat, waiting. "I'm going home with the chief tonight. We'll figure out what's going on at St. Agnes tomorrow. What about you? Do you need a ride?"

"No thanks, Fran. I'll just catch an Uber. But Chief?" Sterling looked over. "I've got you down for our live shots tomorrow morning, right? Exclusive access for twenty-four hours?"

The chief nodded, and all three walked out to the street together.

Lucky stood under a streetlamp, leaning against a car, waiting.

"Goodnight, Stella." Chief Sterling waved, and Fran gave her an encouraging smile. She watched them until they'd disappeared around a corner, then slowly, all vestiges of exhaustion suddenly gone, she turned to face Lucky, her stomach clenching as if she were about to jump off a cliff in the dark.

He tilted his head to the side and pushed away from the car. "Stella. I guess we need to talk."

39

Lucky's bow tie hung undone around his neck, and the top two buttons of his point collar were open. His blond hair was untidy and ruffled, as if he'd run his hands though it a hundred times since she'd seen him last.

He was quiet as he moved to close the gap between them. He stopped a full sidewalk square away and crossed his arms, assessing her with a critical eye.

She ran a hand down her naked arm, she'd lost her bolero at some point that evening. But even though it had to be back down below freezing, only her emotions felt numb. "Lucky, I—"

"No."

Stella's eyes widened. This was it? He wasn't even going to let her apologize? Was this where he decided she was too much work, and he'd had enough?

"No. You've done enough talking for one night, Stella Reynolds. It's *my* turn, and your only job right now is to listen." His eyes were wary as he looked at her. Intense. "We have been through a lot. More than most couples might go through their entire lives together. Some of it because of my job. Some of it because of yours."

The street around them was quiet, and the streetlamps overhead glowed behind Lucky like a halo. He moved a step closer to her and quirked his brow up, asking for agreement. She nodded and opened her mouth again. "I know, and I—"

He held up a hand. "Not yet."

She clamped her lips together, unable to read either his tone or expression.

"I had plans tonight. Big plans." He cocked his head to one side, just a glimpse of humor sparkling in his eyes. "As usual, I should have cleared them with you first. Now that I've had a few hours to go over what went wrong, I see the problem. I was trying to fit us into my job. And that's never going to work out, is it?"

He wasn't really asking, so Stella just stared, her heart hammering in her chest like it was trying to escape.

"Don't get me wrong. Work is always going to be a part of our relationship. I mean, we both have high-profile jobs; there aren't always days off, are there? But our jobs can't be the priority all the time, can they?"

She shook her head, and he took another step toward her, so they were now only a foot apart. He smiled and she lost her breath for a moment at the sight.

The low, sexy note of a saxophone swung up in the otherwise quiet night, but Stella couldn't take her eyes away from Lucky to see where it was coming from.

"I love you, Stella Reynolds, even when you ruin my plans. I love you so fiercely, it hurts, physically *hurts* inside my chest when we're apart." He reached out and carefully pressed her right hand against his chest. He breathed in for a long moment, then raised her hand to his lips and kissed her knuckles. He tilted her chin up and stared into her eyes, his expression earnest, hopeful. "My love for you changes with each passing year. Grows...bigger somehow. I want to make you happy, darlin', and I want it to be forever." He pushed back a step and sunk down onto one knee, producing a small blue velvet box that he held out to her like an offering. "Without any fanfare, no cameras, not a single other soul watching, will you come with me on this journey to put *us* first, to make sure we're always a priority, that we talk to each other, argue with each other, laugh together, and love each other until the end of our days?"

Stella's fingers trembled, the saxophone music dancing around her like a silk scarf, and she found herself, quite unusually, speechless.

Lucky's voice, usually so carefree and self-assured, was hoarse as he asked one last question. "Stella Reynolds, will you marry me?"

Stella hadn't spent time, like other girls might have, dreaming of this moment, planning it out, wondering how it would go, so she was completely unprepared for how nervous and shaky she felt. She stumbled toward Lucky, landing on his raised knee. His arm automatically circled around her waist and she leaned against his chest for support.

"Darlin'?" Lucky's hoarse voice was now almost a whisper, and she realized with a jolt that she was keeping him in suspense.

She shifted on his lap and put her hands on either side of his face, looking deep into his eyes for a long moment before pulling his face close for a long kiss. When they finally broke apart, breathless, she said, "Yes, Lucky, of course the answer is yes!" She held her hand out and he slipped the ring on her finger, a perfect fit. They both admired the sparkling solitaire diamond, set on an elegant, slim gold band.

Suddenly, Lucky whooped with excitement and leaped up, then, sensing that Stella was about to fall over, latched onto her arms again and swept her off her feet, twirling around before lowering her slowly back to the ground and wrapping his arms around her.

"Bear, you've made me the happiest man—and I know that in our lifetime together, there'll be times when I'm frustrated or you're irritated, but know this—know this deep in your soul." He tilted his head down until their foreheads touched. "I'll always be this madly in love with you. Always."

She pushed back a bit and he looked at her questioningly.

"Is it my turn now?"

His eyes widened, but his smile didn't falter. "Yes. Darlin', the sidewalk is yours."

"Okay." She took a deep breath and blew it out. Her emotions were bouncing around inside of her chest like marbles, and she didn't know where to start.

"I cover terrible things for a living. I watch people suffer, I ask them to relive their hardest, worst moments. And this week, it all hit really, really close to home."

The loss of Penelope, and her inability to save the girl, had hit her like a truck; just like from her bad dream the other night. But it also made important things in her life stand out clearly.

"I am sorry that I screwed things up tonight, and I'm sorry that I was so distracted this week. You can't know how much it means to me that you flew out early to surprise me, and how much I've come to rely on having you in my life. For someone who finds joy in racing around a track at breakneck speeds, you are such a steady influence in my life. I don't know what I'd do without you, and I don't want to find out."

"You won't have to."

"I think being together is hard." Lucky's brow lowered, and he looked at her questioningly, but she plowed on. "But it's the kind of hard that's worth it. And, Lucky, you're worth it. We're worth it."

They kissed again, and gooseflesh broke out along Stella's arms, but again, not from the cold. It was like a fire had been lit deep within her soul that might never burn out.

"So...what's next?" Stella asked when they finally broke apart several minutes later.

"I'd like to say it's as easy as we escape for a week on vacation, but..."

"But you have a race next weekend."

"And you have to work."

"Actually, I don't. Kenny is forcing me to take two weeks off, starting Friday. He called it a mental health break, but of course it doesn't start until after I get the shows through this breaking news story."

Lucky's wide smile slipped for a second before he regained his joy. "So you'll be able to rest up before I whisk you away for a week."

"Sounds perfect."

"And you know I have those two vacations booked already. I'll even let you choose which one we go on." He chuckled at her look of mock outrage. "Don't worry, they're both amazing." Lucky took her hand and led her to his car. "But first, I have plans for our night that don't include talking."

He opened the passenger door and she sunk down into the seat. Despite everything, it had been an amazing night, and it wasn't over yet.

40

It was an ungodly hour, even for someone who wasn't still trying to adjust to the time zone. Stella's alarm had gone off at four a.m., and Lucky had barely managed to croak out a nonsensical moan before he rolled over and was back asleep.

Now Stella stood outside of the Rivermoor Police Station, in full makeup, with Art behind the camera and Conrad manning the satellite truck.

"You good?" Stella asked Fran, who stood wide-eyed next to her.

"Sure, I-I'm good. So, walk me through this again?"

Stella squeezed her arm. "Nothing to worry about. I'm going to be with you the whole time. It'll just be like having a conversation with me at a cafe. Ignore the camera, and just answer the questions honestly. No big deal."

Fran's head swiveled between the huge lights flooding the dark sidewalk, the alien-like camera staring at them, and Stella. "Sure. No big deal."

Stella smiled reassuringly, then bumped a switch to turn on the battery pack connected to her earpiece. Her first live hit that morning for the national morning news program was coming up, but that would be just the beginning of her workday. Fran would go home, and Stella would continue on with live shots, interviewing

Chief Sterling and Rebecca Bowen, who was determined to cast her stepdaughter in a good light.

The local stations were all set up nearby, of course; after all, the story was now theirs. Stella might be ready to move on to the next national story, but they would be here covering the case as it made its way through the court system for the next year.

After a scant hour of sleep and a full day of live shots ahead, she was actually looking forward to her "mental health break." But really, after one day to herself, what in the world would she do with so much free time? It would be her longest vacation since the last time she had a summer break from school.

"Stella, we're ten minutes away from the cold open," Art said, adjusting the light behind her.

"Thanks, Art."

Suddenly, Malcolm McCoy appeared at her elbow, his lips twisted into a snarl. "You."

He wasn't alone. His sister Gail trailed about ten feet behind him, her phone raised up, probably recording the encounter.

Stella took it all in as she turned, and though her face was set in a pleasant smile, there was steel in her voice when she said, "McCoy. You're in my space. Step back."

She slipped her phone out of her pocket and scrolled through the list of recent texts, looking for something.

McCoy was still close, and he leaned in, lowering his voice so that no one else could hear. "I just got off the phone with my news director. He's moving me from the downtown newsroom to our bureau in Gary, Indiana."

"I'm sure there's a lot of news that needs covering there," Stella said coolly, still scrolling back in her phone log.

"It's the armpit of Indiana. I refuse to go."

"Then perhaps one of the other stations will snap you up."

"Oh, I doubt that," Sterling said, walking up. "Stella, you said to get here by quarter after seven, but I figured I'd be here for moral support for our Frannie."

Fran's smile was strained as she looked between the adults. She could clearly sense the tension between McCoy and Stella.

"What—what do you doubt?" McCoy asked, trying to reign in his hostility in front of the police chief.

Sterling took a sip from her coffee mug before answering. "I doubt that any other stations would be interested in snapping you up, McCoy. It's not hard to imagine Fran's family suing you and your station—and winning, of course—for your entirely incorrect characterization of her in the story you ran about her being a shooting suspect, when in fact, with her help we were able to solve a heinous crime in our community."

Fran's lips were pressed into a flat line as she stared at McCoy.

"Shame you screwed up the story so completely. Makes you untrustworthy. Fran, is there anything you want to say to McCoy here?"

"Why are they sending you to Gary?" Fran asked.

McCoy scowled. "That's what I came here to ask. What did you do?" He looked at Stella with daggers in his eyes.

"Don't blame me, McCoy," Stella said. "I suspect that if your sources here in the city no longer trust you, that's on you."

Art cleared his throat. "Good news, at least, McCoy. I accepted the job to be your full-time photographer out in Gary. We'll be working together every day." He turned toward Stella. "I've been ironing out the details of my contract the last few days!" he exclaimed.

That explained why Art had been so secretive on his phone that week.

McCoy make a choking sound, then backed away slowly. "You...you—"

"Watch it, McCoy. Hot mics everywhere," Stella said.

"That's right, Stella. Hot mics everywhere," Gail said, stepping closer. Her eyes, so similar to her brother's, narrowed to slits. She opened her mouth, ready to ask a "gotcha" question, but Stella had finally found the number on her phone she'd been looking for. The one that had been sending threatening texts to her all week. She tapped the number, initiating a call.

"Why don't you tell me..." Gail's grip on her phone faltered when it rang. Her eyes slid to the screen, and then popped wider when she looked at Stella.

"You going to answer that, Gail? I'm sure whoever it is wants to talk to you. Tell you that she's thinking about pressing charges against whoever's been sending her harassing text messages all week." Stella turned to Sterling. "Is that a felony or a misdemeanor, Chief?"

"I'd have to forward the complaint to the district attorney's office, Stella, for them to decide. All that's public information, though." Sterling shrugged. "You never know, it might come out in the media that a complaint's been filed."

Gail's face contorted into a frown, and both she and her brother stalked away, nearly vibrating with fury.

"What did you do, Chief?" Fran asked.

"I may have made some calls to other departments about Malcolm's accuracy." Sterling shrugged innocently at Stella's surprised expression. "He's reckless, and that makes him dangerous. It's not my fault if he's been irresponsible with multiple stories. The people I spoke with were more than happy to call his boss to complain."

"Folks, we're live in five minutes. Five away," Art repeated.

Stella blew out a sigh. She couldn't argue with the fact that McCoy had it coming, but she didn't like to think of him out there, angry and hoping for revenge.

Her phone buzzed and she checked the screen out of habit. "Oh. Wow, it's Janet."

"Who's that?" Fran asked.

Stella's lips scrunched up while she thought of the right way to answer the simple question. She finally grinned. "She was my roommate. Ages ago."

"Come here," Sterling said to Fran, and the chief smoothed out a flyaway hair. "Let me give you a few tips for your first live interview..." The two chatted quietly while Stella tapped her screen to answer the call.

Janet didn't even say hello. "This is going to sound crazy, but hear me out..."

Exactly two minutes later, Stella tucked her phone into her bag.

"Everything okay?" the chief asked.

"Yes. In fact, I just agreed to go on a cruise with an old friend."

"Wow, sounds fun. Somewhere warm, I hope?" Sterling motioned to the tiny flakes of snow that had just materialized in the air and floated down around them.

"Yes, somewhere warm. We leave on Friday."

"Well," Sterling said, taking another sip from her mug, "I'd say you've earned it."

Art cleared his throat. "Coming to you in three...two..."

Stella smiled briefly before Art pointed to her just as the light on top of his camera flashed red, then she squared her shoulders to the camera and started talking.

Yes, she had earned a vacation. It had been a long and difficult week, both emotionally draining and uplifting. But in the end, she knew she was lucky to work in a job she loved, with people who loved her by her side. She really couldn't ask for more.

SPECIAL OFFER

The Big Beginning

Cramming for her upcoming exam, college junior Stella Reynolds finds her favorite professor dead in his office. When her roommate Rachel is arrested for the murder, Stella is convinced they have the wrong person. She must set her studies aside to prove her friend's innocence.

The professor was no angel, and a number of possible suspects lurk dangerously close. In the meantime, an unscrupulous local reporter is maliciously fanning the flames of controversy.

When someone sneaks the murder weapon into her apartment, Stella realizes she's in very real danger. Someone has a deadly secret and Stella must reveal the real killer before they strike again.

Go to www.LibbyKirschBooks.com to find out how to get the free ebook delivered right to your inbox.

Now turn the page to check out the first book in Libby's other series, ***Last Call***.

INTRODUCING THE JANET BLACK MYSTERY SERIES

LAST CALL - A JANET BLACK MYSTERY

Janet slammed the drawer of the cash register. By the time Cindy jumped at the noise, Janet had her phone out to make a call.

"Hey, Darlin'," Jason said when he picked up the line. "I was hoping I'd hear from you."

Janet smiled, in spite of her foul mood, and pushed wisps of light brown hair away from her face. Her hand came away damp. She'd been sweating in the Knoxville summer heat since before she even rolled out of bed, and the ancient air-conditioning unit behind the bar couldn't seem to keep up with the soaring temperature. Then she remembered the reason she was calling and frowned. "I just counted—and then I re-counted. Money's missing again." She walked toward the back of the room, away from Cindy and Frank, her bouncer, who'd just arrived for his shift. "This time we're short eighty-two dollars." She couldn't stop herself from turning back to look at her employees suspiciously.

"And?" her boyfriend asked.

"*And* Elizabeth was working last night." She watched Cindy disappear into the back cooler with an empty bucket.

"Anyone else?" Jason asked.

Her lips puckered. Why did he always sound so irritatingly reasonable? "Well, yeah, but I don't think—"

"I'm just saying. Don't fly off the—"

"I can keep my cool, okay?" she snapped, then flushed. She hadn't meant to shout. She lowered her voice to a whisper. "Jason, can you please just check the video? I gotta go." They disconnected, but before she could shove her phone back into her pocket, the screen lit up with a delayed notification telling her she'd missed two calls overnight from the very employee she suspected of theft. She glared at the walls, then realized it wasn't the poor reception *here* that was the problem. She'd been home all night with Jason, and for some reason the incoming calls from Elizabeth were only now showing up.

She tapped a few icons and shook her head. Her youngest staff member hadn't left a message, but the timing seemed suspicious. She learned just days ago that money was missing, and then last night, for the first time ever, Elizabeth tried to call her on her cell phone? Did she know, somehow, that Janet knew about the missing money?

Cindy hobbled out from the walk-in cooler, her gait awkward as she wrestled the full bucket of ice behind the bar. As usual, she was dressed to kill—or at least maim. She had poured herself into a bright pink tube top that ended just above a shiny green belly-button ring. Her tight jeans rode so low that Janet could see her hipbones jutting out, and Cindy had tied her bleach-blond hair back with a teal bandanna. Body parts were spilling from every piece of her outfit.

"You gained a set there." Janet motioned to Cindy's chest. Something had happened when she dumped the ice bucket into the freezer drawer, and her two boobs had turned into four.

"Oh my gosh! They musta come unstuck!" Her twang made the words musical. She bent over and reached into her tube top to rearrange things.

"Come on!" Frank turned away from the bar in disgust and headed for the far side of the room.

Janet watched him walk off before asking Cindy, "What's under there?"

"It's a silicone push-up thingamajig. Sticks right to my skin and pushes the girls up—but I'm so dang hot, they must've slipped down." She wiped beads of sweat from her brow and then smoothed the fabric of her tube top over her restored figure. "You know, I didn't used to need all this business under here, but after Chip, everything just kind of . . . fell."

Chip, Chip, Chip. It was all Cindy ever wanted to talk about. Janet plastered on a smile when her bartender looked up. "Kids, huh? How old is he now?"

"Seventeen, going on forty," she smiled indulgently. "He leaves for college this fall." She turned back to the bar, a towel and spray bottle in her hands, the goofy grin still on her face.

Frank slammed two chairs down from the table in the corner, still scowling. He might not have liked Cindy's methods, but he took his share from the tip jar every night without complaint. Janet only paid minimum wage, but they all cleared more than thirty dollars an hour on a good night, thanks in some part, perhaps, to Cindy's ramped-up double-Ds. Their nice hourly wage made it even more frustrating to discover someone had been stealing money from the register, and if Janet's new accounting program was right, it had been going on for weeks. That's why she'd had Jason install the state-of-the-art surveillance system. She was ready to catch a thief.

"Damn gum," Frank muttered, scraping the tabletop with a flat-edge razor.

He fit the job description for a bouncer—tall and strong—but his light brown hair was smashed flat on one side, as if he'd fallen asleep while it was wet, and his eyes were red and puffy.

Was he the sticky-fingered employee? Though Elizabeth, Janet's other full-time bartender, was her prime suspect, Frank was no prize, so if Jason saw him stealing in the surveillance video from the night before she wouldn't be shocked.

But Elizabeth still seemed the most likely culprit, although Janet couldn't articulate why to Jason. She just had a feeling the other woman was hiding something.

"Anything unusual last night?" she asked lightly as she walked back behind the bar.

"Oh, you know," Cindy said without taking her eyes off the two bottles of top-shelf vodka she was combining, "same old, same old. We had to throw poor Ike out just before midnight, bless his heart. Other than that, it was the usual."

"Did he make a fuss?" Janet already knew the answer, since she hadn't been called.

"Nah." Cindy placed the full bottle of vodka back on the shelf and set the empty one in the recycling bin.

Frank cleared his throat. "No fuss?" He hefted two more chairs off a table and dropped them to the ground with a bang. "He shouted the whole way out the door, 'The man will always find you —he knows,' not to mention the hail of curse words he spewed at Elizabeth."

Cindy shrugged as she took two bottles of well vodka from the bin and unscrewed the caps.

Janet looked shrewdly at her bartender. "Did we call him a taxi?"

"Yes ma'am, we sure did, and didn't kick him out until it arrived," Cindy said, unconcerned.

"Well, shit," Janet said with a shrug that mimicked Cindy's. Really, you couldn't ask for a better outcome.

Cindy raised her eyebrows and looked pointedly at a jar on the counter.

Janet grinned. "Aw, hell, Cindy," she drawled, making a show of pulling not one, but three one-dollar bills out of her back pocket and pushing them into the oversized, washed pickle jar. The swear jar already had five bucks in it from the last hour alone. "I keep forgetting to watch my damn mouth."

Her good humor was tested, however, by Frank, muttering in the corner.

"That's not how you'd have handled it on the force?" she asked.

"It's not a police issue. I just don't know why he's welcomed back time and again." Frank turned his back on the women and kept working.

Janet had hired him a few weeks ago, impressed by his pedigree. She figured a former cop would surely know how to handle the door of her small bar. So far, however, he'd been a disappointment, always ready to escalate a situation and challenge the status quo.

"I suppose you think that kind of behavior is fine?" he asked over his shoulder.

"No, but this is a bar, not a bookstore. It's going to happen." Janet crossed to the back cooler and emerged minutes later with a white plastic bin full of lemons and limes. She looked up at a sudden clattering at the front door. A gray and grizzled man with greasy hair and dirty clothes pulled at the handle. She could practically smell his days-old sweat through the glass.

"Door's broken!" he called, cupping a hand over his eyes so he could see into the bar. "Ma'am? It won't open." He jiggled the handle again, and then, as if he'd expended too much effort, he leaned in, leaving a streak on the glass with his forehead. Janet and Cindy exchanged amused looks, but Frank crossed his arms and stared daggers through the glass.

"We're not open," Frank said, looking at the man like he was the leftover foam at the bottom of a pint glass.

"Not open?" The man smiled, revealing several missing teeth. "How'd you get in?"

Janet chuckled and looked at Frank. "Take care of it." She pointed to the number for the taxi company nailed to the wall behind her, then waited until Frank picked up his cell phone before she took the empty fruit bin to the back room.

There, Janet caught a glimpse of herself in the mirror on the back of the door. She turned to the side to check her boobs. At thirty-one years old and without kids, they were right where they were supposed to be. She smoothed her black T-shirt with the bar's logo on it and tucked it into her jeans before heading to the desk.

She spent a few minutes going over the books. It was Thursday, which meant they could expect a big college crowd thirsty for deals. She squinted through the window into the back parking lot. If the beer truck didn't show, she'd have to change her happy hour special, as her inventory of cheap, crappy beer was low.

Janet looked at the clock on the wall and blew out a sigh. She'd check the cooler to see what would make a good replacement.

But first, she decided to call Elizabeth. The call went straight to voicemail, so she left a message, asking her bartender to call in; she wanted to ask directly about the missing money. Her phone chirped —the battery was low—so she laid it on the desk and called Jason on the landline, leaving him a long, detailed message about her plan for Elizabeth.

Despite the missing money, she liked being in charge. It was freeing to think if there was a problem with an employee, she could fix it.

Buying The Spot a year ago had made her a boss for the first time ever, and she was on a mission to be unlike any crappy boss she'd ever had. She wanted to be calm, be unflappable, and stay the hell out of her employees' personal lives. With a final nod to herself, she logged out of her computer and left the office.

As she cut through the main room, however, her step stuttered and her heart slammed into her chest. What was it about seeing cops that made you feel instantly guilty?

The man and woman in uniform were chatting with Frank by the front door. Cindy was behind the bar, not making eye contact, but Frank looked up defiantly when she cleared her throat.

"Hello, Officers," Janet said. "What's going on?"

***Last Call, A Janet Black Mystery*, Available soon!**

ALSO BY LIBBY KIRSCH

The Stella Reynolds Mystery Series

The Big Lead

The Big Interview

The Big Overnight

The Big Weekend

The Big Job

The Big Mistake

The Janet Black Mystery Series

Last Call

Last Minute

Last Chance

For updates on new releases or to connect with the author, go to www.LibbyKirschBooks.com

ABOUT THE AUTHOR

Libby Kirsch is an Emmy award winning journalist with over ten years of experience working in television newsrooms of all sizes. She draws on her rich history of making embarrassing mistakes on live TV, and is happy to finally indulge her creative writing side, instead of always having to stick to the facts.

Libby lives in Chicagoland with her husband, three young children, and Sam the dog.

Connect with Libby

www.LibbyKirschBooks.com

Libby@LibbyKirschBooks.com

facebook.com/LibbyKirschBooks

twitter.com/LibbyKirsch

amazon.com/author/libbykirsch

bookbub.com/authors/libby-kirsch

goodreads.com/libbykirsch

www.ingramcontent.com/pod-product-compliance
Lightning Source LLC
LaVergne TN
LVHW091120080826
845145LV00008B/1993